NORTH EAST LINCOLNSHIRE LIBRARY SERVICE

9cc

KU-589-983

NORTH EAST
LINCOLNSHIRE
LIBRARIES

CLE		LCO	
GCL	SIB	NUN	
GCR		SCO	
GRA		SLS	
HUM		WAL	I
IMM		WIL	10 11
LAC		YAR	

SPECIAL MESSAGE TO READERS

This book is published under the auspices of

THE ULVERSCROFT FOUNDATION

(registered charity No. 264873 UK)

Established in 1972 to provide funds for research, diagnosis and treatment of eye diseases. Examples of contributions made are: —

A Children's Assessment Unit at Moorfield's Hospital, London.

•

Twin operating theatres at the Western Ophthalmic Hospital, London.

•

A Chair of Ophthalmology at the Royal Australian College of Ophthalmologists.

•

The Ulverscroft Children's Eye Unit at the Great Ormond Street Hospital For Sick Children, London.

You can help further the work of the Foundation by making a donation or leaving a legacy. Every contribution, no matter how small, is received with gratitude. Please write for details to:

THE ULVERSCROFT FOUNDATION,
The Green, Bradgate Road, Anstey,
Leicester LE7 7FU, England.
Telephone: (0116) 236 4325

In Australia write to:
THE ULVERSCROFT FOUNDATION,
c/o The Royal Australian and New Zealand
College of Ophthalmologists,
94-98 Chalmers Street, Surry Hills,
N.S.W. 2010, Australia

Mark Watson is an acclaimed novelist and comedian, best known for his appearance on *Mock the Week*, *Never Mind the Buzzcocks*, *Have I Got News For You* and *Live at The Apollo* as well as the *Edinburgh Festival*. Mark lives in London with his wife and baby son.

www.markwatsonthecomedian.com
www.twitter.com/watsoncomedian

ELEVEN

This is the story of radio DJ Xavier Ireland, who by night offers words of wisdom to sleepless Londoners and by day keeps himself to himself. That is, until a one-of-a-kind encounter forces him to confront his own biggest regret. Meanwhile, a single moment sparks a chain of events that will affect eleven lives across the city, with unstoppable consequences . . .

MARK WATSON

ELEVEN

Complete and Unabridged

CHARNWOOD
Leicester

First published in Great Britain in 2010 by
Simon & Schuster UK Ltd
London

First Charnwood Edition
published 2011
by arrangement with
Simon & Schuster UK Ltd
London

The moral right of the author has been asserted

This book is a work of fiction. Names, characters, places and incidents are either a product of the author's imagination or are used fictitiously. Any resemblance to actual people living or dead, events or locales is entirely coincidental.

Copyright © 2010 by Mark Watson
All rights reserved

British Library CIP Data

Watson, Mark, 1980 –
 Eleven.
 1. Radio broadcasters- -Fiction.
 2. Women cleaning personnel- -Fiction.
 3. Large type books.
 I. Title
 823.9'2–dc22

 ISBN 978–1–4448–0839–1

Published by
F. A. Thorpe (Publishing)
Anstey, Leicestershire

Set by Words & Graphics Ltd.
Anstey, Leicestershire
Printed and bound in Great Britain by
T. J. International Ltd., Padstow, Cornwall

This book is printed on acid-free paper

To Kit

1

A bone-cold February night. London is being pelted with snow. The flakes dance in the neon beams of street lights and settle in scarves around the necks of parked cars.

In a car park around the back of a concrete building in the west of the city, a thin fox scuttles for warmth, leaving coquettish paw-print trails for early risers to marvel over in a few hours. Five levels up, through the steadily whiting-out windows of a radio studio, Xavier Ireland watches the fox seek out a nook in the shadow of a metal recycling unit.

'Well, I'd stay safely inside, in the warm,' Xavier advises his invisible, London-wide audience, 'and keep calling in. Next, we're going to hear from a man who's had three marriages . . . and three divorces.'

'Ouch!' chips in his co-presenter and producer, Murray, in characteristically banal style, flicking a button to start the next song.

'Very pretty out there,' says Xavier.

'It'll be cer, cer, cer, chaos in the morning,' Murray stammers.

In 2003 Xavier was working for this radio station as a runner, making tea, plugging wires into walls, when he saw snow for the first time. He had emigrated from Australia only a few weeks before, changed his name — which was previously Chris Cotswold — and thrown

1

himself into the idea of starting a new life in this faraway country, where he had lived as a baby, but never since. He was impressed, then as now, by how flimsy each individual snowflake was and the sheer number of them needed to coat a street. At the same time, though, the unfamiliar sight and the bitter cold only reminded him that most of the earth was now between him and his home, him and his friends.

Xavier graduated over time from runner to Murray's assistant, and eventually those roles reversed, so it's now Xavier who acts as counsellor to the show's large, sleepless constituency.

'I just wonder what's wrong with me,' says their current caller, a fifty-two-year-old teacher, who lives on his own on the edge of a housing estate in Hertfordshire.

The wavering mobile connection saws off some of his sentences halfway through. Murray runs his finger across his throat, to suggest they move on to another caller — this call is a good three minutes old already — but Xavier shakes his head.

'I mean, I'm a decent person,' continues the depressed teacher, whose name is Clive Donald, and who, after making this call, will claw what patchy sleep he can from the rest of the night, before waking up, putting on a grey suit, and getting into his car with thirty maths books in a weather-beaten briefcase on the back seat. 'I . . . I support a charity, for example. I've got quite a few interests. There's nothing — obviously wrong with me, you might say. Why can't I make a marriage work? Why do I keep making mistakes?'

'It's too easy to assume that everything's your fault,' Xavier tells him, and all the other listeners in their homes around the city. 'Believe me, I've wasted months — well, years — reliving mistakes. Eventually, I made myself stop thinking about them.'

At last Clive, sufficiently consoled to find the will to go to bed if nothing else, thanks Xavier and says goodbye.

Murray punches a button.

'And now the joys of the news and traffic,' he says. 'See you in a second.'

Murray goes into the corridor and props open a fire door, so that he can smoke a cigarette in the stark air. The snow is coming down with an un-British ferocity, like hail or sleet instead of the pretty featheriness of what usually passes for snow. Xavier takes a sip of coffee from a yellow mug with the words *BIG CHEESE* and a picture of a slice of cheese on it. This was a Christmas present from Murray a couple of years ago, and in its rather garish functionality, its awkward size, it somehow resembles its giver.

A few miles away, a shivering Big Ben — just visible from Xavier's studio on a clearer night — strikes two.

'These are the headlines,' reads a woman miles away, her voice, almost completely toneless, appearing simultaneously on syndicated stations all over the UK. 'In a couple of hours, the country will wake to the heaviest snowfall in ten years.'

It's an odd turn of phrase, Xavier thinks to himself, 'the country waking', as if the UK were a giant, silent boarding-school eventually roused by the morning bell. In London alone, as the success of Xavier's four-hour stint testifies, there is a huge, phantom community of people awake at night for all sorts of reasons: work schedules, unusual hobbies, guilt, or fear, or illness — or, of course, simple enthusiasm for the show. Xavier looks again at the clogged windowpane and imagines the still, snowed-on London stretching for miles outside. He tries to picture Clive Donald, the maths teacher, slowly hanging up the phone after the call and boiling the kettle, instinctively taking two mugs out of a cupboard, then putting one back. He thinks of all the regular callers: the lorry drivers fiddling with the dial as the signal fades on the M1 out of London, the elderly ladies with nobody else to talk to. Then in a vague way he considers all the half-million people on London's night-shift, just beyond the boundaries of the car park with its creeping fox, its silent corners and, tonight, the building channels of snow.

One of Clive Donald's pupils, Julius Brown, seventeen years old and an obese one hundred and thirty kilograms, is crying quietly in his room. Despite regular workouts at the gym, he doesn't seem to be able to combat his obesity. He went on medication for epilepsy when he was fourteen; one of the side-effects was a startling weight gain, and although no doctor can really explain it, he continues to expand almost visibly each time he eats. Every school day is full of insults: people make fart-noises as he sits down, gangs of girls laugh in their impenetrable way as he passes in the playground. He's studying three A levels including information technology and wants to design software, but expects to end up manning a helpline for thinner people whose computers won't start up. He senses the snowfall without even looking outside: it was bitterly cold when he got the bus home from the restaurant where he works some evenings. He'd give anything for school to be cancelled tomorrow.

Others are thinking just the opposite, like Jacqueline Carstairs, the mother of a boy a few school years below Julius. She is a freelance journalist with a fast, aggressive typing style like someone playing rock piano. Her husband has agreed to take their son Frankie to school tomorrow morning, so that she can stay up late and finish writing an article on Chilean wine; provided school goes ahead, she will then have time to work in peace tomorrow as well. Sharp-eared from years of parenting, she picks up the tissue-soft, almost undetectable sound of snow landing in the plastic recycling box outside. She punches into a search engine the name of a Chilean actor, now based in the UK, who features in an advertising campaign for the wine her piece is about.

The actor's psychotherapist, Dr Maggie Reiss (pronounced 'Rice'), is sitting on the toilet in her house in Notting Hill. Originally from New York, she has practised in London since 1990, and now boasts a long list of well-known clients from the worlds of entertainment, business and fashion. Two years ago she was diagnosed with irritable bowel syndrome, which she attributes to the unreasonable attitudes of many of her clients: their demands, their self-importance, even aggression, sometimes. Seated beneath a Klimt print which is a reproduction of an original found at the MOMA, she stares out of the bathroom window across the whitening roofs and chimneys. She wonders if anyone uses a chimney nowadays or if they are more or less ornamental, retained by London as part of its renowned package of eccentricities. Maggie's red silk nightgown is collected in her lap. She sighs and thinks about one of her more highly strung patients, a politician who — even at this moment — is amongst the number of Londoners committing adultery. Today, he was particularly difficult in their session, making absurd threats to sue her if she breached confidentiality. He can go to hell, thinks Maggie, her stomach churning and complaining. I don't need to feel like this. I don't care if he lives or dies.

Just a few doors down from Maggie, George Weir, a retired bricklayer, really is dying. The two have nodded to each other in the street several times, but never spoken. As Xavier sips his coffee three miles to the west, George is in the throes of a heart attack, gasping desperately for air that suddenly seems partitioned off from his mouth by some invisible screen. He writhes inch by inch towards the phone to call his daughter, but it's too late, and there'd be nothing she could do in any case. He was born in Sunderland seventy years ago this very week. He had been intending

6

to go to his bowls club tomorrow, although in fact it will be cancelled because of the weather, and then cancelled again next week as a mark of respect to him.

One of George Weir's last thoughts on earth is a memory of having to decline a Latin verb — *audere*, to dare — and, stuck halfway, being hammered on the knuckles by Mr Partridge. More than fifty years late it comes to him how the verb was meant to go. As he fights in vain for breath he also remembers learning that Mr Partridge was dead, perhaps twenty-five years ago, and feeling a certain satisfaction that, at last, the generation of sticklers and sadists who had plagued his school days was dying out. But now George himself, unthinkably, is dying, and he will be as ruthlessly obscured by time as Mr Partridge and all the rest.

Jesus, he thinks — despite never having been a religious, or emotional, man — Jesus Christ, don't let this be it. But this is it. George will enter cardiac arrest shortly, and by the time Xavier and Murray drive home, he will be waiting, head back and mouth frozen open, for one of Maggie's neighbours to find him. In a few days' time a hearse bearing his body will pick its way solemnly through the remnants of the snow to Abbey Park Cemetery, glimpsed momentarily from his living room by Xavier, who for now continues to gaze out of the window at this canvas of tiny, unseen happenings.

'Back on air in fer, fer, forty-five seconds,' says Murray, resettling in his swivel chair and rotating gently back and forth. Xavier thinks for a moment more about his first experience of snow on that night five years ago, and then hastily turns his thoughts to the present: the chilly studio and the callers waiting for his attention.

★　★　★

By the time they drive home, just after four, the snow is thick on the roads. Xavier, a well-proportioned six foot three, sits in the passenger seat, his leather jacket drawn tight around his body, feet drumming on the floor for warmth. Murray, stout and bushy-haired, is ushering the car forward in fits and starts as if geeing up a reluctant horse.

'Good show tonight,' says Murray, nodding his big head of curly hair. 'That man with the three wives was a deadweight, though. Should have lost him quicker.'

'I think we had to keep him on. He sounded pretty lonely.'

'You're a good man, Xavier.'

'I wouldn't go that far.'

There is a somehow weighty silence. Murray clears his throat. The dutiful click-click of the windscreen wipers adds to the impression that he is about to say something important.

'Wer, wer, what do you think about going to a speed-dating night? Tomorrow night. It's in this place in cer, Camden.'

'What?'

'You know, speed dating. You go round meeting lots of women. And then . . . '

'Yes, I'm familiar with the idea. I'm trying to

work out if you're serious about us doing something like that.'

Murray rubs his nose with his free hand.

'I mean, wer, wer, we've both been single for a wer, while.' His stammer tends to gather momentum at moments of embarrassment, as if his voice were an old hard drive trying to download each word individually. 'W' is often the first casualty.

'I'm pretty happy single, mate.'

'*I'm* not.'

The car makes a laboured turn around a skiddy corner next to a postbox, collection times obscured by its new coat of snow.

'I don't think I'm in an ideal position for a singles event. I can't say I'm Xavier from the radio. Imagine how embarrassing it would be if one of the women was a listener.'

'Well, use your old name. Call yourself Chris. What was wrong with that ner, name in the first place, anyway?'

'Well, whatever name I say, they're still going to ask what I do for a living.'

'Make up a job.'

'So, basically, you want me to meet twenty-five strangers and lie repeatedly to all of them.'

'They'll all be lying,' says Murray, 'that's wer, wer, what people do to make themselves attractive.'

Murray carefully snaps the indicator, although there are no other cars on the road, and trundles shakily down the sharp hill towards 11 Bayham Road.

'Do you really think this is the way you're

going to find someone?' Xavier asks. 'Hundreds of brief conversations in a noisy bar?'

'Have you got a better idea?'

Xavier sighs. Nearly anything would be a better idea. It should be obvious to Murray that, with his stammer, he is very poorly adapted to the three-minute date. Naturally, Xavier doesn't want to spell this out to him.

'Well, all right. It'll be good to cross another solution off the list, at least.'

As he pads down the path, his feet sinking surprisingly deep into the wad of snow, like candles into butter icing on a cake, Xavier glances back and exchanges a wave with Murray.

At a broadcasting-industry party last Christmas, an influential producer — short and buxom, in telescopic heels — tried to interest Xavier in leaving Murray and pitching for his own show: something which people have been doing ever since Xavier began to make a name for himself.

'You know, no offence, but he's holding you back,' she shouted, leaning up and breathing cocktail-soured air into Xavier's face. She was the sort of woman who shouted at everyone, as if, being so diminutive, she was used to having to convey her words over a great distance. 'He's holding you back . . . What's his name?'

'Murray.'

'Exactly, babe.' She grabbed Xavier's wrist as if they might be about to dance, or kiss. Not being a regular at corporate parties, Xavier often finds himself taken aback by the ill-becoming intimacies of the people who wield power in his

10

business. 'I was talking about you just the other day in a meeting.' She mentioned a couple of high-up figures. 'You should be looking at TV, I mean it, you'd look great on camera, or if you prefer radio there's all sorts of other things. But you need to be on your own.'

Xavier glanced uneasily across the room at Murray, who was hovering at the edge of a group, unsuccessfully trying to drop a word here and there into a fast-flowing conversation.

'I'll think about it.'

'Do think about it.' She pressed a business card into his hand.

He slipped the card into his trouser pocket, where it still is now, in his wardrobe. He did not, of course, relay the conversation to Murray; as always when these situations arise he said that it was just small talk.

Xavier watches Murray, with his clumsy doggedness, marshal the car up the hill in a series of grinds and jumps.

★　★　★

As he lies in bed in a waiting room between thoughts and dreams, Xavier finds his mind being dragged back to the conversation in the car, and remembers the day he changed his name, two weeks after landing in London. The actual process was surprisingly undramatic, a matter of filling out forms and taking them to a grey office in Essex, and waiting for confirmation by post a few days later. But the infinite choice of new names had been rather daunting.

11

He settled on his new initials, XI, first. A number of things seemed to point in their direction. Firstly, *XI* was a little-known but valid word which he played to win a Scrabble tournament the same week he changed his name. Of course the letters meant eleven in Roman numerals, too, and this is a number he's always been inexplicably attached to: it was no surprise to him to end up living, as he does, at 11 Bayham Road. Xavier was one of the only first names he could think of to fit the bill; Ireland, the surname he chose, had no specific relevance either. But taken as a whole, Xavier Ireland seemed to work quite well — exotic, unique, but somehow plausible.

Changing his name had felt significant because the old one, Chris Cotswold, had had a decisive role to play in forming the key relationships of his life so far. He met his three best friends, Bec, Matilda and Russell, when the alphabetical register threw their surnames together in sequence in Fourth Grade. They were sorted into groups and given one of Aesop's fables to act out. Chris, as he then was, took charge; he cast Bec, well dressed even at nine in tights and red shoes, as the fox: Matilda, hair in plaits, as the sheep; the chubby Russell as the boat which would take them across the river. As they started to rehearse, Matilda's nose began to bleed. He will always remember the ominous drip-drip on the floor tiles, and her small, composed, freckly face a road map of dirty dark blood-trails. She sat, with a nine-year-old's indifference, the drops gliding down her nose like raindrops on a pane.

Chris rummaged in the pocket of his shorts for a scrap of grubby tissue to give her.

'I'll go and tell Mrs Hobson.'

'Don't do that. It's stopped.'

'No, I don't mean I'll dob you in. I mean — she can help.'

'Please don't tell her.'

She clutched his elbow. He stayed where he was. The two of them had just taken their first steps towards their first kiss, at a barbecue in fifteen years time.

The group agreed, with the taciturn efficiency kids sometimes demonstrate, to gloss over the nosebleed by working extra hard on their presentation. That afternoon, Chris and Matilda, Russell and Bec walked to the bus stop four abreast, and nobody else dared to speak to them. Chris was so happy he couldn't sleep; he was in a gang.

The gang of four, as they were later to be called by mutual friends, became an institution. Bec was elegant and orderly, Matilda freckled and scruffy, always in laddered tights, T-shirts too big or small; Russell slow and ponderous, constantly needing Chris's help with homework. Russell and Bec became a couple at age fourteen: Russell's chunky face, from then on, bore the permanent expression of a man who has found a woman far beyond his reasonable expectations. Chris and Matilda took a little longer. They maintained that their friendship was too precious to risk on a romance. Nonetheless it seemed a matter of time, because it was the only outcome that made sense. The four of them went on holidays together, took voluntary jobs together, were routinely invited to parties and even weddings as a group, as if they were one person. They were scarcely out of each other's sight for more than a day in twenty years.

After a short indulgence in nostalgia Xavier manages to drift off to sleep; but, as very often, his dream drags him back to Melbourne. He's in the Botanic Gardens with the gang of four, as well as Michael, Bec and Russell's baby son. Michael takes a few faltering steps, chasing a bird with a long beak; his small legs get in each other's way and he topples over. Everyone laughs, but Michael starts to cry in pain. Throughout this, Xavier is not quite immersed in the dream: even as he watches it, some part of his brain knows it is not really happening, could never happen, and makes a conscious effort to emerge from it.

Eventually Xavier is yanked out of the dream and the disappeared times it shakily presents by an urgent thumping on the door. He sits straight up in bed. The thumping stops and then restarts. Through the drawn curtains comes a subdued white glow, and he remembers the snow last night. Wearing the T-shirt and boxer shorts he slept in, Xavier stumbles to the front door and opens it cautiously.

At first there seems to be nobody there. Xavier looks down and there at knee-height is a three-year-old boy who, rather taken aback by the success of his door-thumping, is wondering what to do next. Xavier and Jamie — who lives

14

in the garden flat downstairs, and will one day develop an antibody against two kinds of cancer — look at each other.

Before either can say anything, Jamie's mother has come up the stairs and onto the landing.

'Come here, Jamie! JAMIE!' she yells, and then, to Xavier, 'Oh, I'm so sorry!'

'That's fine,' says Xavier.

'What are you doing bothering the man?' she reprimands her son, who spiritedly resists her attempts to take his hand, 'Come on.'

Jamie yells something about the snow.

'Yes, we'll go out in the snow as soon as Mummy's parcel is delivered.'

Jamie shakes his head and hits a radiator with his little fist; the parcel is nowhere near a good enough excuse. He moans and skips about like a dog on too short a lead.

His mother, whose name is Mel, grimaces at Xavier.

'I'm really sorry.'

'It's fine,' says Xavier.

They look at each other for a few seconds, uneasy. Mel is embarrassed because this is yet another instance of her having failed to control her son. Xavier feels awkward because, even though Mel knows that he works nights, there is something shaming about having just woken up when the other person has clearly been awake and dressed for some hours. Mel feels like a poor parent because there is no father to take Jamie out in the snow, because her marriage ended in ill will last year, and she hasn't yet stopped feeling that everyone aware of this fact is in

15

possession of a negative opinion of her. After all these embarrassments have been played out in silence, the two of them smile at each other sheepishly and Mel disappears down the stairs with Jamie in reluctant tow.

Jamie has a track record of misbehaviour dating back to long before Mel's husband left; almost back to the night, which Xavier remembers well, when a black cab pulled up outside and the soon-to-be-separated couple triumphantly emerged with their new treasure in a Moses basket. Xavier, who had a night off from the radio show — so it must have been a Friday or Saturday — marvelled at how tiny a human could be, and how this inert thing, his fingernails almost too small to see, could have a whole complicated life mapped out ahead of him. That is, if lives *are* mapped out in advance, which Xavier often likes to believe they are.

Almost from that first night, the new resident of 11 Bayham Road began to make an impression. When Xavier came back from the show at four thirty in the morning, the lights would always be on in the garden flat, and the silhouettes of the weary first-time parents would flicker against the curtains. He would hear the husband, Keith, going leaden-footed to work in the morning, and their tired arguments in the early evening. But Jamie's specific aptitude, beyond mere noise-making, was for mischief. He ate the front page of the newly delivered phone book sitting in the entrance hall. His pudgy little fingers tweaked a dial and reset the electricity meter to zero, baffling the man who came to read it, and eventually bringing a fine on all the residents. He would lie in wait on the stairs and ambush visitors with blows to the knee from a toy power-drill or fire engine. Most alarmingly, he has recently developed a habit of darting outside, whenever the door is open, and making as if to run onto the busy road that runs past the house with its three flats stacked on top of each other.

He is trailed everywhere by his mother, always three seconds behind, scrambling to keep the latest object out of his mouth or impair his progress towards a new hazard, and grimacing apologetically at whoever is there to witness.

There's no going back to sleep now, thinks Xavier, even though he only went to bed so recently. He listens to the cries of children, a little older than Jamie, outside. Most schools in the area are closed. There is no sound from the flat above: Tamara, the council officer who lives there, would normally have left by now, clip-clopping past Xavier's door in her heels. But like more than half of London's workforce, today she will not be going in to work. Today is an unusual day.

The kitchen sink is a nest of unwashed cups and plates, the cupboards contain various food items past the peaks of their careers. Xavier has rented this flat for nearly five years, and in his hands it has, if not deteriorated, then at least fallen into a sort of torpor. Maybe if I had a girlfriend I'd make more effort, Xavier thinks, and remembers tonight's speed-dating arrangement. Boiling the kettle, he rues Murray's

17

persuasiveness, or whatever it is, sheer pathos perhaps. The event, like all singles nights, has an anticipatory ring of grimness about it. Perhaps it'll be called off, because of the weather, but he doubts it: the sort of people bold enough to sign up for dating events are unlikely to be deterred by a freeze, he thinks, even one of this severity.

Early that afternoon Xavier leaves the flat to buy groceries. The sky is just a colourless mass hanging over London, quiescent, as if faintly embarrassed by its outburst last night. The pavements are slick with ice patches between carpets of squelchy, footmarked sludge. The air is cold to the touch like cutlery in a forgotten drawer. Xavier keeps his hands inside the sleeves of his overcoat. The owner of the corner shop, a cheerful paunchy middle-aged Indian man who will die in three years' time, puts Xavier's items into a blue plastic bag before Xavier can say that he's brought his own. Not wanting to seem petty, Xavier doesn't mention it.

On his way back down the hill Xavier becomes aware of a disturbance on the other side of the street. From a clump of black jackets rises a hoarse chorus, the carefully modulated voices of teenage boys, who are collected around what seems to be a package of some sort on the floor. As he gets closer, Xavier can see that the package is actually another boy, wriggling and squirming as five other youths take turns to drop snow on his head. The felled boy, who is slightly smaller than the others, gives a shrill yell and tries to get to his feet, but each time he is pushed back down by one of the bullies. His yells become honking

18

sobs of misery. One of the biggest lads steps away and bends down to pick up a two-glove load of snow, which he packs down between his hands and then dumps on the victim's head. There is a collective cackle. The victim now looks like a dismantled tent spread out at the feet of his aggressors, half-obscured by chunks of snow.

Xavier takes a furtive glance around: there is no one else to intervene here. He advances towards the group. Scrambling for more snow, they pay him no attention.

He clears his throat.

'You should stop that,' he says, his normally resonant voice sounding reedy and hesitant in the cold air.

A couple of the boys look up. Xavier feels a shiver go through him: they're older and more substantial than they looked from across the street, and he'd have very little chance if they all turned on him at once.

'Fuck off,' says one of the kids.

'Leave him alone,' says Xavier.

Now all of them are looking at him.

'What are you going to do?' The ringleader, who issues this challenge, has a beginner's moustache, mean eyes, a slack, contemptuous mouth.

Xavier hesitates.

One of the other boys makes as if to charge him, taking four or five quick steps with his fist outstretched. Xavier flinches and all the boys laugh. Xavier has already had enough of this situation and wants to be out of it. He's well into his thirties, these boys are less than half his age; and yet, he thinks, irritated, I'm afraid of them.

'Just leave him alone,' he says again, but then turns and walks away, his cheeks flushing at the sound of raucous, triumphant laughter over his shoulder.

He leaves the scene as quickly as he can, not looking back to see the continued tormenting of the boy. Reaching the safety of 11 Bayham Road, he slams the door and shakes the snow off the bottom of his trousers and walks up the stairs, past the ground floor flat where Jamie is being pacified by a TV show. 'Here we go, here we go, here we go again!' Xavier hears a woman sing in a strained, hectic voice.

During the afternoon he looks back on the incident with discomfort, feeling he could have done much more. Of course, he could also have done much *less*: he might have ignored the entire scene. But perhaps that would have been better than such a half-hearted attempt. He wonders what state the boy got home in, and then immediately dismisses the speculation. He coaxes the gas hob into a spitting life and puts a pan of soup on to heat.

Perhaps trying to make a dent in the residual guilt left by the event, Xavier devotes a portion of the afternoon to catching up with some of the emails sent by his listeners. He always gives an email address after the show, for the many people who don't get through on air, and his listening duties now extend well beyond the boundaries of the show itself. Xavier always tries to limit himself to one personal reply per correspondent, to avoid getting drawn into long exchanges with people he doesn't really know, because there just isn't enough time; after that, he sends a stock response directing the writer to other sources of help. Again, perhaps he could do more, but on the other hand he could ignore the emails altogether, if he were so inclined.

Monday is the heaviest day for emails: the weekend's expanses of free time can provoke some worryingly detailed confessions, some particularly vivid expressions of loneliness. This afternoon, most of the appeals are of a more practical nature.

Xavier, what would you do if your wife was hell-bent on wearing a bikini, but you wanted to tell her — gently — that she didn't have the figure for it?

I need your help. I have debts of more than £50,000. My wife doesn't know, nor do the kids, nor does anyone.

He challenges the bikini victim to decide whether it is really his *own* vanity that's at stake; he encourages the debt victim to come clean to his wife.

Troubled people have always instinctively sought Xavier out, or he has attracted them by some accidental magnetism. He's the sort of person who always ends up hearing a taxi driver's grievances, nodding sympathetically at the woes of a suddenly loquacious stranger in a lift. Perhaps it helps that women find him handsome (there's often something seductive about confidences, even very awkward ones), or perhaps it's just that he has the rare skill of keeping quiet. In any case, Xavier was accustomed to listening to people well before it formed part of his job — indeed, the habit developed when he was still known as Chris.

Once, in his twenties, Chris talked to a complete stranger in the street for more than an hour. It was an early October night, and Melbourne was tuning up for the long summer ahead. The air was lush with the hint of heat, the sky a gently paling blue, with an even paler moon hanging lazily in it. Chris's arm was around Matilda's back: not yet an official couple, they were in a tantalizing period of affectionate touches, in-jokes and pet names. He could feel the joint of her bra through the old Nirvana T-shirt she wore. At the corner of Brunswick and Johnston Street the three of them went one way and Chris the other, to wait for a tram.

At the stop was a homeless old man, wearing a baseball cap and with a can of lager in his hand. Chris said a polite hello and the two of them stood quietly for a few minutes, watching trams rattle up the other side of the street. A girl was pasting posters for a rock band on a brick wall behind them. Chris thought about Matilda, whom he'd been to watch in a trampolining competition the previous day. Each time she sprang skywards, he imagined leaping up and catching her mid-air. The old man started to sing quietly to himself, glancing amiably at Chris. He seemed like a drunk, but a harmless one: one who'd had so much booze in his life that he could never really get drunk any more, but would never seem entirely sober either.

He winked at Chris.

'Had a good day?'

'Not so bad. Just went to a film.'

'A film!' The old man chuckled. 'Do you know how long it is since I went to a film?' He wiped his mouth with the back of his hand. 'It would be twenty years, I reckon.'

Not knowing how to respond, Chris asked, 'How . . . how has your day been?'

'You know,' said the stranger, 'I'm eighty years old next month. Hell of an age, isn't it!'

'It's pretty good,' Chris agreed.

'When you get to my age, there are a lot of things you don't want to think about. So what I do is, I have a vault in my brain where I put all that stuff. See what I mean?'

He fumbled with a cigarette, his hand shaking as it coaxed a worn lighter out of his jacket pocket. Chris took the cigarette and lit it for him.

'I just say to myself, that's in the vault now,' the man continued. 'And I never let myself go in there. It's locked. It's locked even to me. I don't know where the key is.' He grinned at Chris, showing a surprisingly good set of teeth.

Trams went whirring by. Over the next hour the man told Chris that his wife died young and his brother, an Anzac, was killed in action in 1944. His sons, both of them, turned out disappointingly: one could have been a football player but was too lazy, the other went to France and got into, as the man put it, 'you know, drugs and art'. The man's business, a shop selling groceries, was squeezed to death over the course of a couple of decades by the advent of chain newsagents, 7–11s and all the rest. The man realized as he got into his forties that he was attracted to young boys, and would never be able to satisfy such a craving. He embezzled a sum of money in the mid-seventies, to boost his business, and when it came to light more than ten years later it was one of his best friends who went to jail. And so on.

'Yep, pretty much most things have gone wrong,' the old man concluded with another of his toothy grins. 'And I know it all happened — I just told you all about it, right? But I don't think about it. I don't go in the vault. See what I mean?'

Chris asked, 'Are you ever going to open the . . . vault? Like, to get it out of your system?'

The old man lit another cigarette and coughed and grinned.

'When I know I'm going to die,' he said, 'maybe in the last hour, I'll open it up and have a good think about everything, and I'll think well, it's over now, what the hell was I worried about?'

When the next tram came past, the old man, his eyes suddenly watery and imploring, took Chris's sleeve and asked him for a dollar. Chris gave him a ten-dollar note and boarded the tram.

As the four-way friendship became older and more complex, he was called upon more and more to be the unofficial leader of the gang of four, its most capable pair of hands. Often, it was

24

Russell who needed help: he couldn't seem to stay in a job, not even a job where he had to dress as a carrot and hand out leaflets for a juice bar; he never had any money; Bec couldn't get pregnant. Chris's twenty-year friendship with Russell was, in many ways, good preparation for working with Murray: similar men, slightly overweight, hapless, inspiring goodwill and a certain foreboding, like sporting competitors everyone roots for but fully expects to lose.

In bed one day, Matilda claimed that during their fifteen-year period of platonic friendship, nothing had made her want to tear Chris's clothes off more than — she couldn't find better words — his sheer helpfulness.

'What, you're turned on by me being nice to other people?'

'By you being a nice man in general. Is that so strange?'

'So I could have skipped all the other stuff I did to impress you, all the clothes I bought, and trying to enjoy *Pretty Woman*? I could have just helped old ladies across the street till you slept with me?'

She laughed. 'Please don't spoil the illusion.'

Xavier looks out of the window at the cheerless early evening. The cars, still caked in snow, look like animals mooching in a frozen field. A middle-aged couple, in matching red raincoats which look too thin for the weather, cling onto one another for support, inching along the slippery pavement. Xavier wonders whether any of the women at the speed dating will notice this supposedly attractive kindness of

25

his, and indeed, whether he still has it. He wishes that he hadn't agreed to accompany Murray tonight, and wonders if there is still a chance it might be cancelled after all.

★ ★ ★

But the event is, as he guessed all along, unaffected by the adverse weather. Six or seven people haven't made it, but a handful more have turned up to take their places, thanks to the paucity of other attractions in Central London on this snowbound night: cinemas and restaurants are closed because of staff shortages. The venue is a nightclub with plush velvet sofas and low lighting. A square of tables is laid out on what would normally be the dance floor.

Murray has attacked his dense loops of curly hair with an inexpertly applied payload of gel. He wears a bright red shirt: dark patches are already collecting around the armpits. He looks relieved to see Xavier. The socializers throng awkwardly around the bar until the MC, a good-looking black man in a suit, begins to speak into a cordless microphone.

'OK, guys. You've each been given a number.' Murray is 3; Xavier 8, not 11 as he would have liked. 'In a minute I'm going to ask you to find the table with your number on. You'll be joined by your first date. Each time the siren sounds' — he gives a blast on what sounds like a car horn ripped from its vehicle — 'the guys move on to the next table. At the end of the night you write down the number of anyone you want to

26

see again, and we'll hook you up with them. Who's up for it?'

If the MC is expecting a roar of approval in exchange for this hurried spiel, he's disappointed: the participants shuffle and mutter amongst themselves.

'Good luck,' says Xavier to Murray, patting him on his meaty back.

Over the next hour and a half they make their rounds of the room at the command of the klaxon, which sometimes comes as an interruption to the three-minute date, but more often as a welcome release. Each time it sounds, there is a collective scraping of chairs and a self-conscious mass movement and resettling at the tables. The whole thing feels like a series of pre-written transactions, like a scripted exercise rather than an exchange of emotion: which is probably, when Xavier comes to think about it, precisely what attracts people.

4: So what are your . . . hobbies and interests and things?
Xavier: I play Scrabble.**4:** Scrabble?
Xavier: Yes, in tournaments. Competitive Scrabble.
4: There are competitions for Scrabble?
Xavier: Yes, it's —
4: Isn't it just about who knows the longest words?
Xavier: Not necessarily. There's quite a lot of tactics. Like, for example —
4: I'm not *that* interested.
Xavier: Oh.

27

9: What job do you do?

Xavier: I'm, er, a film reviewer.

9: Cool. What films do you like?

Xavier: Er . . .

9: Have you seen the *Harry Potter* films?

Xavier: No.

9: You should see them. So, anyway, you sound Australian, like me?

Xavier: Yes, I'm from Melbourne. But I live here now.

9: Why did you decide to leave? Prefer it here?

Xavier: It's a bit of a long story. Something happened and I couldn't really live there any more.

9: Wow. So, anyway, do you find people here are really hard to talk to?

12: I'm a professional cleaner. I work two days a week for a hotel chain. I take on one-off jobs for all sorts of corporate clients. And then I also do weekly visits on a private basis. I charge twelve pounds an hour. Which is a lot for a cleaner. But I'm an excellent cleaner. Sorry, I'm talking away here. I'm terrible for talking. Especially with someone new.

Xavier: I need a cleaner. My flat's a mess.

12: I could come on Saturday.

Xavier: All right. I'll text you my address.

12: Terrific.

Xavier: Well, we should get on with the, er . . .

12: I think the horn's about to go.

22: Your voice sounds familiar. Why would I recognize your voice?

28

Xavier: I don't think you would.

22: Are you on the TV or something?

Xavier: No.

22: Oh. To be honest, I actually have a boy-friend. I'm just here to support a mate.

Xavier: So am I.

22: Really? Which one?

Xavier: Over there. In the red shirt. Curly hair.

22: Oh right. I had quite a nice chat with him. That stammer, though . . .

Xavier: I know.

There's a palpable relief in the air when the final 'dates' are over and the event lapses into a conventional singles night, the area around the bar playing host to less constrained versions of the conversations held over the tables. A DJ starts playing club remixes of sixties classics, occasionally interrupted by the compère encouraging everyone to 'get on the floor'. Xavier finds Murray, whose shirt is now unbuttoned at the top. His hair has separated into two broad camps, some of it still held in formation by the gel, other areas springing up in sprigs of resistance.

'And now the joys of the expensive bar,' says Murray.

'How did you go?' Xavier asks him.

'Ner, ner, not bad. Couple of people der . . . definitely interested. So we shall see. We shall see. You?'

'Well, I booked a cleaner. So the evening wasn't entirely wasted.'

It's ten o'clock already and they'll be on air at

midnight. Xavier goes outside to arrange a taxi while Murray queues at the teeming bar for drinks. It won't be the first time they have done their show under the moderate influence of alcohol. Outside on the pavement, Xavier can still hear the bassy thud of the music inside. He thinks of the four hours in the studio that lie ahead and then perfunctorily reviews the events of the day. The argument with the boys in the snow still bothers him, but he tells himself to toughen up and stop thinking about it. He can't look after everyone in London. Besides, it's already in the past.

2

Sometimes, Xavier doesn't feel like going to sleep when Murray drops him off at half past four in the morning. He sits in the lounge in front of the obscure war films shown in the early hours, or tunes into twenty-four-hour news stations and stares at the headline strip running endlessly along the bottom of the screen, with its telegrammatic dispatches: *ECONOMY 'TO GET EVEN WORSE', PRESIDENT'S SURPRISE IRAQ VISIT, TRIBUTES TO FORMER NOBEL WINNER.* He watches the bright-eyed Americans chew voraciously over every morsel of news and hook up with on-the-spot reporters nestling in every war zone in the world. When Xavier tries to picture the Gaza Strip or Afghanistan it's as a hive of reporters and camera crews, jostling for a sight of conflict.

Sometimes he puts on the computer and works in his study. The radio show pays enough to cover the meagre rent of his flat, which has never gone up in the years he's been here: the landlady is married to a millionaire and can barely be bothered to collect the money at all. But as much to keep himself busy as anything, Xavier takes on film reviews for various London publications, and writes regular magazine columns for a nationwide network of worriers.

The habit of staying up at peculiar hours began as a ruse to sidestep the queasiness of being so far from home. He'd taken the job as a runner because it was somehow comforting to know that Bec and Russell and Matilda were awake, back in Melbourne, at the same time as he was; it made the separation less jarring. This was on his mind when he made the remarks which were to seal his place as a regular on the show.

A caller was bemoaning his failure to settle in London, the feeling that everyone else was going relentlessly about their business. Xavier, who was meant to sit there and say as little as possible, couldn't resist chipping in.

'I've had that experience myself. I only moved here recently, and it's been quite lonely. But, you know, nobody in London really feels they fit in.'

He added, 'My dad used to say: remember, mate, nobody in this world knows what they're doing. Everyone is just getting away with it.'

'Wer, wer, wise words!' said Murray joshingly, but the incoming emails showed that listeners *did* consider them wise words, and before long, people were calling in and specifically asking to speak to Xavier. Without ever acknowledging it, the two of them gradually traded places, until it was Xavier who sat in the right-hand chair with the big green microphone, and Murray who flicked the switches.

Xavier has got used to the particular sounds of the night: the gurgling outbursts of Jamie downstairs and Mel's almost instant shushing and placating; the creaks of Tamara or her boyfriend walking to the bathroom and back. Now and again there are more suggestive sounds

32

from upstairs, sobs or short angry cries or thuds and thumps, which he assumes are the couple making love. Then there are the sounds made by the building itself: its creaks, sighs and rattles as the central heating shuts down and comes to life again, as its fibres contract and expand minutely in the cooling and warming air, as if it were an old, mentally absent individual muttering to itself as the night went by.

And then there are the noises from outside, from all London's late-night-and-early-morning people: the odd drunk hollering as he lurches down the street, the purring of the first vehicles — taxis taking businessmen to Heathrow, perhaps, or delivery lorries stocking the area's many grocery shops with faddish vegetables. At half-past seven Tamara's chirruping alarm heckles her out of bed, the shower gushes, her heels clop across the floor. Downstairs Jamie's demands acquire a steely ring with the confidence-boost of the light outside: there are crashes as he hurls things to the floor and Mel pads about limiting the damage. The streets outside fill with tight-faced commuters, buses rumble up the main road packed with people avoiding each other's eyes, and the hyperactive chatter and cackle of breakfast DJs — who arrived at work shortly after Xavier left — pours out of radios citywide. Once his building has emptied and the streets ease into the beginning of their mid-morning rhythm, Xavier, like the other night-people, the heartsick, those with digestive problems or disturbed consciences, finally goes to sleep.

* * *

Calling in to their show that night, to contribute to a new feature called 'For the Very First Time', is an old lady from Walthamstow.

That's how she introduces herself: 'I'm Iris, and I'm an old lady from Walthamstow.'

Xavier and Murray exchange grins.

'May I say first of all how much I'm enjoying your show. I found it quite by accident.'

'Thank you, Iris,' says Xavier, 'and what are you up to at this late hour?'

It's something of a running joke on *Late Lines* that Xavier always acts surprised that his callers are awake, expressing a sort of avuncular concern at their lack of sleep.

'Well, now,' says Iris, ten miles away on the phone, 'I've been reading *The Decline and Fall of the Roman Empire*.'

'And how far have you got?'

'I'm on page 300,' says Iris, 'and so far — '

'Don't spoil the plot!' Xavier cuts her off. 'I don't want to know how it ends!'

Iris giggles — this is exactly the sort of joke his audience likes — and Murray honks his amusement.

'And now, what 'first time' are you going to tell us about?'

'Well, now. I was going to talk about the first time I saw the love of my life.'

'Perfect. When was this, Iris?'

'It was in 1950. I served him in a shop, a grocer's, just down the road from here, I mean, it's long gone, it's a pizza place now. I was

34

. . . well, fifty-eight years ago, so I would have been nineteen. His name was Tony. I plucked up the courage to ask him his name the third time I saw him, when he came in for sprouts. But this first time, I didn't even speak to him. He just watched me put his vegetables in a brown-paper bag. And then, as he was handing over the money, he dropped it on the counter — I remember I couldn't help wondering whether he was nervous, you know, whether he liked me. And we both bent down to get the coins at the same time and our heads banged together! Whack!'

'Ouch!' says Murray.

'And so did you ask Tony on a date in the end,' asks Xavier, 'or did he ask you?'

'Ah, no, bless you, no, we never went on a date.' Iris laughs. 'I saw him several more times and chatted to him, and he was wonderfully funny, and a real gentleman. He came in wearing a trilby once, just to make me laugh. And once, he asked how I was and I mentioned I was gasping for a cup of tea. Half an hour later he comes back with a mug which he's made at home, and brought all the way down the street! There was even a biscuit!

'But then after about three months, he moved away — got a job somewhere, I suppose — and never came back.'

There's a second-long pause.

'But I thought you said he was the love of your life?' Xavier says.

'Well, yes, he was, I think,' reflects Iris. 'I mean, I thought about him so many times, I

35

never forgot him. And in the end of course I married a chap who was perfectly fine, we had twenty-eight years and then he died. Still, I could never escape the idea that perhaps the right man had been this other fellow, Tony, all along.

'But then . . . ' Iris continues.

Murray is grimacing and making his 'wrap it up' signal, which Xavier bats away with a hand.

'Then, last year, I saw him in the street, Tony. Walking along with a stick. You couldn't mistake him! Still a lovely head of hair, bright white now. I said hello and introduced myself and he remembered me. He told me he'd moved to Leeds in 1951 and married and had children and then they'd moved back to London some years later. His wife had Alzheimer's disease, and he had just popped out to get some things for her. We shook hands and that was that.' She coughs. 'But it was nice to see him again.'

Xavier blinks and clears his throat.

'And you didn't find out where he lives, or . . . ?'

'Well!' says Iris, in a sprightly, but rather tight voice. 'It's been fifty-odd years!'

'But aren't you anxious to strike up the friendship again?'

'Oh, well, at my age!' says Iris.

'Nonsense. If you've got time to read *The Decline and Fall of the Roman Empire* . . . '

'Perhaps you're right,' she concedes, amused.

'Well, let's put a call out on *Late Lines* tonight,' says Xavier. 'Tony, if you're listening, Iris would like to see you again. At least for a cup of tea and a biscuit.'

'Thank you, Xavier, ever so much,' says Iris. 'And now, listen, I've taken up enough of your time. Keep up the good work with the show!'

'Let us know how you get on, Iris, and call again soon. This is *Late Lines*. Here are Simon and Garfunkel.'

'Two for the price of one!' adds Murray, who has used this small joke many times.

They sit there in silence for half a verse of 'Mrs Robinson', looking out at the car park. Although the air is still raw outside, the snow has mostly been trodden out of existence, with only a few isolated banks, in shady spots, continuing the fight.

'Imagine having that on your mind for fifty years,' says Xavier.

'Or she could just be delusional,' Murray suggests.

Xavier looks at him and sighs.

'Hey,' Murray asks, 'wer, wer, wer, was there any feedback in your email from the . . . from the speed dating?'

'Feedback?'

'You know. Did anyone get in touch? Any of the . . . ? The girls?'

'Oh. I haven't even checked.' This is true. Xavier had pretty much forgotten the tawdry night in Camden. He did supply an email address for any interested parties to contact him, but one he almost never checks. 'I confirmed a booking with the cleaner, though. What about you?'

Murray tugs his hair and cocks an eyebrow in an attempt at nonchalance.

'Nope. Ner, nothing yet.'

'And did you send emails to any of the women?'

'Nine of them.'

'Nine out of the twenty-five?'

'Got to keep your options open.' Murray shrugs. 'The, the, they've not got back to me yet either.'

The Simon and Garfunkel song reaches its final chorus. After this there will be adverts. Murray mimes drinking from a cup and, when Xavier nods back, goes out to put the kettle on.

Xavier quickly slides into Murray's seat, in front of the computer, and opens the email account in question. Half-buried among transparently fraudulent offers of free money, he notices a message. It's from a girl, the fellow Australian he met at the dating night. She says she thought he was cute; she wonders if he wants to *catch a movie*.

He's had more amorous messages from his listeners, but even so Xavier is momentarily pleased at the idea of being sought out like this. His memory of her is imperfect: she was quite short, with dyed black hair, very white teeth, he recalls, and a short skirt. The wording sounds a faint alarm: Xavier is slightly suspicious of people who talk about *catching* movies, as if they were attractions floating by on the breeze, as disposable as pieces of confetti. And anyway, the message is four days out of date now. All in all, he's not sure he will call the Australian girl, but it's nice to be asked.

As Xavier is reading the message a second time, Murray re-enters, propping the door open

38

with his foot and twisting inelegantly through the space with a coffee in each hand.

'Caught you checking your mail! I knew you cer . . . couldn't be as cool as you made out!'

'Fair cop,' says Xavier, and is about to mention the email, but something in Murray's ever-rumpled appearance deters him: it's all too easy to imagine him at home, opening his inbox with an unshakeable optimism which, deep down, he knows is ill-founded.

'No luck, anyway,' Xavier says, quickly shutting down his email. 'No replies.'

'You and me both, then,' says Murray. 'Wer, what is it about us?'

'It could be the fact we're awake when everyone else is asleep?'

Xavier sees a solitary car winding its way out of the car park, probably driven by a caretaker relieved after a six-hour circuit of the draughty corridors.

'But I only told a couple of people that I'm on the radio. I didn't want them to be freaked out by me being wer . . . well known.'

'Or maybe we're just a couple of ugly fuckers,' Xavier adds, and feels guilty at the gratitude, the complicity, in Murray's laugh.

* * *

Late the following afternoon, Xavier is leaving the house to visit the corner shop when he meets Tamara from the flat above coming the other way. He only really knows her name from her mail, which sits in the communal entrance hall.

Xavier always picks up and leaves Mel's letters outside her door, Tamara's outside hers. Tamara only moved in a few months ago and most of their conversations have been like the one that occurs now:

'Hi there!'

'Hi . . . '

'Just off out to the shop?'

'Yeah.'

'I could have picked up something for you,' says Tamara briskly as if there has been a regrettable logistical lapse.

'Oh, it's fine. The walk will do me good,' says Xavier.

'Up to anything nice tonight?'

'Working,' he says.

Although they've had many versions of this chat, she's never asked what he does for a job, which suits Xavier nicely. He's not sure why exactly he doesn't like people knowing that he is Xavier Ireland, from the radio. Someone like Tamara, a council officer in her late twenties, in bed by ten, with a boyfriend, is unlikely to have heard of him. Anyway, so what if she had? There's something about the anonymity of the show that he values, though: something important about maintaining a division between the people who tune in and solicit his advice, and the people who can hear his choice of TV show, and his bath water escaping through the pipes.

'What about you?'

'Going to stay in and have a quiet one,' says Tamara. 'Telly and a bath. Too cold to do anything else!'

40

'It *is* cold,' Xavier agrees.

Around now is where the conversation normally falters.

'Well, have a nice night!'

'And you!'

And up the hill he continues, while Tamara's heels carry her down to 11 Bayham Road.

That evening, watching a news-discussion show on TV, Xavier feels an obscure but palpable loneliness chewing gently at him. He catches himself daydreaming about Matilda cooking, naked but for a pair of boots, on one of many hot, drowsy afternoons in their apartment in Melbourne. As comfortable nude as clothed, she would drive him mad by wandering around the place with no cover except the gauze of freckles over her shoulders, as she took work calls on the phone. He loved being the only one to know. 'Matilda speaking,' she would say in her best business voice, as if the client were the only thing that mattered to her, all the time looking him so squarely in the eye that *he* felt naked. 'What can I help you with?'

It's a struggle to reverse the trend of these daydreams once they're under way, and later in the evening, somewhat to his own surprise, Xavier finds himself calling the Australian girl who emailed him. The phone rings almost into voicemail before she answers, clearly from a crowded bar.

'Gemma speaking.'

She sounds pleased to hear from him. They make an arrangement. Xavier is reviewing a Romanian film, playing tomorrow night in a tiny

41

arts theatre on Wardour Street, for a high-end cinema magazine. It's not exactly the sort of film you choose for a date, but it is meant to be a comedy, and Gemma sounds enthusiastic.

'So I'll meet you at eight outside the cinema?'

'Awesome!'

Xavier is still not sure, even as the conversation ends, why he's done this. Normally he goes alone to press screenings, or takes Murray who arrives late and crunches his popcorn too loudly. Anyway, it's done. He's not been on any sort of date for four months. You have to make an effort sometimes, he tells himself. Even if you don't think you're looking for romance, you should be open to the possibility. That's the advice he would give on the show. But he doesn't necessarily take his own advice anywhere near as seriously as everyone else does.

★   ★   ★

On the Friday night — one of his nights off from the show — Xavier sets out for his date with Gemma. He wears a suit jacket with jeans and a black shirt; maybe it's a bit formal, but he thinks the combination works well. He glances at the mirror in the bathroom. He is, undeniably, fairly handsome — tall, blue-eyed — a fact he registers without its having any real impact on his morale: good looks, like money, fame, sexual prowess and so on, are a lot more interesting to those who don't have them than to those who do. He sports four days' stubble. Xavier has a seemingly

42

permanent air of health, a residual boon of his outdoorsy, suburban life in Australia. He has very long, delicate fingers, like a pianist, which indeed he was for a while at school, attending lessons with Russell. He gave up quietly after becoming aware that Russell was being made miserable by the comparison between them. 'I'm hardly coordinated enough to sit down on the fucking stool,' Russell complained, 'let alone play a scale.'

Mel smiles at him through the window as he leaves, and moves the tubby arm of a momentarily cooperative Jamie in a wave. Xavier walks fifteen minutes to the tube and gets the Northern Line down to Leicester Square.

At about the same time, Jacqueline Carstairs, the journalist, is setting out from her house in Hampstead to review a restaurant. She waits at the corner for a bus. She had a dinner companion lined up — her husband is away on a golf weekend, her son Frankie being babysat, though at thirteen he hates that phrase — but the friend pulled out, by text, an hour ago. She stands at the bus stop, on an evening which keeps threatening rain without delivering, wishing she had dressed for either a warm or a cold night: she's tried to hedge her bets with a dress and pullover which are unnatural partners, and the whole outfit feels overdone and hot and awkward. Her phone's battery is low, she forgot to charge it before leaving, and this again annoys her. But the real source of her bad mood, which she can feel hovering somewhere close behind her like an overzealous translator rendering every thought into a regret, is what happened to Frankie last week.

She was at home, researching an article, when the call came through from the Deputy Head.

'Are you the mother of Frankie Carstairs?'

For a moment the question sent needles of fear into every exposed point of her skin.

'Yes, I am. What is it? What's happened?'

'Well, er . . . he's been the victim of some, er . . . some bullying, that's all. A group of boys, I'm afraid, roughed him up in the snow. Actually outside the school grounds, but nonetheless, we are dealing with — '

'What do you mean, 'roughed him up'?'

'A bit of pushing and shoving, and — well, we've sent him to A and E.'

'A and E!' Jacqueline felt the needles jabbing at her again. 'Is he all right?' She resented having to ask a virtual stranger for reassurance like this.

'He's quite all right. As I say, the matter's being dealt with at our end.'

'I hope it *is* being dealt with,' was all she could say, petulantly, 'or . . . '

'I can assure you,' the Deputy Head said confidently, having anticipated this and practised his speech, 'we are taking this matter very seriously.'

When she got to the hospital, Frankie was having the first of six stitches.

'It's nothing, it doesn't matter,' he muttered. 'It doesn't matter,' he kept repeating in the back of the Volvo, sitting forlornly next to the giant *A-Z of Britain*, staring out of the window.

'You know if you are being bullied, you must

44

always tell someone . . . '

'It doesn't matter, Mum.'

But it did matter. He locked himself in the bathroom for an hour that night, didn't come down to dinner, and pretended to be sick to get out of school later that week. Jacqueline felt more and more ashamed of herself as the days went by. Hadn't she hoped, on that snowy day, that his school would stay open, so she would have a few extra hours of solitude — even though at thirteen Frankie was perfectly capable of keeping himself occupied? And hasn't she in general allowed her husband to do more than the lion's share of parenting duties recently, citing pressures of work? What kind of mother is so hell-bent on writing 2,500 words on Chilean wine that her son comes home with his cheek split open? What kind of mother has a Writers' Guild award on her mantelpiece with a press cutting praising her *lucidity of thought and prose*, but can't work out what to say to her downhearted son as he sits at the kitchen table toying with a forkful of peas? And is now flouncing off to review a restaurant in Soho — called Chico's, for God's sake, she hates it already — while her son barricades himself in his room? What kind of mother doesn't know what is going through her son's head?

The restaurant's stinging review has in some senses already been written, however hard the chef may be toiling right now over a spatchcock with market vegetables served in a rich jus. It was written when Xavier failed to save Frankie from getting beaten up in the snow.

* * *

Gemma's teeth are very white, like bathroom fittings in a showroom. She is pretty, thinks Xavier, the way the presenter of a TV holiday show is pretty: healthy-looking, symmetrically smiling, clinical. She is doing casual work in London for the year. She says 'anyway' a lot.

'So, anyway, this is pretty cool, reviewing films?'

'Yeah, I just do a couple a week,' says Xavier, 'alongside the, er, other stuff.'

'What else was it you said you did?'

'I work for a radio station.'

'Cool! How long have you done that?'

'I kind of fell into it when I came over here.'

'What did you do in Australia?'

Xavier looks at his shoes.

'I kind of — well, various things. What about you? When you go back to Australia, I mean? What do you want to do?'

'Oh, you know, I'll probably look for something in, like, a bar and see what comes up. I mean, my dream is to be a fashion designer, but, you know, I don't think that's going to happen!'

She laughs, as if the likely futility of her dream is little cause for worry. Xavier feels an internal lurch of unease. They're not well matched. For a second he wants to make some excuse and disappear.

'Anyway, this is a cool place,' says Gemma, looking around the cinema's small bar, its framed posters for foreign-language films with an impressed wariness like someone looking at overpriced rugs in a foreign market. Xavier's mind flickers unavoidably back to the Zodiac Cinema in Melbourne, with its colonial pomp, its plush red velvet curtains across the screen, two grand, semicircular balconies watching over the stalls, and its fanatical projectionist, who would sometimes come out and give an unscheduled talk about the film before it began.

Tonight, Xavier and Gemma are among a very small number of people in the cinema. When the lights go down, Gemma puts her hand on Xavier's. He feels an automatic fluttering, like a flag picking up a breeze, and is almost resentful at how easily it happens.

'No trailers!' she whispers in surprise, as the British Board of Film Classification certificate makes its stately appearance on the screen, the traditional introduction which in a couple of decades will seem as nostalgic, as antiquated, as the captions of a silent movie do today.

The film is called *The Non-Existent Man*, and concerns a man who suddenly finds his friends and family behaving as though he were dead. It's a political metaphor, Xavier half-gathers, something to do with the question of how a human defines himself in a society that discourages individuality.

Around halfway through, and as he's starting to warm to the premise, Gemma begins to pass comment in a series of indiscreet mutters.

'This is a bit depressing! I thought it was a comedy!' And then, not long after, 'What was the point of *that* scene?'

Again, Xavier feels in his stomach the awkward weight of a social mismatch. It's not her fault that he loathes any sort of chat during a film. She is not to know that, once, at the Zodiac, after a campaign of shushing had come to nothing, he stood up and berated a couple who had been keeping up an ironic commentary to impress one another.

'Why don't you just go for a beer!' he shouted. 'This is a fucking cinema!'

There was a ripple of applause and laughter from other punters.

The couple did, sure enough, leave before the end of the film, and the other three formed a cordon around Xavier afterwards, in case the miscreants were waiting somewhere with reinforcements. But the only person they met was the projectionist, who shook Xavier's hand and offered him free tickets for the rest of the year.

That was eight years ago, and nowadays Xavier doesn't challenge anyone, especially the girl he's brought with him on a date, however misguided a date it has come to seem. Gemma gets up to go as soon as the final frame gives way to the credits, slipping back into her bag the phone which she played with for the final twenty minutes.

'So what are you going to say in the review?' she asks as they come out into the stinging air and begin the plod down Wardour Street, where drunk people are queuing at cash machines, staggering out of kebab shops with hamper-sized slabs of meat sweating into white paper packages, and throwing themselves onto the bonnets of taxis, like drowning men at lifeboats.

'Well,' Xavier says, 'I thought it was a clever idea, but maybe a bit heavy-handed.'

'A bit what?'

'A bit, er . . . '

'It was *depressing*,' Gemma says.

Where Wardour Street comes out onto Oxford Street, two men are propping up a girl vomiting on her shoes.

'Are we going back to yours?' asks Gemma.

* * *

Not far away, Jacqueline Carstairs is coming to the end of an unsatisfactory evening at Chico's. Of course, it could hardly have been a satisfactory one, since the snowball attack on her son has been a more significant component than the food or service or décor or any other aspect of the experience. The restaurant didn't do much to help itself, though. On arrival she had to wait for ten minutes in the narrow neck of the room, constantly jostled by waiters on their way past with jugs of sangria, because the manager couldn't find her booking. When eventually seated, Jacqueline dined next to a rowdy table of executives celebrating a birthday, and felt self-conscious on her own; she cursed her friend Roz for pulling out. And then the wait for her peppers stuffed with goat's cheese, followed by the spatchcock, was long and infuriating and not really justified by the food itself, which was tasty enough, but well executed rather than exciting.

Still, as she sips a black coffee and begins to

49

draft the review in her head — *The furore over Chico's only emphasizes the dearth of world-class Spanish cuisine in the capital* — she is aware that it will not really be a review of the fare at the restaurant, but of her own mental soup. She looks around the room as it descends into an aviary, feeling a sudden disgust for the fleshy executives digesting their paella, the clatter of cutlery, the underdressed women yelping over dessert cocktails, the anonymous swipe of the card removing invisible cash, the food and drink swilling around overfed bodies, the waiters directing flatulent men towards the toilets with a weary angling of the head. She thinks of Frankie's cut face again and then, with an almost violent distaste, of the idiotically hyperbolic phrases that have filled some of her past reviews.

A restaurant like this, inevitably, lives and dies by its seafood mains.

This eatery is part of the lifeblood of Notting Hill.

The faux-classical pretensions deal a fatal blow to this unprepossessing joint.

Who the hell cares about food? Why does anyone allow her to write this nonsense, as if it is a matter of pressing importance whether a piece of sea bream has been cooked for exactly the right length of time, as if the quality of the paintings hanging on the wall of some Shoreditch café is a moral question rather than a matter of frivolous

50

taste? Jacqueline gestures in vain to try to get the bill. A middle manager dressed like a call girl totters by, almost catching Jacqueline with her flailing arm, hooting with laughter as she mimes something comprehensible only to the people on her table and barges through the door of the Ladies.

By the time the bill comes on its smug silver plate, Jacqueline has mentally composed the first scathing paragraph of the review which will appear in next week's *Evening Standard*, a review which will be unfair on Chico's, a restaurant that happened to get in the way at the wrong time. But there it will be all the same, in black-and-white.

★   ★   ★

As he sees the flat through the eyes of his visitor, Xavier registers all sorts of mini-squalors. When he first moved in he was quite rigorous about housework, as part of the general new leaf of energy and positivity he intended to turn over by coming to England, but that resolution has flagged. Some mugs haven't seen the sink for many months. There are cobwebs in the kitchen corners; the bin needs emptying, too, and gives off a faint whiff of something rancid. Then there are the cupboards with their resident semi-retired comestibles. Xavier knows there is a scrunched-up towel on the bathroom floor, and the toilet is passably clean at best. Even the lounge, where they sit down with a bottle of wine, is dusty and littered with opened but not dealt with mail. The sofa has needed replacing for years.

They make their way through the wine in the methodical manner of people aware that sex is on the cards. Gemma ransacks her limited stash of conversation-starters and the two of them labour gamely to keep each ball in the air, but they are both grateful for the distraction of an incensed shriek from downstairs as Jamie, having fallen asleep on his small arm, wakes to the impression that it has disappeared. A few seconds later Mel can be heard shuffling around.

Xavier grimaces.

'You don't like kids?' Gemma guesses.

'Sorry?'

'Do you not like kids?'

The question grabs Xavier by the throat and holds him like that for a few seconds. He sees, as if right there in the room with them, Russell and Bec's child Michael, three weeks old, in a tiny one-piece outfit, resembling the cub of some woodland animal.

'Er . . . '

'It's just, you looked like you were thinking, oh my God, that bloody kid.'

'Oh.' Xavier collects himself and the almost-vision fades. 'No, no, I just . . . just feel a bit sorry for the lady that lives down there. She's a single mum and the kid is pretty lively. But no, I do like them.'

'It must be a nightmare being a single mum.'

Xavier agrees that it must be.

'I'm no way ready to do anything like that,' Gemma adds.

That's probably good news, thinks Xavier.

When they get to the bedroom, Gemma

undresses Xavier with a practised ease and then gets him to undress her. Xavier feels what he felt when she first touched him in the cinema: a sort of reluctant arousal. She is an energetic lovemaker, she bites his shoulder and claws at his back, and he, caught up in it all, begins to enjoy himself. For a little while he forgets himself and everything, and is just a person making love to another person, like hundreds of people across the city at this time of night — like Jacqueline Carstairs' friend Roz, who cried off the dinner date to have sex with a man she met last week at her salsa class, or like the Indian shopkeeper's daughter and her boyfriend, who are about to get engaged. It feels to all these people, for a few minutes, as if there is nothing else worth doing in the world. When it's over, Xavier and Gemma lie there for a little while in the silence, listening to miscellaneous noises, the rattle of a lorry on the main road outside, a heated conversation beneath the best efforts of the TV upstairs.

Xavier goes to the bathroom and when he returns, to his surprise, Gemma is sitting partly clothed on the edge of the bed.

She pulls her top over her head and looks, coolly but without acrimony, at Xavier.

'I think I should go.'

'What? Why?'

She shrugs.

'You know . . . '

'Did I do something wrong? I'm sorry, I can be a bit . . . '

Gemma spreads her hands in a wry, rueful gesture.

'No, no, it was great, but you know.' She shakes her head vigorously, whether to express something or to reanimate her hair he's not sure. 'We haven't got much in common.'

'Well, maybe not, but . . . '

'I've had a really nice time but — you know, we both did it for the sex. We're not soulmates or whatever. So I don't really believe in staying the night and then having that whole awkward thing in the morning over breakfast. So, anyway, we should leave it there.'

He starts trying to argue, out of politeness, and then realizes that he is relieved. He gets dressed and walks Gemma down the stairs to the door, as if he had just shown her around the flat as a prospective buyer. He offers to call her a cab, but almost at the same moment she spots one at the lights, fifty metres down the road, and sticks an arm out with the confidence of someone whom taxi drivers rarely ignore.

'It was really fun,' says Xavier, and now that it's ending so suddenly he does indeed look back on the encounter with some affection.

He kisses Gemma on the cheek. She slips nimbly into the back of the car.

Although half an hour ago she had his penis in her hand, this is the last time they are ever to see each other. She will return to Australia in eight months, sleep with ten more people, then meet and marry an orthodontist named Brendon. She will have two children and work part-time in a tanning salon once they have grown up. She and the orthodontist will retire to Tasmania and die within a few weeks of each other. Xavier watches

54

the cab disappear, a streak in the dark, and turns back to the house.

★ ★ ★

Only after lying sleepless in the disarranged sheets for a couple of hours does Xavier fully feel the distinctive emptiness familiar to those who take part in one-night stands more regularly, the jolt of the transition between strangers and lovers and strangers again. Since relocating to Britain, most of Xavier's sexual encounters have been much like this, even if it's a bit unusual for time to be called quite so abruptly afterwards. There was the girl from the British Film Institute bar who approached his genitals like crockery to be cleared away, firmly but without sentiment, even muttering, 'Sorry, love,' at one mishandled manoeuvre. There was the travel agent Murray introduced him to at a party: neither of them could quite relax during sex and afterwards they admitted they were both thinking of Murray, and giggled, and then felt very guilty.

There have been others, too, but it's all been much like this: as Gemma said, no question of any connection of souls or anything nearly so dramatic; not even a *physical* connection of anything more than a few moments' duration. The final, overriding impression is of having made little more impact on each other than if they had simply shared a train carriage. He knows that it's his own doing, this incompleteness; that he holds something back, refuses to be entirely immersed, the same policy as he applies to the rest of his life these days. He knows that it's out of some reverence for old times in Melbourne, a subconscious refusal to admit that all that is really over, and he knows too that five years is an awfully long time to be so perversely disengaged with one's own life. If he were advising a caller on the radio show he would talk about 'moving on', 'living in the moment', valuing the present over the past, no doubt, and a fair number of people across the city would nod at their radios.

But, again, it's much easier to know these things than to act on them, and as he sleeps, Xavier finds himself trapped in the most revisited memory of his former life.

It was a summer party at Bec's parents'. Russell, big and square-shouldered, in a shapeless T-shirt, stood by the barbecue. Bec, tall, graceful, in a vintage grey floral skirt, was here and there among the kids, building a tower of bricks with one, carrying another to sit on the wall and look into the neighbours' garden.

Russell watched her, his eyes mournful.

'She's so good with kids. She just always has been. Even when she *was* a kid.'

It was true: as a thirteen-year-old Bec directed Matilda in schoolyard games where they ran a crèche, or were Girl Guide leaders. She would wade in her stately way into fights between slightly smaller boys and cuff the surprised aggressors, comfort the weaker ones. Her mind had been on starting a family since they were all teenagers. This was deeply unfashionable among their peer group, full of aspiring rock stars, world

56

travellers and dedicated drifters, but so were many of Bec's tastes: at school she had earned funny looks by snacking on salami or raisins instead of chocolate, she wore long skirts even in the heat of summer, she did yoga. More than anyone else Chris had ever met, she appeared to know precisely what she wanted, and not to care how her desires struck the rest of the world.

Russell swigged from his beer.

'It would just break her heart if we couldn't have one, mate.'

Chris patted him on the back.

'Of course you'll have one.'

'It's been three bloody years.'

'It takes a lot longer than that, sometimes.'

'But it's just — you know. Typical of me.' Russell's tongue flicked out fretfully over his wide lips.

'Bullshit. It's pure luck. It's nothing to do with you.'

Chris fought back the chastening memory of last summer's camping trip, how he and Matilda had joked at the ungainly sounds coming from the next tent.

'I don't think this is going to be the night,' he had whispered. 'Shall we just make a baby and give it to them?'

She'd laughed back: they were still not an official couple. There had been so many jokes about Bec and Russell's failure to conceive, and only now was it becoming apparent that this was not a joke at all.

'I just worry I'm not doing it right.'

'How can you not do it right? Are you

accidentally putting on a condom?'

Russell stared at the ground.

'They say it's — it's more likely if she has an orgasm. I don't think she normally does.'

Chris ruffled Russell's hair.

'They say a lot of things. It's all crap. It'll happen when it happens, mate. I don't reckon it'll be long.'

He wandered over to the other end of the garden, where Matilda stood clutching a cocktail glass and gazing skywards. She grabbed his elbow and pointed.

'Hey. Look.'

In the sky, which was a cloudless, almost gaudy blue, a plane, buzzing in a determined little arc, had begun streaking a cotton-wool trail. The letter C hung in the sparkly air above Melbourne.

'It's going to be your name!' said Matilda, jiggling his arm playfully.

Chris laughed.

'What, it's a C, so it's going to be *Chris*? Why the hell would someone write *Chris* in the sky?'

'Why would anyone write *anything* in the sky?'

'Well, it'll be an ad or something.'

'You're so unromantic. What will you bet me that it doesn't say *Chris*?'

'Unless you commissioned it yourself, I'll bet you whatever you like.'

'All right.' Matilda grabbed and shook his hand. 'If it says *Chris* you have to do whatever I say. If it doesn't, I'll do whatever you say.'

The pilot sliced horizontally through the air to join two upright lines into a pair of rugby posts, and Matilda cooed with pleasure.

'CH!'

'Are you sure this isn't a set-up?'

Matilda grinned.

'Where would I get the money to hire one of those guys? How do you even get in touch with one?'

Behind them, Russell and Bec were holding hands, there was laughter over a spilled beer and shouts from inside the house where a football game was on. The late afternoon was warm and good-natured and everyone else was oblivious to the tiny airborne drama.

The next letter was an R. Then an I.

'This is the best thing that's ever happened,' said Matilda, raising her glass to the spirited sky writer, hundreds of metres above.

'It could still be an advert.'

'You idiot.' She landed a series of light blows on his arm.

As the plane began the single helix that was, at a moment's glance, obviously bound to become an S, the two of them began to laugh euphorically, the way they might have laughed ten or twelve years ago, when making fun of the world still felt like an idea that they were the first people ever to stumble on.

'What are you going to make me do?' asked Chris.

She put a finger over his lips. He stiffened.

As the pilot completed his swivel into the final gentle incline of the S, Matilda took his face in both hands and said quietly, 'Kiss me.'

'What?'

'I said kiss me. Not like friends. Kiss me properly.'

Chris looked at her, her eyes huge and vulnerable as if she had caught herself doing something rash, her hair in uneven pigtails. He stared at her old-man's shirt and baggy jeans, the pretty constellations of freckles painted, as if with flecks from a fine brush, across her arms and neck and nose. He could feel himself trembling. He had known her fifteen years. She dropped her hands to her sides and looked straight back at him.

Far above them, the pilot swooped again, and on the ground the two of them turned involuntarily to see him complete a new letter: T.

'Christ!' they both said.

They watched, holding hands, for three long minutes as the far-off calligrapher finished off his message: *CHRIST LIVES*. After the tension of that first S, the second was full of bathos. Chris imagined the pilot landing the plane, hauling his cramped limbs out of the seat, looking back up at the already faded contrails of his handiwork.

'Well,' said Matilda, raising her eyebrows, 'so, I guess *I* have to do what *you* say.'

And he grabbed her and kissed her, the two of them kissing there on the porch until everyone was watching and applause broke out, applause and whistling, and all their friends saying that this really should have happened years ago.

★ ★ ★

When Xavier wakes, it takes a few moments, as ever, to realize that Matilda is not here, that she is in Sydney with her fiancé; and a few more moments to remember what happened last night.

He gets up, thinking about anything to dispel the dream: Murray's rather subdued mood over the past week, the kitchen does need a bit of a clean, the way Gemma tore her nails into his back last night, the argument between Tamara and her boyfriend upstairs — or did he dream that too? It's half past eleven. He goes into the bathroom. The crumpled towel is still lying in the corner like a tramp in a doorway.

The shower runs, capriciously veering between hot and cold as it always does at first, as if it were a performer low on confidence, needing to settle into a rhythm. As he's about to step into the tub, the doorbell rings. He withdraws his foot with a short sigh and stands, listening. There's an external bell for each flat. Xavier's and Tamara's simply read *First Floor* and *Second Floor*, respectively: Mel's, which once said *THE CARPENTERS*, now defiantly reads *JAMIE AND MEL*. Mel, of course, normally ends up answering the door for everyone, as she's on the ground floor, and sure enough Xavier can hear Jamie crashing around excitedly as she comes out into the hall downstairs. It will be a parcel or something, he thinks, and Mel will sign for it, and I can stay right where I am. Or a Jehovah's Witness, in which case Mel will say I'm out. But to his alarm, after a conversation — he hears a strongly accented female voice alongside Mel's — there are footsteps on the stairs. He pulls his boxers back on (the shower, slighted, keeps going as he leaves the bathroom) and is wearing

61

a shabby ensemble of clothes, like a temporary display in a shop, when he answers the door.

A woman stands on the threshold of his flat with a huge blue-and-yellow-chequered laundry bag on her arm. She has shoulder-length hair so blonde it is almost white. Her breasts are large and pendulous, making themselves known even through the shapeless raincoat she's wearing. She has a collection of pale freckles which give him a strange flashback to Matilda and the recently dissipated dream.

'I'm here to do the cleaning,' she says.

'Oh!' says Xavier. 'Yes, I mean — '

'Did you forget I was coming? My name's Pippa, you probably forgot that too, what with all the comings and goings that night, it was chaos, wasn't it, and that bloody DJ afterwards, what a racket!'

As she comes in, Pippa keeps talking, and Xavier takes a step back, like a boxer on the defensive.

'It was a bit of a waste of time, wasn't it, no time to meet anyone, but then what do you expect, it's the social aspect that people go for, isn't it?'

She's about his age, perhaps a little younger, which Xavier finds faintly embarrassing: it feels somehow decadent to engage a cleaner who could have been in the same school class as him. She has a Geordie accent which rips the consonants off the ends of words, and sometimes kidnaps them from the middle. Even after a few years in Britain, Xavier has never stopped being amazed by the diversity of accents he hears on the show. Pippa is standing in the kitchen doorway, casting what he can only imagine are appraising professional looks around the ill-tended flat.

'Yes, to be honest, I, er, did forget you were coming, so the place is, er, pretty messy . . . '

'Well, that's why you hire a cleaner!' says Pippa brightly. 'You don't go to hospital if you're well, do you!' He feels it's a line she has used before; everyone probably apologizes for the state of their houses. 'Where d'you want me to start?'

Xavier remembers the shower running.

'Well, I was just in the bathroom actually, so perhaps don't start there . . . '

Pippa laughs raucously as if this were a much dirtier joke than it is. She is already unpacking from the laundry bag an arsenal of spray-bottles and cans, detergents and polishes.

'I can assure you it wouldn't be anything I've not seen before! Cleaning in a hotel, you see everything!'

'I'm sure you do,' says Xavier.

'Only the other week,' she continues, the anecdote arresting Xavier as he attempts to leave the room, 'I had to clean a room a rock band had been in. They had an all-night party after their show, booze, drugs, there were probably forty people, mostly girls, of course, those pathetic creatures who attach themselves to rock stars, as if there was something impressive about poncing around with long hair and playing the guitar . . . ' (Doesn't this woman ever breathe when she's talking? Xavier wonders.) 'I go in the next day

— at two o'clock, mind, they check out two hours late, to be extra difficult, and you cannot imagine. Pools of vomit. Condom-wrappers. Bottles everywhere, I mean *everywhere*. They'd damaged the table. There was shit on the floor of the bathroom, I mean, if you're going that close to the toilet, why not go the whole hog and use it! And they'd done graffiti in the hotel information pack.' She says this as if it is the most damning offence of all. 'Drawn penises on it.

'And *then*, of course, I go down and complain . . . ' (This word, rather than being shaved down by her accent, is drawn out to a considerable, indignant length, *com-PLAY-ahn*.) 'And do you know what they said? You're the cleaner! We expect you to clean the room!'

'You didn't, though?'

'I did.' She rolls her eyes. 'I can't afford to lose the contract. But I can tell you, I was mentally punching the hotel manager in the face the whole time, believe me.'

She looks straight at Xavier.

I do believe you, he thinks.

'Anyway, I must stop chatting away, just ignore me, I'm terrible with a new person. I'll get cracking on this.'

Xavier has an idea.

'Would you . . . could you start with the study?' He indicates the little room to the left of the front door. 'It's just I'm going to be working in there this morning, afternoon, I mean.'

'Right you are, pet,' says Pippa.

She gathers up the cleaning materials in one grab, accommodating a seemingly impossible amount in each hand. Xavier makes a sort of grateful shrug and retreats finally to the bathroom where a lot of now hot water, he realizes guiltily, has sloshed away.

Standing in the shower, Xavier is relieved that he asked her to start in the study: he can shut himself in there and write the review of the Romanian film, and not become the audience for what may be a two-hour stream of consciousness. Or will it be even longer than that? He can't remember if they arranged a specific duration for Pippa's visit, he assumes she just keeps going until everything's done, but then, how long will *that* be? It occurs to him, although it's unlikely, of course, that the woman could actually be mad: he's only got her word for it that she's a cleaner. What if she goes around doing this wherever someone is rash enough to let her in? There are many unhinged people out there. Don't be so stupid, Xavier tells himself, she's got just as much reason to think *you* are insane. Look at the state of your kitchen.

When Xavier returns to his study, it has been swiftly and uncompromisingly cleaned, scattered books returned to shelves or neatly piled in corners, the laptop set up on the desk for work instead of languishing on the floor — and, he realizes after a few moments' disorientation, surfaces dusted properly for the first time in his tenure. Pippa has pulled back the curtains, revealing a hazy, pleasant early afternoon. Jamie is riding a toy fire engine in the garden, noisily impersonating a siren.

'This looks great!' he almost calls to the

kitchen, where Pippa has commenced a more serious battle; but he changes his mind — it would seem patronizing, and besides, he might be inviting another of her verbose replies. He puts the computer on and tries to start the review of *The Non-existent Man*.

Over the next couple of hours Xavier makes little progress: his memories of the film are tainted by his date's off-putting restlessness, and it's odd trying to work with someone else in the house. Pippa can be heard pummelling implements with brushes and cloths, spraying air fresheners like a policeman with tear gas. When she goes into the bedroom he experiences a renewed series of qualms, picturing her attacking his saggy pillows, folding and tidying and arranging, either side-stepping his stray underwear or (more likely, he thinks) manhandling it into the laundry basket. Once or twice he quietly inspects a room while Pippa is working on another, and the results are astonishing. The kitchen boasts an almost pained sheen as if it were a patient still weak from an operation: the surfaces look, superficially at least, like the untouched worktops seen on display in IKEA. The bathroom too is like a scruffy boy scrubbed up for a school photograph, grimacing sheepishly in new clothes. The overall atmosphere in the flat is healthy, glossy, but there is a sense of exhaustion, as if the inanimate objects are in a kind of shock at their treatment.

Pippa seems as energetic as ever when he offers her a cup of tea towards the end of her two and a half hours. She is in a long, faded black

66

T-shirt commemorating a youth athletics event.

'This is great,' says Xavier awkwardly, as Pippa, squatting on strong haunches, scrapes away at some tiny blemish on the skirting board.

'I've just done the basics,' she says. 'I'll do more of a job next week.'

So there's a next week, thinks Xavier, who — if he considered it at all — thought he was making a one-off arrangement with her.

'Have you got a Hoover, pet?'

'Yes — well, no. The lady downstairs has got one. I normally borrow hers.' The sentence exaggerates his familiarity with Mel's vacuum cleaner: it's probably a year since he last borrowed it.

'I met her before, shall I pop down and get it?'

It's at this moment Xavier realizes he has no cash in the house.

'I'll go and get it,' he says, 'but also I'm going to have to go and, er, get some money out for you, so I can pay you. I can't remember how much . . . '

'Well, I charge twelve pound an hour. So, two and a half hours, say thirty? Is that all right?'

'Yes, of course, of course it's all right,' says Xavier, ill at ease with the whole subject, with the reminder he is paying someone to do his household chores. 'I'll be back in ten minutes.' The corner shop has a cash machine, which charges £1.75 per withdrawal, the sort of modern impertinence callers bemoan on the radio show.

'Right you are,' says Pippa, rising to her feet. She's tall, only a few inches shorter than Xavier.

67

She dries her hands on her T-shirt. 'Only some people, you know, when it comes to actually paying, they get very funny and start saying things like, 'Well, I never agreed to that!' Or they just look at you like you're being greedy or something or taking the piss by asking for money at all. There's this woman I clean for in Hammersmith, right, so it takes me an hour and a quarter to get there for starters, and this woman is a bloody Pilates teacher, right, which means . . . '

Xavier hears Mel bringing Jamie in from his stint as a fireman, and senses an escape route.

'Hey, listen,' he says, 'that's Mel coming in now, so I'll . . . I'll just go and ask about the Hoover.'

'Grand.' Pippa is still tinkering, dusting the rim of the fruit bowl which houses a solitary orange. 'Don't mind me, pet. I'm terrible for talking.'

Again, Xavier has to remind himself that she is only his own age, she could be even younger, this eccentric, powerful, garrulous visitor who talks a little like a pensioner. He makes another vaguely apologetic gesture and slips out of the door.

★ ★ ★

As he listens to the whirr of the cash machine's innards preparing to spew his cash, Xavier feels rather drained. But the flat, he remembers, looks wondrous. His spirits rise at the thought of going back and having the whole day to himself in his rejuvenated home. Maybe it *would* be a good idea, after all, to have Pippa round once a week — if, indeed, he has any choice in the matter. But next time, thinks Xavier as he rounds the corner back onto Bayham Road, perhaps I'll make sure I'm out.

3

They confirm the next appointment in a brief phone conversation, during which Pippa finds time for remarks on the new American President, her sister's operation, and an account of a conversation she overheard this week: Woman one — you're sure this will go no further? Woman two — relax, there's no one here but the cleaner. Woman one — what if she turns out to be a well-connected cleaner? Then, sniggering.

'And what were they talking about?' Xavier asks, reluctantly interested, as with her story about the rock band.

'I didn't listen. Fuck them, excuse my language. I'm not giving them the satisfaction of being eavesdropped on by someone they don't think is capable of understanding them.' After a pause she adds, 'I did find out one of the women has eczema, though. Anyway, I'm rattling on, but see you at the weekend, love.'

'Look forward to it,' says Xavier vaguely.

He has a Scrabble tournament that Saturday, and will have to leave keys for Pippa to let herself in, but explaining this over the phone might open the door to another ten minutes of conversation, which is a tiring prospect. He decides to text her with the news nearer the time.

On Monday morning, Xavier is woken early

by Jamie running up and down the stairs shouting something about bears. Xavier decides to go for a walk, feeling fresh though he's had barely four hours of sleep: it could be his imagination but the bed feels more comfortable since its encounter with Pippa. He comes downstairs to find Mel apprehending her son, and outside her flat the two of them conduct their traditional exchange of abashed smiles. Xavier wonders what she thinks of his having a cleaner. Mel wonders if he noticed what a bad condition the Hoover was in; she can't really afford a new one. Xavier thinks she might have heard him having sex with Gemma last week; Mel feels bad, as usual, about his being woken up by Jamie.

'How are things?'

Mel turns a grimace into an unconvincing smile.

'He's being a little terror. The car's broken down, and he wanted to go to . . . anyway. Fine. How are you?'

'Not bad at all . . . '

The phone in Mel's flat begins to ring, offering them a reprieve from further efforts to muddle through a conversation. Seeing the look that the sound brings to her face, the look of someone eternally tackling one more chore than they can manage, he is struck by a fleeting desire to go into her flat, pick up the phone and relieve her of one tiny problem by taking a message. Perhaps there would be other things he could help with, while he was there. The idea immediately seems presumptuous and silly. This

71

isn't the radio show; his mandate to help people doesn't extend to poking his nose into his neighbours' lives. He doesn't know anything about her. Almost certainly it would seem very patronizing, and he could easily end up doing more harm than good.

Just as Mel makes as if to go and answer the phone, a door slams two floors up and footsteps thump above their heads. Mel and Xavier follow the sounds with their eyes. A man comes into view, thundering down the stairs so quickly Xavier worries he will trip over. It's Tamara's boyfriend, a short man, a regular visitor to 11 Bayham Road, and someone they are both on small-talking terms with. Today, there is no speaking at all. He forces himself through the space between Mel and Xavier, almost walking straight into Jamie, without acknowledging any of the three of them. He shuts the front door behind him so hard that it bounces open again, and Mel hastens to shut it before Jamie can seize his chance to run outside.

'Gosh!' says Xavier.

'Bit of a fight, I suppose,' ventures Mel.

And it probably was just that, but there was something in the urgency with which the man left, and the menace in his eyes as he glanced at them, which makes both of them uneasy as they part.

For the rest of the week Xavier sees nothing of Tamara, though he hears, as ever, her to-the-minute showering routine and clip-clopping out of the door. But he more or less forgets the incident, distracted by another puzzle: Murray's unusually downbeat demeanour.

In the years they've worked together, the spectrum of Murray's moods as witnessed by Xavier has been a fairly narrow one, stretching from euphoric (fairly often) to bubbly (his default position) and only down as far as what most people might call 'pensive'. In the course of the large amount of time they've spent in the studio and away from it, Xavier has seen Murray contend with difficult events — the death of his mother a couple of years ago, for example — without seeming to suffer any lingering upset. It could even be said that Murray's cheerfulness is his greatest talent: his ever-ready guffaws have got Xavier through some long stints on the radio, even if Xavier's fans mostly regard him as an unwelcome distraction.

But all this week Murray is noticeably quiet, on the drive to and from the studio, and in the shows themselves. On the Monday, when Murray normally overcompensates for the listeners' start-of-week gloom with a particular outpouring of good humour, he barely musters a single remark. Tuesday isn't much better, and Xavier begins to feel something is preying on his friend's mind. The stammer, always a yardstick of inner unrest, flares up again and again: while they are chatting during the 2 a.m. news break, it takes Murray nearly half a minute to get through the phrase 'completely changed my mind'. This in turn discourages him from chipping in on air, and Tuesday's show is so lacklustre that Xavier is almost embarrassed to think of people listening to it.

On the way home on that night, Xavier tentatively asks, as they glide down the hill to 11 Bayham Road, 'Everything all right, Murray?'

'Of course. Wer, wer, what wouldn't be all right?'

Xavier considers inviting him in for a nightcap, but doesn't quite go through with it, in the same way that he didn't quite go through with answering Mel's phone earlier in the week.

It isn't until Thursday afternoon that Xavier thinks back to this exchange and ponders the apparently throwaway question, 'What wouldn't be all right?' Really, there are so many things, in anyone's life at any given time, that might not be all right. That's one of the reasons Xavier feels at home on the radio show, where he can sample people's problems for five minutes, like a speed-dater of the counselling world, and then send them on their way with his best wishes. Outside the five-minute format, problems are far less tractable, turn out to have clauses and caveats, change shape like ink in water. It's better not to get involved at all, he thinks, than to dabble, to prod a sleeping dog into life if you don't know how to handle it once it's awake. Of course, this could be just another excuse Xavier uses to justify the number of good turns he seems not to do these days.

That night they take another call from the maths teacher with three failed marriages: that's his phrase, though Xavier tries to argue him away from it, in the process sounding — even to himself — uncomfortably close to a clinical therapist, rather than the persuasive amateur he prefers to be.

'I reckon it's quite damaging to talk of these three marriages as failures, Clive.' They're on first-name terms now; Clive has become a regular caller. 'I mean, if you look at it like that, you're not far from dismissing twenty or thirty years of your life as a failure.'

'Well, perhaps they were.'

Murray is about to say something, but Xavier, not trusting his sidekick's navigation of these dangerous waters, gets in first.

'I don't think you can ever say that, Clive. I've definitely felt like that myself before, but it doesn't get you anywhere.'

In the next commercial break, Murray, toying with the corner of a sheet of paper, says quietly, 'A mate of mine saw you with a girl, the other night.'

'A girl?'

'You were on a date.'

'Oh. Yeah. Aussie girl. I took her to a film. It didn't go too well.'

'Did you . . . der, der, did you . . . '

'Did we sleep together? Well, we had sex. It didn't get as far as sleeping. She left in the middle of the night. As I say, not a success.'

'Wer, was it someone you knew from before? From Australia?'

Xavier grins.

'No. Tiny as Australia is, we somehow hadn't run into each other before.'

But Murray, quite uncharacteristically, seems put out by the joke. 'Well, I don't know who you knew in Australia, do I? You never tell me anything about wer, what happened before you

75

came here. You cher, change the subject every time.'

Xavier puts down the BIG CHEESE mug and looks at his friend. An oversized pair of headphones sits lopsided on Murray's head, the right one lower than the left.

'Are you all right, mate? What's on your mind?'

Murray rubs the edge of the paper between his fingers.

'You ter, told me no one got in touch. From the speed dating.'

'Well, no one had at that point.'

'I'm just surprised you wer, wer, wer, wer, went on a date and didn't mention it.'

Xavier is taken aback to be on the defensive like this; again, this is all very unlike Murray, this sort of polite reproachfulness, and the stammer's little outbursts suggest that Murray is conscious of this himself.

'I'm sorry, mate. It kind of slipped my mind. Like I say, it was over pretty quickly. We're not going to see each other again or anything.'

'No apology ner, necessary. I'm just not quite my usual . . . oh, back in twenty secs.'

And before he can elaborate — if he was going to — they are back on air.

On the way home Murray chats about the blossoming career of the tennis player Andy Murray — his sort-of-namesake — and about a new scheme to fill London with electric cars, and seems, all in all, just like his normal self.

★ ★ ★

76

Having left keys in a flowerpot and money in the flat, and informed Pippa by text, Xavier leaves on Saturday morning for the Scrabble tournament. These events, a monthly fixture in Xavier's life since his first week in London, are held in a church hall in Islington, rented out by the churchwardens who need £40,000 to repair a roof which shelters a steadily diminishing number of worshippers. The Scrabble tournaments are open to the general public, in theory, but it's the same twenty or so people who always show up, and the winner (who gets £150 in cash) is almost always a Sri Lankan gentleman named Vijay. The runner-up is almost always Xavier.

At least half of the players have no chance of ever winning the competition, but enjoy taking part just the same. The players are quite a disparate bunch. One is an accountant who plays to avoid spending Saturday with her husband, one is a professor, one a plastic surgeon. There is an attractive young couple whose other interests include kayaking (Xavier knows this because the man once played the word *KAYAK* against him, for 16 points; it was a bad move, but the man's fondness for the word overcame his tactical sense). There is also a formerly well-known pop singer who had a big hit in 1987, and who now ekes out a living making appearances in clubs specializing in kitsch. Nobody ever alludes to this, or to any professional matters: one of the functions of the Scrabble group is to provide an escape from Monday-to-Friday business.

Only an A4 sheet on the door of the church

hall announces the Scrabble competition: it's not the sort of event that exerts itself to attract new customers. Xavier shakes hands with Vijay, and the kayakers and the entirely bald man who organizes these tournaments. He pays his admission money: the bald man puts it into a Tupperware container. Pretty soon Xavier is only thinking about Scrabble.

★ ★ ★

There are two main ways to play Scrabble.

The first is the way ninety per cent of people play, at Christmas when the old green box is excavated from the loft, or when a family get-together outlasts the duration of all the family's collected reminiscences, or when a rainy day destroys a summer fête. Quite simply, it involves politely tacking word after word at angles to one another: the E of a horizontal *SNAKE* becomes the base of a vertical *AGREE*, which branches out into *GREAT*, and so on, a succession of mild 10–15-point words, the players casually totting up the scores, until one of them inches in front by happening almost apologetically upon a triple-word score. This is the generally understood method of playing Scrabble, almost as a collaborative exercise in word-building rather than a contest. If you play this way against a serious player, you will always lose, as Murray found when he challenged Xavier once in a hotel, and lost five times in a row.

Xavier, as a serious player, understands the

78

second method of playing, which is to treat it as a battle of strategy, not vocabulary. The main ways to win a game of Scrabble are to make sure you score at least one Bingo (a 50-point bonus for using all seven letters at once), and to milk X, Z, Q and J for as many points as possible — these are the heavyweights of the Scrabble board, Scrabble being a sort of inverse universe in which the alphabet's least useful letters become its most precious. A player who plays a pretty word like *ICICLE* for 12 points will invariably lose to a player who puts down *JA* or *XU* or *ZA* on a triple and collects 50. Which brings us to the key to Scrabble: the two-letter words. A real Scrabble player knows them all, all fifty or so, including *JO* (a companion or sweetheart), *QI* (a word from Chinese philosophy, describing a life force, or energy), and *XI*, defined by the Scrabble dictionary simply as *a Greek letter*, and a potential match-winner all by itself.

★ ★ ★

The afternoon passes more or less as expected. Although almost all the players there are at least aware of the two-letter words, not many can match Xavier's speed: in competitive Scrabble you only get a minute to move, before the electronic timer, with an accusatory series of bleeps, cuts you off. Xavier's other main weapon is his knack for the seven-letter anagram: indeed, *ANAGRAM* (61 points, with bonus) is one of the blows with which he fells an opponent in the

79

second game; others are slaughtered by *GECK-OES* and *LIMINAL*. As time passes, Xavier can see his chief adversary Vijay making his way through the competition with similar ruthlessness on the other side of the hall. At half past five the two of them sit down together for the final. The customary £150 is at stake. The defeated players, with a couple of exceptions, crowd around the board to watch this finale: the Xavier — Vijay showdown is as much a traditional part of the afternoon as their own involvement in the earlier games.

The final is a best-of-three match. Xavier and Vijay study each other across the board, with the affection of old rivals. In the first game, Xavier gets the luckier hand: a blank and an S in the same crop of tiles allow him to spell out *ROCKETS* early in the match for a 50-point bonus. Vijay eventually assembles a retaliatory Bingo, but too late. When they shake hands, Xavier is one game up, and needs one more for the overall victory.

The second game is a far more defensive affair. Vijay holds a slender advantage from an early J which he turned into 40 points, and now begins to close down every possible scoring square. Xavier is forced to scrape short words here and there, unable to place a Bingo because Vijay's strategy congests different parts of the board until there's no room for one. Xavier shuffles in his chair, feeling hot, partly because of the pressure of the game, and partly because of the church hall's rudimentary heating system: the bald organizer errs on the side of clammy

80

warmth, rather than the dispiriting cold which church buildings of all kinds are noted for.

The crowd around the board maintains an attentive silence. When the faded pop star's phone goes off, he takes it outside to answer it. Emergency-vehicle sirens wail outside: there has been a car accident, caused by someone speeding down the hill parallel to Bayham Road. Vijay completes his suffocation of Xavier's prospects and the game is his. As usual with these two players, it will come down to a decider.

There is a brief pause for everyone to 'stretch their legs', as the bald organizer invariably puts it. The spectators chat in low tones — even though there's no need for quiet in this intermission, a certain solemnity always seems to surround the latter stages of the competition. Xavier and Vijay remain at the board, talking amiably.

'How's the studying?' Xavier knows that Vijay is researching something to do with artificial intelligence, at UCL.

'Baffling, as usual.'

Vijay is in his forties, has a boyish smile and always wears denim shirts. He's the sort of person who will be connected with academic establishments for his whole life.

'And how is everything with you?' asks Vijay.

'Not bad at all, thanks.'

This is as deep as they ever delve into one another's lives, which suits them both perfectly.

In game three, Xavier gets his nose in front and is still comfortably ahead with about thirty tiles remaining. Then, Vijay begins to swap his tiles.

At any point before the endgame, a Scrabble player may trade between one and all of his seven tiles for fresh ones, in exchange for forfeiting his turn. Everyone knows this, but most casual and even some advanced players only do so if completely confounded by their letters (all vowels or all consonants, perhaps), regarding the forfeited turn as too great a price to pay. Even Xavier only does it as a necessary measure, rather than as a way of striking out ambitiously in the direction of a new word. Vijay, on the other hand, thinks nothing of it. This is the principal difference between their approaches to the game.

As this decisive match advances, Vijay takes the seemingly untenable risk of swapping his tiles again and again. He always spends the first forty-five of his sixty seconds pondering the board, his eyebrows low over his eyes, and then with a slight lilt of one brow he nods at the bald organizer who passes him the velvet bag.

'Swapping two,' says Vijay, and delves into the bag for new tiles.

It is unsettling for any player when his opponent keeps declining his turn. Xavier can only concentrate upon building up a bigger and bigger lead, shutting down the board as clinically as he can, and hope that Vijay is either bluffing, or heading down a blind alley. For a while this does seem to be the case. Xavier collects 20 points, 23, 20 again, while Vijay keeps trading, examining the new letters with eyes that give nothing away, fingering each tile meditatively as it comes out of the bag. Some of the more studious spectators walk behind one player then the other, in turn, to have the benefit of seeing both racks of tiles, like tennis-watchers turning their heads to and fro. Xavier suspects that Vijay has the X, or J, neither of which has appeared yet, and is waiting until he can muster a seven-letter word including one of them. This is going to be difficult even for him. Xavier keeps amassing modest words until his lead is a commanding 70 points. When Vijay elects to swap yet again, there is an undercurrent of incredulous giggling, even though everyone has seen him play this way before.

But just when Xavier begins to believe he might be able to reach the finish line from here, Vijay serenely lays down the word *BANJAXED*, hooking onto the D of *PLAID* and sliding like a slick of toxic oil across a triple-word square which Xavier had thought inaccessible. With both J and X involved and the 50-point bonus, it is worth a crushing 122 points. There's a collective intake of breath and then applause. Vijay doesn't smile or crow or gloat, acknowledging the acclaim only with a very slight nod. Xavier feels a momentary plunge of disappointment in his belly. The game's as good as over now. There is more applause when Vijay confirms his victory and the bald organizer hands him the £150 in ten- and twenty-pound notes.

'Good game,' says Xavier.

'I was beginning to fear my tactics were too ambitious,' Vijay admits, pocketing his spoils.

He puts a jacket on over his denim shirt and

invites everyone for a drink at the pub, which he always does, despite not drinking alcohol himself. When Xavier wins, he too extends this courtesy to the other players.

They have one drink in the Crown and Anchor. Some people discuss the day's football results. The kayaking couple lead a conversation about Bulgaria as a holiday destination or a good place for an investment property. As usual, all the talk is general and superficial. This is one of the reasons Xavier feels comfortable among this group; even if, as is perfectly possible, one or two of them recognize his voice from the radio, the subject is unlikely to come up.

After the drink, everyone decides they should get going, and at around eight o'clock Xavier gets on a number 19 bus. He picks up a creased *Evening Standard*, which has circulated between passengers since the day before, when a shopper left it on the seat. With vague interest he studies the first thing to catch his eye: a very negative review of a restaurant in town called Chico's.

★   ★   ★

The mean-spirited write-up has an impact upon everyone at Chico's, from the insulted head chef right down to Julius Brown, the overweight teenager who, for £5 an hour, washes up in the teeming kitchen.

Julius leaves for work at 7 p.m.; it takes him an hour on a combination of buses. He'll wash up until one in the morning. He'd like a job nearer home, but every time he walks into a place to ask for an application form he sees straight away the disapproving eyes of the manager taking stock of his flabby bulk. He's tried for jobs in IT, in technical support, in call centres, jobs in places where nobody has to see you; but those, being well paid, are in demand, and as he's still at school he can't commit to full-time hours.

It has been a tiring day for Julius even before he gets to work. He managed a full two hours at the gym: an hour on the treadmill, plodding gamely above the whine of the moving platform, sweat discolouring his grey T-shirt, collecting behind his knees, in the crooks of his arms, the small of his back. He ignored the glances of people going twice as fast on neighbouring machines. Then he did two circuits of the weights, a programme of bench-presses, and finished with a series of warm-down exercises. Feeling as though his limbs were full of wet sand he trudged to the changing rooms and waited for one of the private showers, not wanting to stand in the open-plan ones, with his blancmange of a body laid bare to the critical eyes of the fitness freaks who make up most of the gym's regulars. He weighed himself; there was no change since last week.

On the way out, the attendant reminded Julius that he needed to pay for another month's membership on his next visit. She looks amused every time he appears. As he walked down the street Julius caught sight of a pretty girl from his maths class at school, a girl called Amy with tortoiseshell glasses, chatting to another girl outside the cinema: he lowered his eyes as he went by. He could hear them laughing behind him.

When he gets to the kitchen, Julius is warned that the restaurant's manager is in a 'terrific bad mood' by his slightly better paid supervisor, Boris, a Ukrainian. There is even more shouting than usual. The splenetic chef harries waiters furiously to clarify muddled orders. 'What the fuck does that say? Is that a two or a three? Fuck's sake!' The sous-chef, octopus-armed, frantically tosses vegetables in one pan, cajoles skewers of meat in another, inspects a tray of caramelized desserts and shakes his head, swearing. In and around the huge sinks, a mountain of soiled dishes is already taking form.

'Going to be a terrific bad night, man,' Boris predicts gloomily.

He's saving money to send home to his over-extended family, wishing that one day he could bring them here to see how people in London eat.

★ ★ ★

When Xavier gets home, he immediately feels unsettled: something is not right. More gingerly than usual and without any specific reason for his caution, he walks up the stairs ('Here we go, here we go, here we go again,' exhorts the lady on the TV from behind Mel's door) and enters his flat. The unease lasts a couple of minutes as he slings his coat on the bed and goes into the kitchen. Then the realization dawns: it's not that something is wrong, but something is different.

The flat has had another vicious going-over from Pippa. He'd forgotten she was here this afternoon.

Even though the place was still in pretty good shape from the improvements she made last week, its appearance has risen several more notches this time around. The stairs leading up to the flat have been vacuumed; the worn, dated carpet is almost springy under his feet. The study is spotless, everything in its perfect place. The bedcover is as smooth as the surface of a lake, and beneath it the sheets are like new paper. Gradually, still more of Pippa's efforts begin to emerge. There's a vase of flowers on the kitchen table. The vase, now scrubbed clean, had been in a cupboard since Xavier moved in; the flowers she must have brought with her. There's a bar of soap beside the bathroom sink; again, unless she dug it out of some nook he's never discovered, Xavier has the impression that Pippa supplied this herself. When he looks in the cupboards, he sees almost all the food has been rounded up and disposed of.

It's here that Xavier finds a handwritten note from Pippa. She's used a pad of paper from the study and the writing is large, full of loops, voluptuous — somehow reminiscent of her.

I have taken the liberty of binning quite a lot of your food. It was quite seriously out of date.

Over the course of the next hour, Xavier discovers more notes.

You need to buy some more mugs. A couple of these can't really be saved, not even by me.

You ought to get a lavatory brush!

I'm not sure this is any of my business, but there have been some odd noises from upstairs while I've been working. Quite a violent argument, I thought, by the sound of it. But you would know them better than I do.

There are a couple of products I'd like for next time, so that I can do some more specific cleaning. I will text you the names, if that's all right. The flowers were a cheap bunch, £4, you can pay me back next time if you agree they're a good addition. The soap is a present.

Only hours later when he climbs into bed — at a normal time for once, about midnight — does Xavier find inside the fold of his bedcover the final note.

I'm sorry if it is a bit OTT (over-the-top) of me, leaving all these notes. I've only just realized that it might seem like I'm mad. Anyway, see you next time, if you haven't called the police.

Xavier grins.
He thinks back to the two occasions he's met

Pippa, the now almost forgotten speed-date, and then last week. He tries to visualize her face, but is more successful remembering her very fair hair and imposing breasts. He wonders whether joking about being crazy isn't exactly what someone would do if they *were* crazy. It's unsettling to think she has his mobile number and is blithely talking about texting him. She seems the sort of person who might phone in the middle of the night on no pretext at all. Of course, Xavier is normally awake in the middle of the night, but even so.

He thinks for a while about the Scrabble tournament, wondering if he could have won it, had he been more daring and done what Vijay did, gambled for a bigger score, rather than trying to chip away and win by attrition. Or was it always meant to be Vijay's day, was it somehow etched into whatever scheme of things there is? But then, if there is a scheme, why did it bring Xavier here, and was everything before this a series of red herrings? Before he can begin to indulge himself in the sort of introspection he tries to warn his callers away from, Xavier reaches for the paper he salvaged from the bus and tries to immerse himself in something else. It's still folded to the 'Eating Out' page. *The furore over Chico's, it says, only emphasizes the dearth of world-class Spanish cuisine in the capital.*

★ ★ ★

Some time between midnight and 1 a.m. in the steamy kitchen at Chico's, the weary Julius

89

Brown has the strange experience of falling asleep several times while standing up, just for a few seconds, before snapping back awake. In each interval of sleeping he sees a split-second image, like a shard of a dream which has been broken off from the rest, like a single frame torn away from the millions that make up a film. He is huge, stepping over buildings. Then awake. He's back in the gym, plodding as fast as he can, but somehow he knows that the treadmill is about to speed up and send him flying off it. Then awake. He is sitting in front of a computer, with someone waiting for him to fix it, but he can't work out how to change the operating language into English. Awake again, with a plate still in his hand, streaming suds and water. Boris, the supervisor, is grabbing him by the arm.

'Hey man, tired?'

Julius nods.

'Me too.' Boris grimaces. 'I work at garage this afternoon then I'm working here tonight, then I'm back at garage tomorrow morning.'

Further forward in the building — being at the back of a restaurant is like being below stairs in an Edwardian household — the owner of Chico's, Andrew Ryan, sits in the main dining room. The flamenco guitarist who plays on Saturday nights has packed his instrument away and gone home to Hackney with an envelope full of cash. Patrons, full of meat and garlic and oil, have been sent away in cabs. Andrew Ryan is drinking whisky. He gestures to Pascal, head waiter for the night, to refill his shot glass.

Andrew Ryan, forty-eight, with leathery skin

and a yogahoned body, is angry. The review was just my fucking luck, he thinks. That bitch Carstairs. It was the same with the fucking West End play he put money into, that turned out to be a piece of shit, and now Dubai is haemorrhaging money, Jesus, and then there's Hayley costing him a fucking arm and a leg with her travels. Gap year, my arse, thinks Andrew Ryan; no one under the age of twenty-five ever does a stroke of work nowadays. Why is it that everything I have touched this past year has turned to shit, he wonders, gulping his whisky and getting up unsteadily to wander around the premises.

'You know, in Kiev, still terrific cold,' says Boris, loading another clattering rack of the industrial-size dishwasher. 'This cold is nothing. There is guy in Kiev, he pisses in the street, he is drunk, you know, and it is so cold his dick freezes to the . . . '

Julius's eyelids feel like soft cheese. Again he stumbles into a scene too brief for him to perceive; he's dimly aware of being chased around his school, late at night, by someone, maybe Liam Rollin who calls him 'Sumo' and makes farting noises whenever he passes.

'Hey, man, watch it!'

Julius jolts back to the kitchen. A plate falls from his hands and it smashes on the hard floor with an echoing crack that reminds him of the breaking of a bone.

'Man, you got to wake up,' the supervisor chastises Julius.

'Sorry.'

91

Julius is on his hands and knees, scrabbling for the jagged pieces, when a figure appears in the doorway. Julius's ears burn. He hears slow, uneven footsteps advancing towards him; Boris lets out a series of short, panicky breaths.

'What the fuck is going on in here?' demands Andrew Ryan, steadying himself with an arm propped against the wall, four paces from Julius.

Julius, feeling his shirt clinging to his back, looks up at the restaurant owner, whom he's only seen once before in his time here.

'Sorry,' he mumbles, 'I'm sorry.'

'Do you think this is a fucking game?' Andrew Ryan enquires, looking with contempt at the fleshy item crouched below him. How did this fat bastard get a job in my joint? he wonders.

'No,' mumbles Julius, collecting up the shrapnel, not looking up.

'Is it any wonder,' Andrew Ryan muses, his innards sloshing with viscous, directionless anger, 'is it any wonder we get a bad fucking write-up when we've got a bunch of clueless fucking . . . clowns in the back room?'

Neither of his subordinates, standing as if at a military court martial, ventures an answer.

'I mean is there anyone in this place that can actually get the fucking job done?'

There'll be no answer to this, either. Andrew Ryan's rage grasps for a victim. He points a nicotine-smelling finger at Julius.

'What's your name?'

'It's Julius,' Julius informs him in an undertone.

'It's what? Julie?'

'Julius.'

'How long have you worked here, Julius?'

'Eight months.'

'Look at me, you little freak! How long?'

'Eight months.'

'Any chance of calling me 'sir', what with me being the owner of this establishment?'

Andrew Ryan will look back on this, twenty years later, from a hotel room in Hong Kong — not having thought about the incident once in the intervening period — and will reflect with surprise that his younger self was an absolute arsehole sometimes, what with the drink and the drugs. He'll be an awful lot calmer in his old age; he'll wonder what happened to that poor kid. But that's twenty years away. For now, his only instinct is that of a bully.

'Sir.'

'Listen, Julius,' says Andrew Ryan. 'How much do we pay you to smash my crockery back here?'

'Five pounds an hour.'

Ryan nods, reaches into his pocket, pulls out a worn twenty-pound note and drops it onto the floor in front of Julius.

'There you are. There's a bonus.'

Julius looks up at him, uncomprehending.

'And don't come back next time. You're fired.'

'Sorry, sir?'

'You're fired. I'll speak to your manager. Your services are no longer required.'

Andrew Ryan puts his hands on his hips and shakes his head importantly. He reaches into his pocket for a stick of chewing-gum. Julius swallows. His throat is dry. He feels so tired that he could fall straight through his clothes.

'Please don't fire me.'

Ryan, who has half turned away, reluctantly looks back.

'What?'

'I need the money.'

'I can't hear you.'

Julius swallows again. He feels as if his Adam's apple is a snooker ball.

'I need the money, sir.'

'The money!' Andrew sneers. 'Do you know what, Julius, we all need the money. Some of us work very hard for our money just for some bitch to stitch us up in the papers after we bust our fucking balls to get a restaurant on its feet. Tough life, isn't it!'

Andrew Ryan is vaguely aware that he is talking as if he thinks he's in a Mafia movie, or one of those films from the eighties with businessmen in braces. He casts a final look at the doughy, abject form in his kitchen, the distraught young man he will forget the next morning and not remember for two decades, and storms through the kitchen door.

Julius Brown has lost his part-time job because Andrew Ryan got drunk and lost his temper, because Jacqueline Carstairs wrote a vicious piece about his restaurant, because her son got beaten up on a snowy day a few weeks ago, because Xavier failed to step in and help. But as far as he or anyone knows, he's simply been sacked for dropping a plate on the floor.

4

On Sunday morning Xavier lies in bed, thinking about another Sunday morning, just under six years ago, when Bec went into the labour ward at St Vincent's Hospital.

Chris and Matilda spent seven hours in a café down the road from the hospital, having lunch, coffee, then dinner, with still no news. They tried to talk about other subjects; one by one, each ran out of steam.

'Not even *I* would stay here as long as you guys,' remarked the owner, 'and it's my place.'

But as the sun began to cast long shadows over Melbourne, Russell appeared in the distance, running, limbs flailing, looking like a buffalo charging unstoppably down a ravine.

'Jesus,' said Chris.

'Fuck,' said Matilda, 'I hope everything's — '

'Boy,' gasped Russell, his shirt dark and heavy with sweat, his face glistening. 'It's a boy, it's a boy. She had a boy.'

They grabbed him, and the three of them jumped around there on the chequered linoleum floor, next to their plastic table with the latest half-drunk coffees, watched indulgently by the proprietor who, having owned a café next to the hospital for fifteen years, had seen it all before: news of births just like this one; the shell-shocked, inert faces of the newly bereaved.

He gave them a cheap bottle of champagne on the house.

'You've already spent enough for me to have a holiday.'

Russell's hand was shaking so hard that Chris had a hard time filling his glass. The gang of four was now five. Chris put his arm around Matilda's waist and they raised their glasses in a toast, feeling drunk already.

The wind brings a faint, plaintive sound of church bells from half a mile off, and Xavier grips the memory, as if physically, before he lets it go.

★ ★ ★

Not far away, the overweight teenager Julius Brown sleeps in late, only momentarily interrupted by the sound of his mother, Simone, leaving for her supermarket shift. On Sunday she works from ten till four. She divides her time between the deli counter and the checkout. (That's how she put it on her most recent CV, as if talking about summer and winter residences in different hemispheres.) When he hears the door judder shut, setting off short-lived yelps from the Alsatians next door who are pent up and hungry for drama, Julius returns gladly to unconsciousness.

Around one o'clock he sits up in bed, watches ten minutes of a documentary on wind farms, puts his computer on and then, without looking at it, rolls heavily onto his side and pulls the covers over his head.

At four thirty Simone returns from work. The shift was all right, apart from a frosty exchange with a customer whose idea of 'three thick slices of ham' was different from hers.

'You haven't been in bed all this time?'

'I'm ill.' Julius coughs, not unconvincingly. He feels as if a huge, invisible paperweight is pinning him to the bed.

'How was work last night?'

He hasn't actually thought about it until now.

'I got sacked.'

'What?'

Simone Brown takes a step into the room and surveys the bundle of her overgrown son, like a hibernating thing in its burrow. She is wearing the supermarket's regulation blue cardigan and underneath it a T-shirt which says *OUR PRICES ARE MAD AS MARCH HARES*. The marketing manager wanted checkout staff to wear novelty rabbit-ears for the month, but his suggestion was rejected.

'I got sacked.'

'Oh, Julius.'

'I didn't do anything.'

'You must have.'

'I dropped a plate and it smashed.'

'They sacked you for that?'

'Yeah.'

Simone hears paws scraping imploringly at the inside of her neighbour's front door, and the dogs begging in peppery yelps to be taken out, the neighbour — a retired postman — telling them to pipe down.

'They wouldn't just sack you for that.'

97

'They did.'

'You must have given them some cheek.'

'I didn't say anything.'

Simone looks helplessly at what can be seen of her son.

'Have you got any washing?'

'I can do it myself. It's all right.'

★ ★ ★

A petulant wind welcomes Julius to Monday morning and blows rain in his face as he walks to the bus stop. There's only room at the bus shelter for about half of the pale people awaiting the 436. Julius wonders why the numbers go up so high: he bets there aren't that many bus routes in London. He realizes that two women are discussing him and gets a suspicion they are annoyed with him for taking up so much space in the shelter. He shuffles out into the rain and the two women take his place.

The bus is damp and crowded and restive, like a suitcase full of wet clothes after a failed weekend break. The already stuffed-in standing passengers survey the trail of new arrivals without enthusiasm as they press their cards one by one against the sensor. The driver listens to the muted bleep-bleep of the sensor, which reminds her of some machine in a hospital. She used to work in a haematology department but was seduced by a campaign by Transport for London to attract more women to the job. It was the worst mistake of her life.

The bus chugs along in grinding stops and

starts. Every crunch of the brakes throws passengers into one another. They get stuck behind a bus which is returning to the depot; on the front it says *SORRY I'M NOT IN SERVICE*. As they finally pass, Julius glimpses the word *SORRY* and imagines the bus is apologizing for detaining them. As he is thinking this, the driver has to brake and Julius hurtles back against a small black woman with shopping bags. She gasps at the weight of him; a stranger takes her arm and looks accusingly at Julius. A few people meet each other's eyes in amusement. Julius's size is a visual joke, it's as if merely by appearing in public he is performing a stunt for a hidden-camera show. On the back seats he is aware of Amy, the pretty girl with glasses, giggling with an entourage of her friends. Julius feels very hot.

In maths he's aware of her all the way through the lesson, particularly when Liam Rollin makes one of his signature farting noises as Julius sits down: a trick which Rollin has been doing for almost four years without growing tired of it. As soon as the lunch bell goes, Julius heads for the school gates, hoping to avoid the scrum of his fellow sixth-formers in their straggly ties. Carting his school bag over his wide back, he ignores the witticisms that break out behind him. 'Where are you off to in such a hurry, Brown? KFC?' He hears someone else mutter 'Brown Trousers' as he barges his way through the gates. As Julius reaches the gates, head down, he nearly runs into Clive Donald, his maths teacher, who also has his head down; the two unwitting partners in melancholy mutter apologies.

It's still raining. From fast-food shops comes an onslaught of delicious smells which make Julius's stomach thunder with longing. He passes without looking in. He buys a low-calorie sandwich from Boots; the woman serving him looks as though she is on the point of asking whether that will be enough for him. He eats it almost without noticing it on his walk back to school, which takes him past the supermarket where his mother Simone is slicing Wye Valley Cheddar and half a dozen of his classmates are buying snacks and beers. No one at school, thank God, knows that the lady on the deli counter is his mother.

On the way to the gym after school, Julius has to walk past Amy, on her own this time. She's using a cloth to clean her glasses. She gives him a look which is, he thinks, not unfriendly. He wonders how it works as you get older, how people eventually find someone to marry. I have to lose weight, thinks Julius, there is no way that someone could hold my hand as we walked down the street. There's no way a girl could point to someone looking like me in a club and say that's my boyfriend.

At the gym, he swipes his membership card and pushes against the turnstile, but it refuses to yield to his bulk, as if someone had put an arm out to stop him. He tries it again.

The sardonic girl looks up from the computer screen.

'You need to pay. Your membership's expired.'

Julius feels his insides sag.

'I thought,' he says feebly, 'I thought it wasn't till the end of this week.'

'No, it's now. You need to pay another £67 for this month or you can pay £400 to take you up to the end of the year.'

Julius is almost one hundred per cent sure that she only talks to him this way because he's fat and doesn't look like he ought to be in a gym. She wouldn't speak like this to the lean man in a rugby shirt who nudges him out of the way to get through the turnstile and shoots her a flirtatious wink.

Julius has £32 in his bank account — or rather, minus £968, but an overdraft facility of £1,000. In his pocket are the remains of the twenty which Andrew Ryan dropped in his lap while firing him.

'Can you just let me . . . ?' mumbles Julius.

'Sorry?' The girl glances at the phone on the desk, which she would rather be answering.

'Can you just let me through this once and then I'll pay next time I'm here?'

'That's not possible, I'm afraid,' says the girl.

Julius feels for a second that he could throw himself against the turnstile, just crash through it, like an elephant crashing through a bush, and be on the other side before she knew what was happening.

'Please. I need to . . . I'm in a routine. I need to train.'

'It's not doing you much good so far,' he can almost see her struggling not to say: not to spare his feelings, but out of a professional instinct that it might lead to trouble. Sometimes, being able

101

to read what people are trying not to say, seeing the insult they are tiptoeing around, is almost worse than if they had actually said it.

'I'm afraid it's just not possible,' says the girl again, as if allowing him in is beyond the limits of what humans can accomplish. She answers the phone on its ninth ring, spelling out the name of the gym, and the conversation is over.

On the way home Julius fantasizes about Amy, but the gulf between them is too great for his imagination to bridge with even the most far-fetched scenario. Perhaps Julius is too literal-minded, too mathematical, for fantasies; they start to collapse under the weight of reality almost as soon as he starts to conjure them up. All that's left is brutal fact. I have to lose weight, I have to get back in the gym somehow, I have to get some money.

★ ★ ★

As Julius sleeps fitfully a few hours later, his maths teacher Clive Donald again calls Xavier's show, where the topic of the night is 'If You Could Live in Any Era'. Clive begins by talking about the 1920s, but soon returns to the subject of loneliness, until Murray cuts him off.

On the Tuesday afternoon, on his way out to the corner shop, Xavier runs into Tamara, who is sticking a notice up on the board at the foot of the stairs. On the notice is a picture of a teenage girl executing what seems at first to be a spectacular dance move, but is actually a horrible mid-air contortion after being hit by a

102

car. It's one of a series of images released by the Mayor of London to raise awareness of road accidents. Tamara's T-shirt rides up, exposing a tranche of flesh, as she stretches to affix the top-right corner but it flaps away again.

'Can I help with that?'

Xavier arches a long arm and secures the corner, flattening the ball of Blu-tack against the board.

'Thank you.' Tamara steps back like a painter to look at the poster. 'It's a petition about speed bumps.'

'Speed bumps.'

'We need speed bumps for this street. Don't you think? People come down here at sixty, but it's a residential street. Don't you think?'

Xavier is surprised to see her animated by this subject.

'Well, yes, I suppose you're — '

'I've set up an online petition,' she says. 'If you could sign it that would be great.'

'I will,' he promises. 'I definitely will.'

As if a whistle has blown, they both sense the conversation's imminent slowdown.

'So, anything on tonight?'

'Working,' says Xavier. 'You?'

'Boyfriend's coming round,' she replies.

'Should be nice.'

'Yes.'

'Well, see you!'

'Remember to sign the petition!'

Xavier has every intention of looking up the website and putting his name on the petition but, even as he walks up the hill to the corner

103

shop and rashly driven cars swish by at potentially lethal speeds, the task is quickly filed in a minor drawer of his mind, and forgotten.

★ ★ ★

Murray comes to 11 Bayham Road for a drink on Thursday night to celebrate the end of another block of shows, and is immediately struck by the cleanliness of Xavier's flat.

'Are you sure you haven't got a wer, wer, wer, wife all of a sudden?'

'Just a cleaner.' Xavier pours the remainder of a bottle of Cabernet Sauvignon into two bulbous glasses. 'But she's a very good one.'

'Looks like she is. I'm scared to touch anything.'

'Wait till you meet her. Then you *will* be scared.'

'Is she crazy?'

'She's just quite . . . she's a character.'

When Murray leaves, his breath puffing out in white wisps on the doorstep, it's just after five, and Xavier feels little inclination to sleep: he can hear the stillness of night already giving way to the familiar overtures of the early morning. A fire engine, sirens off, trundles down Bayham Road. In an hour, a couple of fanatical joggers will begin their patrol, and soon after that Tamara, and any number of other workers, will be awake. Xavier puts his computer on and begins to wade through the backlog of emails from listeners.

Xavier, I have terrible skin. I don't just mean a few spots. This is the real thing. I'm like a cactus or something.

104

I have a very strong crush on my aunt. I know it probably sounds like a joke. I've been trying to decide what to do ever since I realized, which was four years ago. She came down to breakfast after a family get-together, just in her nightie, and I was alarmed to find that I felt . . . I mean, I'm twenty-nine and she is forty-eight. I know I can never do anything about it. I just have to tell someone. I feel like the only person in the world who is in love with their aunt!

Frightened of death. I keep waking up in the middle of the night and I can't think of anything else. Just the idea that all this will disappear and there is nothing beyond it. It's silly because all I'm doing is working in a café. But the thought of not existing! I know it shouldn't matter because I won't know anything about it. But that's why it's so frightening. Like anaesthetic.

Xavier — Clive here. We've spoken a number of times on your show, which I enjoy very much. I'm the one whose three wives . . .

These are the most difficult ones, the ones that tempt him to break the one-reply rule. Xavier imagines Clive refreshing the web page in the hope of a reply, and thinks of the filing cabinet of photos and letters and cards, the creaking mental storehouse of dashed hopes, the sense of defeat

105

which makes up Clive's whole relationship with his past. Eventually Xavier feels he has no choice but to stop thinking about Clive altogether. He returns to the other emails. He tells the acne sufferer that there are many good treatments and sends a link to a website. He assures the amorous nephew that crushes on family members — especially outside the immediate family — are remarkably common. He agrees that death *is* frightening, but points out that, as we get older, our bodies and minds develop a familiarity with the idea, even a welcoming readiness for it. Whether this is true, or a comforting myth, Xavier isn't sure, but he likes to think the former, and it has tended to go down well.

Downstairs, Jamie stirs in his sleep and gives a sort of monosyllabic half-cry like a tenor warming up his voice, but then seems to fall asleep again. It is on this day in twenty-three years' time that he'll submit a Ph.D. proposal leading to the work which achieves a small breakthrough against two types of cancer. The twenty-four-hour news continues its relentless pursuit of the just-past, the slogans haring along the bottom of the screen (*MORE JOBS AXED ON WALL STREET, EARTH-QUAKE LEAVES HUNDREDS HOMELESS*) like text messages from an excitable, omniscient source.

★ ★ ★

On Friday night, after going to see a middling biopic of an American artist which he'll review tomorrow, Xavier finds himself cleaning the flat

106

in preparation for Pippa's visit. He is well aware that this is the stuff of middle-aged jokes, although the cleaning he does is superficial, especially compared with the severity of Pippa's operations. He goes through the cupboards to make sure everything is in date; runs the shower to clear the bath of small fugitive hairs; goes to the corner shop to buy new flowers, replacing the now flagging ones Pippa bought last week. I'm like a student cramming for an exam, thinks Xavier with a half-grin to himself.

As he goes to bed that night Xavier can hear Tamara upstairs arguing with her boyfriend. He briefly remembers the online speed-bump petition and mutters to himself for forgetting to sign it. He lies awake for a while listening to rain on the corrugated-iron roofs of the garages at the bottom of Mel's garden, a sound which reminds him of his mother typewriting letters to old friends in England. Tap-tap-tap-tap-tap. He thinks — again, briefly — about the lonely Clive and the man with the terror of death and then tries to decide whether he is looking forward to Pippa's visit tomorrow.

★   ★   ★

When it gets to a quarter past twelve the next day with still no sign of her, he has a queasy sensation that something might be wrong. Unreliability doesn't seem to be in her character, but then anyone can have an off-day. The flat seems to be holding its breath. Another ten minutes pass. Xavier picks up his phone to text

107

her, but straight away the doorbell rings. He jumps, either in spite of, or maybe because of, the fact that he has been awaiting this sound.

As he heads down the stairs he can hear Mel saying to Jamie, 'No, darling, we don't have to go, it's not for us.' He opens the door and takes a step back in surprise. There stands Pippa, with her blue-and-yellow laundry bag, covered in splotches of mud that beat a roughly diagonal path from her boots all the way across her raincoat, like toppings on a pizza. There are smears of mud on her face and mucky dots all over the bag.

'God! What . . . ?'

'Well, am I coming in, or what?'

Before they are up the stairs she's given him most of the story.

'A fucking — excuse my language — a bloody lorry — '

'Fucking is fine,' says Xavier.

'A fucking lorry,' she resumes, 'a big fuckin' thing, comes past me at the bus stop, and literally, he could see me standing there, I swear to God, right, he literally decides to drive right into the puddle and splash me. He literally decided to do it. I could see him laughing as he drove away.' The words are wrapped in her accent like bundles held together with black sticky tape. 'I tell you what, the things I shouted after him would have made a miner blush.'

'I bet they would,' Xavier agrees.

She stops decisively on the threshold of his flat.

'So just to let you know what I think we

should do. What I've got in this bag, luckily, as well as all my cleaning stuff, is, in another bag, I've got my running kit because I was going to go for a run after this, you might not think it, but I'm quite a runner actually. So if you'll allow me to use your shower I'll have a shower and then change into my kit, which will look a bit funny but never mind, and then I'll clean as normal and clean the bathroom extra well, what do you think about that?'

'Sounds fine,' says Xavier. 'Would you like a cup of tea? Afterwards, I mean. I mean, after your shower.'

'That would be lovely, pet.'

Pippa sits on the floor with her legs stretched in front of her, peeling off her mud-splattered boots with a rueful sigh. Xavier goes into the bathroom and cranks the shower into life. The decision to pay attention to the state of the place before her visit suddenly seems an inspired one.

As he busies himself in the kitchen, Xavier is irresistibly drawn to the thought of Pippa peeling off her clothes, tossing them unceremoniously on the floor; it's a while since his bathroom floor had a bra to contend with. He pictures just for a second her large breasts set free, and her powerful thighs, and her bare feet on the base of the tub. He's surprised at how intimate a feeling it is to have someone naked elsewhere in the flat. When the shower stops, he realizes he never offered her a towel, but undoubtedly she has helped herself to one on the way. This is odd, too: being aware that she knows where

109

everything is, everything he owns, even though they've barely met. He isn't sure if he likes the thought or not.

They sit in the lounge with their tea.

'You've kept the place nice since last week,' says Pippa. She is now wearing a white T-shirt and tracksuit bottoms, and her wet hair is tied back.

'I've done my best.'

'I could be out of a job soon!'

'No, I . . . I wouldn't expect so.'

It's quiet for a moment. Jamie yells downstairs. Despite the steady drizzle, a gang of kids skateboards defiantly down Bayham Road, the smallest boy struggling to keep up. Xavier isn't sure if this is a companionable silence or an awkward one.

'So you go running?'

'Three times a week. That's as much as my knees can do now. If I didn't do it I'd get fat as a house before you knew it. My body was so used to exercise and then, when you stop, you just become a balloon. I used to run every day.'

'Really?'

'Well, yes, I mean, I had to, did you know I used to be one of the top young athletes in the country?'

How could I possibly know that? Xavier thinks, in amusement.

'Athletes . . . ?'

'I was a discus thrower. You know the discus?' Still holding a mug in one hand, she makes a sweeping arc with her right arm, tossing an invisible object over her shoulder.

'Yes, but — well, I've never met anyone who — '

'That was all I wanted to do. I represented Newcastle upon Tyne Schools. I was in the British under-eighteens. I was being talked about for the Olympics a few years down the line.' She counts off these distinctions on her strong fingers, as if they were all counter-arguments to something Xavier said. 'My personal best was sixty-one metres. The British record for a woman is sixty-seven. And nearly all the records for things like discus were broken in the eighties and now they're suspect because everyone knows the athletes were all doped up to the tits.'

She pauses at last for breath.

'So what, er, what happened?'

'Six years ago I was twenty-two. I know I look closer to forty but that's what cleaning toilets does for you. So anyway. There I was on the verge of an athletics career and my knees packed up. Arthritis. I remember sitting in the doctor's surgery. He said you've got arthritis. I said be honest with me, is there any way I can keep competing? He took my hands and said Pippa, if you do, you'll get to thirty and you'll be in a wheelchair. We sat there and I started to cry. That was the only time I've cried with someone I didn't really know.'

Unsure of what to say, Xavier glances down at her knees.

'So you just had to stop and . . . start from scratch?'

Pippa smiles.

'Aye. I had hardly any qualifications. I'd put

everything into athletics. I'd earned fuck-all money, excuse my language, actually, don't, we've covered that, haven't we? Athletics pays fuck-all till you get to a very high level, especially the less glamorous events. What money I had, I'd lent to me sister, who'd been left high and dry by this man, I'd cut his bollocks off today if I saw him, and she could never pay me back. I had nothing. I started doing cleaning jobs. Me and my sister were going to move back up to Newcastle, then I got a few contracts in London, you can charge more here, so we live together here, and we've not got a pot to piss in but I said to myself if all I can do is be a cleaner, I'll be one hell of a cleaner.'

She breaks into coughs as if the supply of words had finally overwhelmed her vocal cords.

'You *are* one hell of a cleaner,' says Xavier.

'Thank you,' she says, and blushes a little, momentarily thrown by the compliment. She puts her empty mug down briskly and stands up. 'Well, that was a lovely cup of tea for an Australian.'

'I was born in England,' says Xavier. 'Next time, I'll have the kettle on when you get here.'

'I'll bring biscuits,' Pippa says. 'Now, let's get on with it. You're not paying me to sit on my arse as it gets bigger and bigger.'

She heads for the door.

'To this day, when I see little plates, I get this urge to chuck them forty metres or so.'

Xavier laughs and allows her to lead him out of the room. He glances at her muscular backside and imagines her for a moment in a singlet and shorts, on some bitterly exposed field in the North-east, on a nasty afternoon much like this one, taking the discus in her hands with an expression of concentrated fury, crouching and rotating in an intricate little circuit of steps, and then, with a shout, hurling the thing into the distance. A smattering of spectators applaud as it lands and a man marks the point with a pin and notes the distance, and another competitor gets ready to do the same.

★ ★ ★

Pippa leaves at three o'clock with an envelope into which Xavier considered trying to put a tip, but decided against it on the grounds that it might be patronizing. She buys vegetables and rice from the corner shop — the Indian proprietor beams at her, a new customer — and takes them home on the bus. At half past six, with fatigue beginning to grasp at her joints, she begins cooking a risotto for herself and her sister, who is on a cleaning job at a hotel in Holborn.

Shortly after Pippa puts the rice on, Julius Brown leaves home, his heart beating furiously, and heads through the rain for the dark, ill-maintained National Rail station half a mile from his home, rather than the restaurant as on thirty-four consecutive Saturday nights before this one. He has a kitchen knife in his pocket. His hands are trembling and his stomach feels as if it could fall out of him, whole, onto the pavement, at any step.

Over the past few days Julius has tried every avenue which might have led from his current circumstances to quick money, and found them bricked up. He didn't even like to ask his mother; indeed, he backed out of the conversation almost as soon as it began.

'Mum?'

'Yes, Julius?'

'If I asked you if you had any money I can borrow, you wouldn't have any, would you?'

'How much money?'

'About sixty-seven pounds.'

'Sixty-seven pounds! What for?'

'For the gym.'

Simone looked sadly at Julius.

'You know, darling, I honestly can't afford at the moment to — '

'I know. It's fine.'

'I can give you maybe thirty?'

'No, no. It's fine.'

He tried his brother as well, but Luke, as usual, was evasive.

'I got a few things to take care of at the moment. How about if you ask me in a few weeks, yeah?'

From time to time Luke seems to be moved by sudden fraternal urges towards Julius; he turns up and takes Julius for a drive in his throaty-engined sports car, or he sneaks him into a corporate event in some dark bar, and introduces him almost aggressively to people — 'This is my brother.' But in between these high points, there are lengthy hiatuses during which Luke doesn't come round, doesn't reply

114

to text messages or return calls, continues with whatever 'things' he is always 'taking care of'. Julius isn't sure where he works, somewhere in Kent, something to do with cars. He wears gold chains and suede jackets with jeans.

Julius tried a few places for another job, trudging up and down the high street after school, wary of being spotted by classmates. He tried seven shops, the last a pet shop, smelling of hay and rabbit's piss, where a macaw screamed at him as soon as he set foot inside.

On Thursday, Julius's name was read out in assembly, as one of five people picked to represent the school at the London Schools' Maths Olympiad, Mathdown, in Kensington. When the Head read his name, a whisper of amusement crept around the room and his ears reddened like glowing coals. Teachers, including Clive Donald, glanced across at the giggling students in half-hearted rebuke; most of them feel that for kids this age, compulsory assembly is a waste of time. Julius picked out Amy's self-confident undertone among the sniggerers and he felt as if some chemical change had taken place in him, some decision had just been made.

Even so, when he woke up this morning, he didn't think he would go through with it. He lay with the covers over his head while Simone scanned vegetables in the supermarket and Pippa got splashed by the lorry and London went about its business. He stood for a long time in the shower, watching his globular belly disappearing slowly behind the steam patches on the mirror. He drifted through the afternoon. It was almost as if carrying out instructions that he took the kitchen knife and left the house, and began the walk which ends now, in quickening rain, at the station.

Julius's bass-drum heart keeps a manic time. He tries to stop himself breaking wind, out of some sense of pride in the face of his absent tormentors. His stomach feels like a cage with an animal thrashing around inside. A train will arrive in seven minutes. He heads to the back of the station, to the exit which only a few people use.

★ ★ ★

Xavier sits in front of the TV, a newly plumped cushion behind his back. In one of her final flourishes Pippa lined the three remote controllers up in length-order on the coffee table. *Muriel's Wedding*, starring Toni Collette, is on one channel; Xavier watches for a couple of minutes, remembering the hype that had eventually persuaded the gang of four to see it at the Zodiac fifteen years ago. They were in their early twenties, full of fashionable cynicism, and secretly hoping to sneer at the film, but in the end it made Matilda cry, which made Chris want to kiss her even more than he normally did.

He flicks through another few channels and settles on a rugby match. The action stops as a player receives treatment for an injury and Xavier looks out of the sparkling window — he hadn't realized how dirty it had been — at the rain on Bayham Road. He thinks about Pippa

116

and wonders whether he should have tipped her, after all.

★　★　★

One of the £10 notes Xavier gave Pippa has, at various moments in its three-year life, been in the possession of a dozen people in London. Xavier received it in his change from the Indian shopkeeper earlier this week. The Indian shopkeeper took it, as payment for a packet of cigarettes, from a loss adjuster who got it at Boots in Chelsea, where it was brought by a student, and the chain of London owners goes all the way back to an estate agent, Ollie Harper, who brought the banknote to the capital last summer, having come by it in Edinburgh where he was attending the Festival.

Ollie is now on a train about to pull into a station about a mile from 11 Bayham Road. He's had a long day at work, but it was worth it. He did eight viewings and, although three or four were hopeless — you can tell immediately from the over-polite things they say — two were promising. In one case, he convinced the potential buyers that the flat was already as good as sold, but 'there might be a chance' if they were to put in a bid on Monday. This is a common tactic but he could see that the young couple fell for it; they're getting married soon and love the idea of moving into their first home as soon as they come back from honeymoon. Ollie remembers feeling like that with Nicola.

Nicola will be almost asleep when he gets

home, even though it's only eight o'clock; she won't last beyond ten. Pregnancy hasn't made her sick but tired, tired, tired. There'll probably be a tetchy exchange about the fact he's chosen to work a Saturday again, but this is how he gets the edge over his colleagues, this is how his sales are up so far this year when everyone else's are down. This is how the baby, when it's born, will have a dad who's got a safe job when everyone else is about to lose theirs. Ollie imagines it will be a boy, although he'd secretly like a girl, a tiny version of Nicola, a portable beauty. The thought makes him smile as he steps down onto the station platform. His umbrella springs open to keep off the rain. The weather's been shit recently, he thinks, but at least it's not so cold now. Unlike the handful of other passengers who disembarked here, he makes for the quicker, darker, rear exit.

'Stop where you are and give me your money,' says Julius.

It sounds ridiculous out loud, the line that he practised hundreds of times in his head, and he senses that his intended victim is in danger of not taking him seriously. In the dusk, the two of them look at each other; Julius, ten years younger, more alarmed than the man he is trying to mug.

'What?'

'Give me whatever you've got.'

Ollie screws up his eyes to look at his mugger. The kid is huge. If he turned and ran now, he would surely get away. But there could be more of them.

118

'Or what?'

Julius is sweating.

'Just give me your money.'

Ollie wants to get home. He still doesn't regard this as a threat, just an inconvenience.

'Look, get out of my way, would you?'

'Give me your money.'

'What are you going to do?'

Julius looks at Ollie's impatient, puckered face, and has a strong sense that Ollie is what Liam Rollin will be like in ten years, that Ollie, in fact, would be one of his school tormentors, were it not for the fact of their decade-apart birthdates. A dam bursts in his mind and he seizes Ollie's wrist violently, his other hand bringing the knife out from under his jacket. Ollie cries out in pain or surprise. Julius brings the knife close to his victim's chest. The knife is almost comically big, like one you would slice crusty bread with, but a blade is a blade, and he can feel his victim's wrist stiffen in fear.

Ollie's free hand begins to fumble in his pocket. He brings out a pair of rumpled notes.

'This is all I've got.'

Julius hasn't thought any further than apprehending someone. He certainly doesn't want to negotiate over how much he gets. But this is nowhere near enough. He thinks he can hear footsteps.

'Give me more.'

'This is all I've got, for fuck's sake.'

'Well, give me your phone.'

Ollie sighs and looks at Julius with what still seems like irritation — even now, Julius registers

119

at the back of his mind, even with the knife I'm not getting respect. He tightens his grip. Ollie's eyes waver between the knife and his whitening wrist. Finally he gives in, remembering how a barrister was killed by a fourteen-year-old at this station a few years back. He reaches around with his free hand and fishes his BlackBerry out of his pocket. Julius takes the BlackBerry and clasps it in his shaking hand. Their eyes meet for a second before he lets go of Ollie and starts to run for the other exit, in wide, awkward strides, his eyes bulging like a cartoon character's.

'I'll have the police after you, you fat cunt!' Ollie calls after him.

Julius careers, like a runaway trolley, down the nineteen steps to the main station concourse and out through the deserted ticket office. Panicking, he dumps the knife into a ragged bush by the taxi rank. He regrets it straight away. The bush is barely thick enough to hide it, it will probably be visible in daylight, they'll get it out and fingerprint it, they'll check everyone somehow. Gasping for air, his body awash with sweat, Julius lurches for home, not daring to stop. He is barely conscious, for once, of the surprised or amused looks of the night-walking lovers as he steams past. The screwed-up banknotes scratch together in his pocket. He feels as if nobody has ever done anything as bad as this.

5

Three nights later, as Murray and Xavier address their mid-week audience, Julius flits between wakeful shuffling and dreams of being interrogated or chased. He exchanged the BlackBerry for £100, no questions asked, at a place in Kilburn that cheerfully buys and sells almost-certainly-stolen goods. Added to Ollie's cash, it covers another couple of months at the gym, which buys him time to get a job. Whenever a teacher looks directly at him, or he walks past a policeman, Julius expects to be confronted with evidence of what he did at the weekend. He mutters disjointed, uneasy phrases in his sleep, and casts his arms about as if to ward off a series of attackers.

'Continuing our sideways look at the . . . world of the news,' says Murray.

One of Murray's strategies for dealing with the W problem is to pause shortly before the troublesome consonant, and then, after a deep breath, sail through it, and the next few syllables, all in one movement. This can give his sentences an odd cadence, like the jumpy phrases which answering machines piece together from pre-recorded fragments, but it's better — anything is better — than those agonizing stops and starts.

'Now, our next story is that our esteemed leader is meeting the American President this week. I was trying to picture the scene in the

121

wer, in the wer — '

'In the White House,' Xavier puts in helpfully.

'Exactly.' Murray's curly head bobs up and down. This is his favourite part of the show. 'And I imagine it might go a bit like this.'

Xavier stares out of the window at the car park as Murray adopts an unconvincing American drawl. The thin outline of their resident fox emerges from behind the recycling units. Murray almost trod on the fox last week as they left the studio; it has become so composed around humans that, rather than scuttle away, it gave the pair of them a cool, contemptuous look, its black eyes like tiny stones.

Beyond the limits of Xavier's gaze, nocturnal London, the shadow London, is halfway through its shift.

On Bayham Road, Xavier's neighbours are asleep, although Jamie will wake at 6 a.m., and resist all Mel's gummy-eyed attempts to negotiate another hour or so of peace. Maggie Reiss, the psychotherapist, is asleep too, next to her stock-broker husband; she hasn't been bothered by gastrointestinal problems at all this week. A few postcodes away from her, Frankie Carstairs still has a prominent scar from the stitching, which the doctors say will fade. His mother's uncharitable review of Chico's won praise from her editor, who is always delighted if a section as irrelevant as 'Eating Out' can create some controversy. Ollie Harper sleeps next to his four-months-pregnant wife Nicola. He didn't tell her about the mugging — why make a drama out of things; the doctor told her to avoid stress. He

122

got a temporary phone on Monday, it'll be a week till his BlackBerry can be replaced. The young couple made an offer, which he's pretty sure they can't really afford, on the flat.

Murray lumbers to the end of his skit about world leaders and moves on to his second prepared piece of topical comedy, about a Somali pirate ship which has made headlines by taking a crew hostage somewhere in the Indian Ocean. Xavier musters a couple of encouraging chuckles and snorts, and looks forward to the syndicated news bulletin which, with its precise, non-negotiable timing, will put an end to this awkward comic interlude.

Julius's teacher Clive Donald is in his back garden in Hertfordshire, staring absently at the sombre bare trees in the moonlight, which make him think of arms reaching up through the earth, their fingers trying to grasp the sky. Earlier he took a sleeping pill, which has had no effect. Also medicated, and cruising far above London, is Andrew Ryan, the restaurant owner, coming back from Hong Kong where he lost a couple of thousand pounds at the races. His seat reclines to become a bed, and can be fully shut off from the rest of the cabin by means of a curtain, but these comforts are wasted on Ryan who knocked himself out with two pills before take-off. Unknown to any of the passengers, the hold of the plane contains the corpse of a formerly high-ranking government official who died of a stroke last week. Meanwhile, George Weir lies placidly in Golders Green Cemetery. His daughter, a council worker specializing in road safety, laid fresh flowers on his grave at the weekend.

'That was 'Murray's Musings', and if you've had a bit of a giggle, text in and let us know. Now, the joys of the news and sport.'

'And after the break,' says Xavier, 'we'll be asking you to tell us about a moment that haunts you. Something you'd like to put right, if you could turn back time. And we might just play a song on that very subject.'

Murray flicks a switch and the toneless, crystal voice of the newsreader begins.

'Nice work,' says Xavier. 'The bit about pirates was good.'

'Just something I ner, ner, knocked up on the way here,' says Murray. 'Coffee?'

As Murray shoulders his way out of the door, Xavier thinks, I really should stop him from doing these bits. Or at least reduce the length of them. Or the frequency. One a week would do. A couple a week. Not every night.

Murray has found all sorts of ways to sidestep any suggestion of dropping his comedy segment from the show. He proposes ideas to 'punch it up' or 'give it an extra kick'. They moved it nearer the beginning of the show because 'the audience will be fresher then', and then back towards the end because 'the audience will be more in the mood for light relief then'. When from time to time Roland, their executive producer, suggests removing it altogether, Murray always rolls his eyes and accuses him of 'underestimating what a bit of laughter can do for a show'. Xavier keeps his opinions to himself. Murray works hard on the jokes, and often arrives with several handwritten A4 sheets, dense with witticisms scrawled in his stunted handwriting, which seems as strained as his speech.

Tomorrow evening, Xavier is taking Murray to a premiere in Leicester Square. The film stars Nicolas Cage, who goes out for revenge on someone, or someone goes out for revenge on him; Xavier can't quite remember the details of the press release. He was invited initially by email, which was then followed up with a glossy note in the post — a sign that the producers are not expecting much press interest in the movie, are chasing up anyone who might give them a quote, like party organizers casting the net wider and wider into the pool of their casual acquaintances.

Murray sets down Xavier's coffee in the *BIG CHEESE* mug. He checks the incoming emails and texts. There are very few from people claiming to have 'had a giggle' at the last part of the show, and at least a couple report a contrary reaction.

Murray brushes these aside, as ever, with a goofy smile.

'Some people never lighten up.'

The ensuing half-hour is certainly not conducive to lightness, as callers tackle 'The One Thing You Would Change in Your Life'. One man says he should never have left his wife, who went on to win the Lottery.

'But if you'd only have been with her for the money,' Xavier consoles him.

'No, I think I really loved her,' laments the caller.

'So why did you leave her, if I can ask that?'

'Because I'm an idiot,' the caller answers matter-of-factly.

There are other people who have dropped out of university or shouldn't have gone in the first place; turned down a great job, or were crushed by a dismal one for thirty years; missed the last chance to say goodbye to a loved one. The regrets fizz across the city from their various custodians to the meeting point in the studio in West London. There are lighter recollections, too: someone in Belsize Park merely wishes he had never bought his current toaster.

'If that's the worst thing you can look back on,' Xavier reasons.

'I didn't say it was the worst. Just the one I'm telling you.'

'Well, fair enough, and maybe I won't tell you *my* worst one, either. But here's one of mine.'

The expectant hush when Xavier begins a story, Murray always thinks, can be sensed from the studio as clearly as if all the listeners were sitting rapt in the same room.

'I was about eleven, and we were on holiday by the sea. I had a kind of dinghy, shaped like a big fish, which me and my dad were floating around on. Suddenly this boy, about my age, tried to climb on board.

'My dad was trying to shoo him away. The kid kept saying is there room for me? Is there room for me? And looking at us with this very pleading face. He didn't seem to have a parent or anyone with him. I didn't know what to do, I was frozen, but my dad told him pretty roughly to go away.

He kept gesturing: get lost. And eventually this boy swam away, looking very hurt, or just disappointed, as if he'd really set his heart on getting on that fish. After he'd gone, my dad said the kid had mental problems. There's nothing you can do for people like that, he said.

'He wasn't a bad man, my dad, he just . . . he didn't really understand other people that well. Anyway. If I could turn back time I would at least try to get him to let the kid on board. I sometimes wonder where he is now.'

'Maybe he drowned!' Murray starts to blurt out glibly. He means it as a relief from the taut atmosphere, but it's a terrible error.

Xavier, quick as ever, covers for him, anticipating the sentence and blocking it with one of his own, like a goalkeeper instinctively smothering a shot with his body.

'So let's lighten the mood . . . any even sillier regrets than the one about the toaster? Thanks to Nigel for that, and we'll take more after this — the song you've all been requesting.'

'You're listening to *Late Lines*,' says Murray redundantly, grateful for his reprieve. The polished chords of a popular soul ballad emerge from the speakers. Murray reaches across and pats his partner's hand by way of a thank you. Xavier is surprised at himself for telling the story: an episode which he hadn't thought of, as far as he can remember, for many years. When he looks out of the window again, he can see, as clear as a photograph, the boy's troubled, imploring face, and his stiff, sad shoulders as he turned and swam away.

127

* * *

On the night of the premiere, Leicester Square is sulky with drizzle and the red carpet looks dog-eared and damp at the edges as a selection of the best available stars trots dutifully across it, posing, arms around whoever, for the rapid-fire snaps of bored photographers. There's a model, the winner of a recent TV talent show, a game-show host; not many people, tellingly, from the actual film. The director is there with his much younger girlfriend and a gut which imposes itself through an inadequate tuxedo like somebody mooning through a gap in curtains.

As Xavier waits for Murray near the optimistically signposted VIP entrance, his mind goes back irresistibly to another premiere, years ago at the Zodiac. The picture was a much anticipated art film about an orphan, locally produced and set in Melbourne. The gang of four had secured tickets by being loyal Zodiac customers. The director, a jolly-looking man with an uncle's beard, sat a couple of rows ahead of them. The Zodiac had been built before the clinical comforts of today's multiplex were ever dreamed of; the rows were crammed together and the intimacy between patrons was one of the things that gave the place its particular heightened atmosphere.

With the start of the film imminent, Matilda tapped Chris's knee.

'Hey. Look.' She pointed to the director in front of them.

He had seemingly worked himself into a

remarkable state of anxiety. He continually wiped his sweaty hands in his lap, jiggled his legs up and down, and glanced to his left and right as if in hiding from some enemy. At one point he swivelled all the way round to survey the full room behind him, and his large, alarmed eyes peered at the four of them for an uncomfortable moment as if appealing for help.

'Fuck! He looks terrible!' Matilda observed in a clumsy whisper.

Chris rolled his eyes and dug her in the back, in case the director heard them.

'He'll just be nervous. Imagine making a film and everyone knowing it was yours. Well, imagine making a film at all,' said Russell.

'He does look unusually worried, though,' Bec chipped in.

'By unusually do you mean — ' Matilda began, but at that moment the lights dimmed.

Before long they had a possible explanation as to the director's distress, because the movie, of which so much had been expected, turned out to be terribly slow-moving and dull. As the scenes wore on, the disenchantment of the once-excited audience became almost palpable, like a sickly smell blown in from outside. From time to time Chris stole a glance at the hunched figure of the film-maker. His movements had become less frenetic, more resigned; he rested his head wearily in his hands once, and several times shook his head, as if unable to believe what he was seeing.

Towards the end — at least, they hoped the end was near, but the film was too long on top of everything else — a particularly ill-judged piece of dialogue brought an incredulous snigger from sections of the audience. The director rose from his seat in a violent motion and crashed his way through the row of legs to the aisle. As he hurried away, the gang of four could see that he was crying.

The friends exchanged rueful looks. Chris felt a sudden impulse to go after the man, though with no idea of what he hoped to achieve if he found him. He allowed a couple of minutes to pass and then, as inconspicuously as possible, slid out of his own seat.

Of course, there was no escaping Matilda's notice. Her eyes widened in surprise: Chris had almost never, in anyone's memory, missed a moment of any film.

'Where are you going?'

'Bathroom.'

She didn't buy it, he knew, but he edged his way to the end of the row and out into the lobby, where the dark-red walls were hung with autographed pictures of long-dead MGM stars. After a brief scan of the lobby, Chris went into the Gents, and found the director, leaning as if drunk, with his head against the hand-dryer.

'Are you all right?' asked Chris in the end, not knowing what else to say.

The director turned to glance at him through his teary eyes, seemed to weigh up the question, and then said decisively, 'My film's a pile of shit.'

Chris's wish to console the man competed with his integrity as a cinemagoer. Compassion won the battle.

'I thought it was pretty good.'

'You're just saying that,' the director protested, and then, in a sudden burst of fury, repeated in an angry, pointless shout, 'You're just saying it!'

He thumped the hand-dryer, which had the unfortunate effect of setting it off and drowning out the next part of his lament. As the machine roared out its air, Chris inched closer to the man and laid an arm, gently, on his shoulder. The director turned and almost threw himself at Chris in despair, burying his head in Chris's chest and continuing to sob.

'A hundred thousand dollars. Eighteen fucking months. And the thing's no good. The thing's no good. I knew all along.'

Chris, knowing that the screening was about to end in the auditorium, quickly steered the bedraggled auteur out of the toilets, and — acting on instinct — up the ladder into the projectionist's box.

'This is the only place you can get some privacy,' explained Chris, who had been coming here for so much of his life that he knew most of the staff by name.

The big man, as feeble as a child, followed him. The projectionist, with his black T-shirt and long, lank hair, looked up in surprise and irritation at the sound of approaching footsteps, but relaxed when he saw Chris's familiar face, only to revert to surprise again at the sight of the director.

'He's depressed about the film,' Chris explained. 'I'm trying to tell him it's all right.'

'It's a pile of shit,' muttered the director.

'It is actually passable,' ruled the projectionist helpfully, 'just not the film it could have been.'

Shortly after this, once the final credits had rolled and the muted applause had died away, the projectionist went downstairs to oversee the after-show party preparations, and Chris was left with the director, who had by now stopped crying, and was staring, with a mixture of sadness and relief, down into the ghostly, empty auditorium and the blank screen where his disappointing work had played itself out.

'See,' Xavier said, 'in the end, it's OK. It's just a film.'

'Sure,' the director agreed, sniffing. 'I'll get to make another one.'

They sat there for a good few minutes in silence, Chris's arm on the director's shoulder, the director thinking he had made a fool of himself, Chris thinking that Matilda would be wondering where he had got to. But she had guessed and, when he came down from the projectionist's box with the sheepish director in tow, her face softened into a signature smile — somehow sentimental and knowing at the same time — whose meaning he knew very well.

The weekend that followed was full of joyous, emphatic sex; when he turned up on Saturday night, she answered the door naked, standing there for a few moments in full view of anyone who might be passing, and led him to the bedroom, arms pinned behind his back, without saying a word.

The memory of Matilda's face, that shaky column of freckles, and its sister pattern of tiny moles all the way down her belly to her thighs, sends a strange hybrid of sexual electricity, wistfulness and something almost like grief through Xavier. Cut it out, he tells himself, scanning the Square for the inelegant figure of his friend. Toughen up.

When Murray eventually arrives, exactly a minute before the scheduled start, he is not only panting and sweaty but wearing a red tie. The event is strictly black tie — even a modest premiere has to keep up some sort of appearances — and everyone else here has a bow tie on.

Xavier gestures helplessly.

'What the hell . . . ?'

'I couldn't find a ber, bow tie.'

'Could you not hire one?'

'I didn't realize I didn't have one.'

'So instead you went for a red tie? Not a black tie, say?'

'I thought any tie would be better than no tie.'

'No. A red tie is *worse* than no tie. A red fucking tie!' Xavier shakes his head in a combination of chagrin and reluctant affection. 'Look, take mine.'

'How do I put it on?' Murray's big fingers fumble with the prissy object as if he were a walrus grappling with a mobile phone.

'It's a clip-on one, Murray. You clip it on.'

There is an announcement: the screening is about to start. Xavier grasps Murray by the lapels and fixes the bow tie, then takes his sleeve and guides him towards the auditorium. Halfway into the darkened room with its modest buzz of

133

anticipation, Murray turns back, trying to grab a glass of wine from a tray, and causes a logjam of latecomers around the main doors which will still be straightening itself out as the lights go down for the start of the film.

★ ★ ★

The film is watchable but bland, roughly on a par with the level of expectation. At the end, there is a mass chirping and bleeping, like an electronic dawn chorus, as hundreds of mobile devices are switched back on at once. By the time they get to the reception, the queue is three-deep at the free bar, and Murray goes off to battle it. Xavier is watching a PR representative for the film flirting with journalists when someone tugs at his sleeve. It's the TV producer he last met at Christmas. Now, as then, she is supported by a pair of long, pencil-thin heels; it must be like trying to walk on crabs' claws, thinks Xavier. Her non-champagne hand grabs his and she leans upwards for a kiss on the cheek which he feels obliged to give.

'How are you?' he asks politely.

'I'm great. Who are you here with, the girlfriend . . . ?'

'No, I'm with a friend,' he says, gesturing to the bar.

The woman — he can never remember her name, it's something like Hannah or Hayley — glances over her shoulder and, as if politely, stifles a chuckle at the sweaty Murray, bow tie askew as he hefts himself, drink in each hand,

134

between two skinny girls in low-cut dresses.

'Your sidekick.'

'Yes.'

'Still enjoying the radio show?'

'It's fun.'

'Good for you,' she says. 'Well, when you're ready to move on, remember, just drop me an email. I've been speaking to a couple of people about you.'

'I will.'

Xavier makes his excuses as Murray returns.

She whips out her BlackBerry — people all over the room are doing this each time they move between conversations, as if the gadgets contain instructions on how to move — and stilt-walks away, tugging someone else's sleeve as Murray hands Xavier a glass of wine.

'Is that Hannah Woodrow?' Murray looks back at the miniature woman, already immersed in a new conversation.

'Yeah.'

'What were you talking about?'

'Just about the film.'

'I should try to talk to her. She's a good person to get in with.'

'What do you mean, 'get in with'? For what?'

Murray shrugs.

'You never know. It's always good to have options. I mean, at the moment, the show is perfect, but we've got to look ler, ler, ler, ler, ler, ler, ler. Long-term.'

'I guess.'

Murray fingers the ill-becoming bow tie.

'You just concentrate on the show. Leave the

tactics to me. I've been in this game a while.'

Xavier watches him move, heavy-footed, to the periphery of the producer's new group, where he waits with his hand poised to shake hers, like an autograph-hunter hoping to catch a passing star. Xavier is surprised to find himself wondering about Pippa: where she is at the moment, what she's doing. Watching TV, he supposes, or maybe out with her sister; she seems like the sort of person who could work all day and then go out at 4 a.m. She could be doing anything — jogging in the dark, country dancing, life modelling, playing the kazoo, nothing would be a surprise. But then, she could just be relaxing. He briefly imagines her in the bath, pink knees rising imposingly from a cloud of suds, and is surprised at himself again. He reaches to loosen his bow tie, but it's not there. Murray, with Xavier's bow tie drooping around his neck, is still at the corner of a conversation, his smile flagging at the edges.

★　★　★

Ollie Harper spends the following workday grappling with irritations. His replacement phone suffers from an unwieldy keypad, and of course contains none of his clients' numbers, so he's spent quite a lot of this week so far just making up lost ground. He hopes something bad happens to the fat fuck who stole his BlackBerry. His only consolation has been exchanging flirtatious texts with his colleague Sam, who sits on the other side of the office all day twirling her hair, answering the phone — 'Hello, Frinton'

— and grilling callers for personal details. It's a Frinton rule that every caller, however casual, is logged on a database with a mobile number and, if possible, an email address which will receive details of available properties for years to come. 'Even if they don't end up buying with us this time, or renting with us this time, there'll be a next time,' as Roger, the boss, points out tediously often. He is so obsessed with the database, Ollie sometimes thinks, that he'd be happy if they never completed a sale again, as long as they had ten thousand people's email addresses.

This morning Roger gave the staff a typically laboured talking-to about motivation. With the 'current financial problems faced by the globe' — as he grandly put it — everyone had to work twice as hard, but he'd been getting the impression some people were working *half* as hard. He looked straight at Ollie as he said this.

Ollie has never liked Roger and the dislike is, he assumes, mutual. Roger has foul breath, as if years ago he ate something which still haunts his mouth; he's short, balding, and lacking in charm. Ollie and Sam have been batting insults about him back and forth between their phones, insults which are becoming increasingly rude given the increasing level of sexual tension. Ollie knows that Nicola, pregnant back home, would be appalled if she knew he was compulsively texting another woman, but she's lucky, really, he thinks; if he wasn't getting it out of his system this way, he'd be actually fucking someone else, like half his mates, like most men deprived of sex

137

in a long-term relationship.

Sam wears short skirts and coloured tights, red, or even purple on occasion, an eccentric choice by the standards of a high-street estate agent. From time to time Roger makes a half-hearted attempt to talk her into greater conservatism, but it's a battle he has no stomach for.

While he considers himself slightly better than her as an all-round agent — and the figures bear out his opinion — Ollie has to admit that Sam is very good, and she's only been in the business a couple of years. She's got excellent phone technique (it's almost impossible to end a conversation with her without surrendering details to the database) and he bets she's great at viewings, too, persuasive without seeming to be pushy, never allowing a door to close: *Well, if you change your mind . . . Well, if you want to have another look . . . I happen to know they will take a lot less . . .* using all the agent tactics people believe they are wise to, but cave in to nonetheless.

And she's a good texting partner. He likes seeing her eyes flicker in amusement over the screen of her mobile, even as she's putting on a grave voice to placate a disappointed vendor on her desk phone. He likes the anticipation as her fingers trip nimbly over the keys to send a reply up into space, only to land ten metres away on his screen. In a sense, Roger was right to lecture them — they probably *could* be doing more — but it's flair that sells homes in a climate like this, not graft alone.

The phone rings.

'Frinton, Ollie speaking.'

It's someone calling about one of the properties in the window, a nice place with a double garage and decent garden, actually sold some weeks ago, but kept on display in the hope of luring customers in from the stagnant high street towards other purchases.

'Let me check.' Ollie pretends to shuffle some papers on his desk. 'Yes, now that one has actually been sold already, I'm afraid. But we do have a couple more places which have very similar — ' He's cut off. The caller has heard this kind of shtick before. The invisible could-have-been-client wriggles off the hook of the database. Sam, who's on the phone herself, gives him a hard-luck raise of the eyebrows, but this is immediately cancelled out by Roger, who looms behind him.

'What you want to do, Ollie, in that situation,' says Roger, 'is be more proactive. Ask them to come in and talk to you about the property. Then when they're here, *then* you tell them, oh, it's sold, but here are some more. Much more difficult then for them to get away, if they're sat right here.'

'Thank you, Roger,' says Ollie in what he hopes is a tone of acid sarcasm, 'you are very wise.'

The phone barks at him again.

'Hello, Frinton. Briars Road? Let me see. Yes, now that one has been sold. But we do have some other very similar details.' To hell with Roger; Ollie is going to do it his own way. This time, the caller is snagged: Ollie can hear it. 'So if I could just start by taking some details? Could I get your name?'

It's as simple and quick as that, when it works, the flipping of the conversation so that the caller, having rung up in search of information, ends up feeling it is quite natural to part with it, instead. From here, it's easy. Ollie can do the patter without engaging his brain, which is instead put to work tapping out a message to Sam on the unwieldy face of the replacement phone he's still fucking stuck with. *If he comes and breathes anywhere near me again I'm going to vomit . . .*

He sees Sam's phone light up for a second, reads the amusement in her grey eyes. This is the kind of thing you miss when you're married, he thinks: making someone grin, seeing them react to tricks which your partner has seen a thousand times. Freshly minted emotions, the rawness of it. A message comes back from her. *His breath is incredible, it's like he ate shit!*

Ollie almost snorts at this, but manages to keep his tone neutral.

'Right, and can I take an email address that I can send details to? And then we'll move on to talking about your specific requirements.' He takes up the baton of her last text. *Maybe that's what he's into . . . some people are . . .* Somehow it makes it more enjoyable that they're spelling words in full, no abbreviations, no stupid little icons and pictures; it gives a full-blooded quality to the flirting, makes it feel less teenage. He sees Sam smirk and begin work on her response. He's hoping she'll pursue the topic of

140

kinky habits, but she simply writes: *You're going to make me throw up! His poor wife!*

'Right. So you're looking to pay, ideally, around £250,000. Now I'm going to ask you a question. If I found your *ideal* home — your absolute dream place — how far could you stretch? Two sixty? Two seven five? Just to give me an idea of parameters.'

Ollie has the receiver tucked under his chin. He is inputting the caller's data with one finger and trying to compose a new text to Sam with the other hand, though first he has to read a message from someone else. He laments, once again, this stupid temporary phone, with its over-clever way of pre-empting words, its baffling menu system. *If you were Roger's wife you'd have only yourself to blame for not bailing out when you smelled his breath . . .*

The caller is becoming slightly tetchy — is this going to take much longer? As he rolls his thumb around his temporary address book, Ollie is forced to concentrate on the conversation again.

'OK, David, listen, instead of me grilling you over the phone like this, what about if I book you in for an appointment and we — '

His heart jumps. It feels for a moment as if it has actually dislodged itself and is rattling around like a cog loose in a machine.

He's sent the text about Roger *to* Roger.

Ollie concludes the conversation as fast as possible, puts the receiver down. His hands are shaking. Sam can see the change in his face. Ollie paws helplessly at the mobile, the stupid shitty fucking excuse for a phone whose alien

141

workings confused him into this disastrous short-circuit of the brain. And it even included his name: not even Roger can fail to understand it. Ollie curses himself, the phone, the fat piece of shit who stole his BlackBerry, Roger, Sam, Nicola, but mostly himself again.

He thinks wildly of trying to steal Roger's phone. One of them could distract him while the other one nicks it and deletes the message, but no, Roger will have it in his pocket as always, his fucking trouser pocket, those trousers which are slightly too short and ride up to give glimpses of his bony white ankles, he'll have the message in his pocket right now, it's a time bomb. Ollie feels sick. He dabs his lips with his suddenly dry tongue and wonders if there is any miracle way of getting out of this one.

★ ★ ★

Xavier is woken by a raucous scream from Jamie downstairs at nine thirty on Saturday morning, and goes to buy a few groceries from the corner shop, along with some extra varieties of tea, in case Pippa turns out to have a preference for peppermint or something. He's not sure whether he is really trying to be a good host or just hoping to amuse her with the formalities. He returns home and begins the superficial pre-clean for her arrival, but in truth not much needs doing: over the course of her few visits the flat has reached a tipping point of tidiness. This poses the question, of course, of whether he really needs her to keep visiting on Saturdays. He

142

can't entirely remember how this became the firm routine it already feels like now.

At about ten to twelve, the bell rings. Xavier pauses: he was just about to put on a slightly less rumpled shirt than the one he's wearing. She always seems to come a bit early or a bit late. But when he goes down to the door, it's not Pippa. Another woman is standing there, fake-tanned, in a black T-shirt, with some sort of photo ID around her neck and a clipboard under her arm.

'Hi,' she says. 'I'd love to just take a few minutes of your time to tell you about a great way to help people less fortunate than yourself. Have you ever considered helping people less fortunate than yourself?'

'Er . . . ' says Xavier.

Just out of the University of Melbourne, he sponsored a child in Ghana, paying $25 a month, but that came to seem a pitiful gesture, a drop in the ocean, so for a while he also gave $30 a month to a homeless shelter, and then went and worked there as a volunteer with Matilda some Saturdays. That in turn led to a stint working for an AIDS charity, and so on for a couple of years, each piece of do-gooding only highlighting to the still impressionable Chris how many more deserving causes there were. In the end, a period of financial hardship put an end to these charitable commitments and he now looks back on the whole thing with a certain embarrassment.

'I'm kind of . . . I kind of . . . I'd rather not . . . ' falters Xavier.

The fund-raiser, with her shiny skin and

143

imploring eyes, has been trained to expect lukewarm responses; indeed, her rehearsed spiel is custom-written to incorporate them.

'Now I know what you're thinking, money's tight at the moment, I need to look after number one first and foremost.'

Xavier has the disconcerting impression that the girl is scarcely aware of the words she's saying, like a high-school actor racing through a chunk of Shakespeare.

'It's not that, really, it's just . . . '

In his peripheral vision Xavier can see Mel approaching down the hill, with Jamie stooping to pick up some filthy item from the pavement, indifferent to her coaxing. She slows up as they near the front door. Xavier is now standing with Mel on one side, the fund-raiser right in front of him, and Jamie scampering around, throwing his new toy — a leaf — out in front of him, stooping to pick it up, throwing it into the air again.

'Don't go in the road, Jamie,' says Mel.

'So anyway, what I wanted to say to you today,' the fundraiser tries to resume.

'Sorry, am I interrupting?' Mel asks Xavier.

'Actually, this is something you might be interested in as well,' says the girl, turning the beam of her eyes upon Mel. 'I've just been talking to this gentleman — I don't know your name yet — '

'Xavier.'

'I've just been talking to Xavier about a great way to help — '

'JAMIE, MIND THE ROAD,' yells Mel, her voice ragged. She turns to the girl. 'Listen, I'm

144

sorry, but I've just had to sell some of his books on eBay for fifty pence each.' She points to Jamie. 'I don't think I can.'

'OK, that's cool,' says the girl hastily; she's already decided Xavier is the one to concentrate on. She turns back to him. 'So would it be possible to come inside and tell you a bit more about this?'

Xavier stands, irresolute.

'I'm, er . . . '

At the top of the hill Pippa appears, on a bicycle, her patterned dress streaming out on either side as her strong legs ease off the pedals for the descent. All three of them turn to watch her. The dress, with its pattern of daisies against a green background, was bought by Pippa's gran on the King's Road in 1956, during what proved to be her only ever visit to London. She has a black cycle-helmet on, but even this seems like some kind of antique: it is comically, impractically large, sitting on her head like a dinosaur's egg; beneath it, her hair gusts about in wild tufts. She wrestles the bike to a screechy halt, jumps nimbly from the saddle and surveys the group on the doorstep.

'Christ knows why I ride this thing about with my bloody knees the way they are,' Pippa says to no one in particular, and then to everyone, 'What's going on here then?'

'I was just telling everyone about a great way to help,' the girl begins yet again, somewhat uncertainly; this has all become more complicated than she imagined.

'You're trying to sign them up for donations?'

asks Pippa, removing the helmet. Her hair is a tangle of straw, her cheeks flushed from the ride.

'Well, what we do . . . ' the girl says, faltering at the sight of this tall, big-bosomed woman, who brushes down her dress and looks straight at her with pale blue eyes.

Pippa points at Xavier.

'Do you want to sign up or not?'

Xavier shifts his weight from one foot to the other.

'I'm not entirely, um . . . '

'All right.' Pippa addresses the fund-raiser. 'Do you have a website?'

'We do,' says the girl, 'but — '

'All right,' says Pippa again. 'He'll have a look at the website and get in touch if he wants to sign up, how about that?'

The girl is already looking to the next door, the next street; this one has been enough trouble for now. She supplies the web address in a quick breath and departs, clipboard under arm, while Pippa leads Mel, Jamie and Xavier inside.

'Thanks,' Xavier mutters. 'I'm not great with those sort of people. It's hard to say no.'

'It's not *that* hard,' says Pippa.

'Well, yes, you made it look pretty easy.'

'Don't forget your post.' Pippa stoops to pick up a couple of letters from the floor; Xavier glances momentarily at the line of her wide thighs beneath the vintage dress. 'Honestly. I don't know what you do when I'm not here.'

★   ★   ★

They drink tea in the lounge. Pippa drains hers in three gulps.

'It's thirsty work, biking about.'

'How was your week?' asks Xavier, bringing in the teapot to refill her cup.

'Oh, up and down. Me sister's ill with something so I've had to look after her and me mum's all upset about me uncle who's a bastard. But it's been all right.' She looks at Xavier over the rim of the mug. 'So, is she in love with you?'

'Sorry?'

'The girl downstairs with the mad kid.'

Xavier feels his cheeks warming, but he doesn't turn away; he doesn't want this ridiculous idea to gain credence from his reaction. 'We hardly know each other.'

'She looks at you in this doe-eyed way,' Pippa observes coolly, 'and she talked about you sort of fondly when I borrowed the Hoover that time. I've seen it a lot, single mothers. Anyway, it's none of my business, pet.'

'I don't think . . . I mean, she seems nice,' says Xavier. 'Not sure we're each other's type.'

'What is your type?'

He takes Pippa's empty-again mug from her hand and it clinks together with his. 'I don't know. I don't know if people have a 'type', even. My last proper girlfriend, I suppose, in Australia, was kind of . . . I probably shouldn't use the phrase 'my ideal woman', but that kind of thing.'

'What was she like?'

Xavier is surprised by how easy it is to slip into an intimate discussion with Pippa; something about her blunt style of questioning

147

reminds him of Australians, maybe.

'She was . . . I don't know. It's hard to describe. We knew each other all the way from school, from nine years old, so I almost didn't stop to think what she was actually like.'

'Well, tell me five things about her. Then I'll start cleaning.'

'OK. She was — well, very foul-mouthed. Always swearing.'

'Worse than me?'

He grins.

'About the same as you. But just coarse in general. Like, we had these friends, Bec and Russell, who were trying to get pregnant for ages, and Matilda would always ask them how the sex was going, in all kinds of, er, crude ways. Until we realized actually, maybe they had a problem, and then she eased off.'

'That is the danger with jokes about sex,' Pippa agrees.

'Um, apart from that . . . ' Xavier considers. 'Well, she often walked naked around the house. I suppose that goes in with her rudeness. She was a very good cook. She had a lot of freckles.'

'More than me?'

'Far more. English people don't know what freckles are. She did trampolining as a hobby. She used to get nosebleeds sometimes. Will that do?'

'That will do,' Pippa says, unzipping the blue-and-yellow laundry bag and assembling her infantry line of sprays and scourers. Xavier retreats to the study and listens to the now-familiar sounds: running water, bottles puffing out detergents,

148

objects being pummelled and scraped and coerced into neatness.

Xavier has never found it easy to concentrate whilst Pippa is cleaning. Today, he ought to be writing his tepid review of the film, and dealing with emails. There is another email from Clive Donald: in this one, he uses the phrase *mounting desperation*, and implies that Xavier's show is one of his only sources of comfort. As always, Xavier has little choice but to remove the teacher, however guiltily, from his thoughts.

Near the end of Pippa's stint, he goes into the hall, and finds her standing there before a rarely accessed cupboard, a photograph in her hand.

'I was kind of running out of things to do,' says Pippa, 'because the place is quite neat already, so, I, er . . . ' She gestures at the cupboard, in which Xavier stashed a motley collection of belongings when he first moved in; boxes, bags, useless but not quite disposable things, all of them dormant beneath a curtain of dust.

'You're brave to venture in there.'

'Nothing escapes me,' says Pippa. 'One of the people I clean for, I've got him to change his phone plan.' She counts the tasks up on her fingers. 'I've sorted out his Sky TV, I've organized his contents insurance. And I'm going to get rid of his girlfriend for him. You're getting off lightly if I just tidy your stuff up a bit.'

'When you say 'get rid of' his girlfriend,' Xavier begins.

'I don't mean kill her!' They both laugh. 'Yes, he's too much of a coward to chuck her even though she's a sponging bitch. I'm going to engineer a situation and have a word.' She rubs her nose thoughtfully. 'If that doesn't work then I will have to kill her.'

There is a pause as she sees Xavier glance at the photo in her hand.

'Can I be really nosy, pet? Is one of these Matilda?'

He studies the picture, which he didn't know he still had; it must have fluttered out of some box or other. It's of Chris and Matilda, Bec and Russell, at York Minster, during their grand tour of Europe in the summer of 2002. They're all gazing down at the ground, as if from a great height, although they are obviously just standing in the nave of the enormous church. Bec wears a dress from Harvey Nichols. Russell's round face, beneath a baseball cap, looks as if it might crack with the width of his smile. Chris has two weeks' beard. Matilda — he points to her — is wearing a tiara they bought for a joke at Harrods, and a low-cut vest top.

'That's her.'

'She's very pretty.'

'Yes.' Xavier coughs. 'The reason for the photo is . . . those two, Bec and Russell, like I said, they always desperately wanted a baby, and it took years, and the day before we went to York, Bec found out she was pregnant. We were all going to climb the tower in York Minster and then she said casually: oh, I'd better not, being pregnant and all. That was how she broke the news. Matilda and I went crazy.

'So then we were all on a high and we got

150

someone to take this photo of us, pretending we'd climbed the tower and we were looking at the view, even though we weren't. It was kind of funny at the time.'

Pippa looks more closely at the photo and Xavier remembers the four of them in the restaurant in York, just after Bec's revelation.

'I just thought there was something wrong with me,' Bec said, 'I thought it was never going to happen.' She swallowed hard, several times. There was a pause.

'Hey, is this where you cry?' asked Matilda. 'We've never seen you cry.'

'This is the best chance you'll ever get,' Chris chipped in.

Bec began to laugh, but it was a high, slightly hysterical laugh.

'Shut up.'

'Come on, you monster,' Matilda persisted, jabbing her. 'This is the biggest moment of all our lives. Cry.'

'Shut up, Mat!' Bec, uncharacteristically ruffled and even slightly pink, grinned into a menu, hiding her face.

They continued the joke all the way through dinner until Russell said, 'Oh, I'll just poke her in the eye, shall I?' He leaned indelicately across with his fork and upset a carafe of wine, and with Chris's help a thin-lipped waiter mopped up the damage as the group held back raucous laughs.

The sudden, rather heavy silence between Xavier and Pippa — though it could be that he imagines the heaviness — is broken by a staccato series of machine-gun screams from Jamie

151

downstairs. The two of them glance at the floorboards, which feel as though they are only just holding back the noise, as if Jamie's piercing, one-note voice were the shaft of a drill about to come boring through the floor and attack them. Mel's voice rises in a plea for quiet.

'Do you ever think of going down and lending a hand?'

'I do, actually, but, you know, it's none of my business.'

'You do tend to keep your nose out of things, don't you?' Pippa remarks.

'I don't go butting in, no.' Xavier feels a pressure to defend his inactivity. 'I tend to think, you know, things will kind of take their course.'

'That's a nice way of saying you can't be arsed.' She says it with gentle mockery.

'It's not about being . . . arsed. I just think — well, I don't know. People often overestimate how much difference they can make.'

'I think people *under*estimate it. You can change someone's life without even knowing it.'

'Well, yeah. But if you didn't then it would probably change anyway.'

Pippa's hands reach down to touch her knees.

'I can't do that. If I just said oh well, I'll let events take their course, I'd just have to accept that I'm a failed athlete with shit knees, condemned to be a cleaner until I retire or die from exhaustion.'

Xavier doesn't know what to say.

Pippa makes a wry face.

'I'm sorry, pet. That was OTT. I mean, I *like* cleaning. I like being the best at it. I'd try to be the best at whatever I was doing.'

'I admire that,' says Xavier quietly.

It has been an oddly weighty conversation and, before there can be another pause, he hands her the envelope, which he prepared earlier, no awkward foraging around for cash this time. They hesitate; for a strange second it feels as though they might shake hands.

'I'll see you out,' says Xavier, and the two of them go down the stairs.

As Pippa mounts her bicycle, he experiences a flickering regret that she is leaving.

'Same time next week?'

'Same time next week.'

He watches her, upright in the saddle, her dress threatening to get caught in the spokes as she ploughs uphill, the arthritic knees, her thighs, haunches and buttocks flexing like components of an engine as she works the pedals, almost standing up fully at the steepest part of the incline. She stops at the top of the hill to let a speeding car past and glances back. Xavier waves and wonders where she's going next.

6

The following Wednesday is showery and full of nasty winds like most of its month-mates. Pippa has to go from her little flat in North-east London to Marylebone; Maggie Reiss, the psychotherapist, has to travel in the opposite direction. The day turns out to be difficult for both of them.

Pippa's problems begin at three in the morning, when her sister Wendy wakes her up, complaining of nausea. She has a particular dread of being sick, which dates back to childhood, when she once vomited up the walls of her bedroom: dark walls which seemed to close in on her. Pippa makes her younger sister a pot of tea and the two of them sit at the kitchen table, half listening to a radio show where someone has called in to say what he would do if he had three wishes.

'We should call in,' says Pippa.

'I don't know what I'd do with three wishes.' Wendy frowns.

'Well, you could kill Kevin with the first one.'

'And then . . . ?'

'I don't know, kill him again with the second one. Third one, you could maybe get us a popcorn-maker or something.'

They laugh. Pippa grips Wendy's arm. Unlike Pippa, Wendy is thin, rather wasted-looking, with delicate features. Pippa chats to her about

154

anything she can think of. By half past four, Wendy's feeling better, and feels ready to trust herself to sleep. Pippa is so tired by now that she can't even muster the energy to take off her dressing gown: she slumps on top of the bed like a suitcase someone has dumped there.

Maggie Reiss sleeps well, waking at seven thirty. Today she will present a paper to a conference in the Soho Hotel, attend a Pilates class and, of course, see four clients: the first, a supermodel, at the model's home in Muswell Hill; the other three in the office. The model pays extra for the privilege of a home visit. Maggie leaves the house feeling reasonably optimistic about the next few hours. This is, however, to be the last day of her professional career.

Pippa is up again at eight, ready for the day's first job, carpet-cleaning for a landlady whose last tenants, by the sound of it, befouled the place in ways she dreads to imagine.

Wendy is already sitting at the kitchen table, fully dressed.

'Pippa?'

'What are you doing up?'

'Will you come with me to the doctor on Saturday?'

'Of course. Why?'

Wendy doesn't say anything but looks down at the table, or rather, as if she can see straight through it to the floor.

'Oh Jesus.'

Pippa sits down next to her sister and wonders who it was, that guy from the blind date,

155

presumably, the Scottish lad. You fucking idiot, she thinks, but says nothing, just slides her hand over Wendy's, and leaves it there.

'How . . . ?'

'I forgot to take a pill, I think. Maybe two.'

'Wendy — '

'I know.'

'Have you told him?'

'He's not answering his phone.'

The clock ticks on. Pippa is going to have to cycle like mad and probably turn up all sweaty and have the landlady look askance at her as usual.

'Well,' says Pippa, brightly, 'maybe you'll . . . maybe you'll not be, after all. Maybe it's just late or your clock's all fucked up or who knows what.'

Wendy nods, but then looks her sister in the eyes.

'I am, Pippa. I know it. I know I am.'

★　★　★

Pippa and Maggie cross paths on Archway Road, Pippa on her bike, Maggie in the back of a cab. Maggie briefly registers Pippa's large, egg-like helmet through the window, before returning to the client notes spread out in her lap.

Her first client of the day, the supermodel who's suffered from depression for four years, hasn't done any of the exercises Maggie recommended last week: all she wants is another big dose of her usual prescription. She goes through the session as if she is being put out by

156

it, as if Maggie is an interviewer from some poxy local paper, granted a few minutes in the presence of the celebrity. Maggie's second client, the MP cheating on his wife with a married TV star, is equally obstreperous, as usual: all he really wants is for Maggie to keep telling him that he's doing nothing wrong. To him, she is a priest in a confessional. Her third client before lunch is twenty minutes late, so Maggie doesn't eat until half past two. She bolts down a tuna salad before her Pilates class.

As Maggie hurries down the street towards the gym, Pippa is trying to work out why the vacuum cleaner isn't working properly. She squats down next to it, presses the button a few times, removes and reattaches the tube, tries again. She feels as if her thoughts are having to wade through a layer of wet cement to reach her brain.

The landlady clears her throat.

'You've forgotten to plug it in.'

Pippa rises slowly to her feet, reddening.

'So I have.'

The landlady smiles politely, but peers through her spectacles at Pippa as if wondering whether she might be dangerously incompetent.

'I'm normally a bit better than this!' Pippa laughs.

The landlady smiles another thin smile, nods like a primary-school teacher with a lagging child, and moves away into her entrance hall, with its richly carpeted staircase and huge, bowl-shaped Regency chandelier. Pippa wishes she had eaten something for breakfast, or for dinner last night.

Maggie gets out of the Pilates class slightly

later than expected — it's one of those days when the time is always ahead of where it ought to be — and arrives flustered at the Soho Hotel for the afternoon conference. Even though she's been to this hotel before, she walks past it once in each direction before finding it, tucked down a little mews off Dean Street. The wind is swatting at passers-by, and there are spots of rain in the grey air. She is meant to be speaking on 'New Developments in Neurolinguistic Programming', which is an alarmingly wide brief, and she's going to have to bluff it as best as she can. There hasn't been much time to prepare it; there's never time for anything.

The delegates are thronging in the hotel lobby; many of them have already filtered through to the airless conference room. Maggie sees her name on the agenda for the afternoon, up on a laminated notice, and her intestines draw themselves into a loose knot. She finds the Ladies, but it's packed, there is a queue of five silent, sullen women, there isn't time. She should have done this after Pilates. She retreats from the bathroom, brings her flimsy notes out of her bag and heads for the conference room, forcing a smile onto her lips as someone important grabs her arm in greeting.

★ ★ ★

Xavier is taken by surprise when Pippa calls in the late afternoon — he thought it would be Murray ringing to 'run some stuff by him' for 'Murray's Musings'. He looks at the name

158

flashing on the display: *PIPPA CLEANER*. Probably time to remove that suffix, he thinks. I don't think I'm going to forget who she is.

'Pippa?'

'Hi. Sorry it's so noisy here. They're doing monster trucks. They're just getting the trucks in.'

'What?'

'You know monster trucks? Where they, like, drive all these massive trucks around an arena and sort of smash them into things, or make them do tricks, or race them, or drive them up ramps, or — '

'Yes, monster trucks,' Xavier manages to cut in, 'but what are you doing there?'

'I'm cleaning the meeting room for a lunch for the big bosses, the people who own the trucks. I've just dived out for a second.' There is a mechanical whine in the background, and a roar of air. 'It's fucking chilly today, eh!'

'I've not really been out,' Xavier murmurs.

'Anyway, to come to the point, love, I need to go to the doctor's with me sister on Saturday morning, so I don't think I can make it.'

Xavier registers a small but definite inner plunge of disappointment.

'That's no problem. Did you want to reschedule it, or . . . ?'

'The trouble is, I'm just so booked up. I mean all I've got is Saturday night, but — '

Xavier says, 'Saturday night's fine, if it's fine with you.'

She hesitates for a couple of seconds.

'I thought you'd be out somewhere glamorous, or — '

159

'Why would I be anywhere glamorous?'

'I don't know, or working, or — '

'I don't work Saturday nights.'

It's a date, of sorts. They are both surprised they've agreed to it. As soon as the call ends, Xavier thinks about calling back and claiming to have remembered an appointment. It's one thing for her to come at lunchtime, but Saturday night! He doesn't call back, though: he just sits, turning the phone over in his hand, and eventually deletes the word CLEANER from next to her name.

★ ★ ★

At the same time, Maggie is leaving the Soho Hotel. Her talk was all right, no better than that. They pronounced her name 'Rhys' instead of 'Rice' and some people sniggered as if it were a deliberate barb. There was some old bastard asleep in the corner, his face lolling down over his lap, and every time she tried to look around the room as her public-speaking coach told her to, her glance caught the discouraging dome of his bald head. There were some half-hearted congratulations and handshakes afterwards and she left without even a drink in the bar: she has to get back to the office for her last appointment. She has texted the client, Roger, to let him know she'll be late, but he hasn't replied. Roger is the managing director of an estate agent, Frinton, and sees her to talk about self-esteem issues. He has awful breath. She wishes this day would end.

She sits in the back of a cab which advances

160

fifty yards in fifteen minutes. Why didn't she take the tube, at this time of day? She checks herself in her pocket mirror: she looks awful, tired, the stylist ruined her hair, there are pouches under her eyes. She looks closer to sixty than forty. Her insides churn mutinously. She shifts about in the seat, tries to lower the window, but it seems to be locked.

The cabbie, like many London drivers, purports to be amazed by how much traffic there is around, as if the car were still some rare, newfangled form of transport.

'Unbelievable,' he mutters, gesturing at the stock-still vehicles on all sides of them, shaking his head at the perversity of other people. 'Unbelievable.'

Roger Willis sits in Maggie's office, waiting impatiently, trying without success to interest himself in one of the magazines provided, a men's monthly, with articles on must-have gadgets; women; the top one hundred clips on YouTube; more women. He glances at the text from Dr Reiss — *So sorry, ten mins* — but even doing this reminds him of the mis-sent text he received earlier from Ollie, who he thought liked him, or respected him, anyway. But no, Roger reflects, obviously Ollie and Sam are always laughing at me. My breath. What the hell do I have to do? I have a mint about every ten minutes. I brush my teeth three, four times a day. I've used sprays, chewed gums, everything. I've got Brenda to stop using garlic, spices. What do I have to do?

Of course it's typical, this wait. Roger glances

161

irritably at the receptionist with her fingernails tap-tap-tapping the keyboard, and she returns him an insipid condescending smile. He can handle Dr Reiss knowing he's depressed, it's her job, but to have these women staring at him, the prim girl at the desk, the cleaner, the other patients, even . . . clients, not patients, they refer to them as clients. Everyone who sees him in this building knows that there's something wrong with him. Imagine if someone recognized him, a big vendor or another agent or client, imagine if they saw him coming out of a shrink's office.

Yes, it's typical, this wait. Everyone thinks Roger Willis is a soft touch. He's someone you can send text messages about and laugh at in the lunch-break. His hair is falling out, and then there's the breath. Roger can feel himself yielding to an undertow of self-contempt, exactly the sort of thing Dr Reiss tells him to avoid; separate out your worries, one negative thought leads on to another and another and it's an avalanche. Well, all very well for Dr Reiss to talk, she's *still* not even here, twenty minutes late now. Roger grits his teeth. He can feel his heart beating. He pictures Ollie's sneering face. Someone is going to be sorry for the way everyone treats me, thinks Roger. Someone is going to be sorry soon.

★   ★   ★

'The reason it's such a problem for me,' says Roger, as Maggie nods patiently, 'is because my job is all about respect. Do you know what I

162

mean? Without respect I can't do my job. I can't tell people what to do if they think I'm stupid. And that feels like a big failure. To be a man in his fifties. And not be . . . not have authority. Do you know what I mean?'

Yes, Maggie thinks wearily, she does know what he means, because they have this same conversation every week. She's not surprised that his employees send texts about him. How has he ever been thick-skinned enough to make it as an estate agent? she wonders.

'I think *failure* is a word you need to think about very carefully,' says Maggie, thinking, oh, I'm going to burst, I'm actually going to explode unless I go to the bathroom. There are still twenty-five minutes of the session to go.

'See, the reason this text message has particularly affected me,' Roger continues.

'Text message'! Why can't he say *text* like everyone else in the world! He probably still refers to *VHS* and the *television set*. Maggie knows she's being unfair but she is suddenly sick of people's problems, their snivelling. Not even suddenly. She's been sick of this for years. Glazed-eyed models. Narcissists. Sex addicts.

'The reason it's particularly affected me.'

He has this maddening habit of restarting sentences, restarting paragraphs, even, and each time she has the horrid feeling that the clock has also been wound back. Incredibly there are still twenty-five minutes left; the hand seems glued to the number on the clock face by some magnetic force, as Roger winds up his subject again.

'It's affected me because, well, to overhear

163

something, you see, it makes it all the worse, because, you see . . . '

This is another thing he does, making some point like 'It's worse to find out indirectly that someone hates you,' or, 'It's embarrassing to be undermined,' as if he was the first person to discover it. In fact they all do it, everyone comes into the office and talks as if their neuroses are startling, as if they are in possession of remarkable insight into the human condition, none of them aware how many times a day Maggie hears the same phrases word-for-word, the same rehashed problems. Jesus. Her congested bowels sit impatiently; her stomach feels like a bowl of hot soup. At moments like this she becomes unpleasantly aware of the word *bowel*.

'Now, I know you told me to avoid the word *failure*, I know it creates a bad set of associations, and I have been thinking about it, and trying to sort of address things in a more, a more positive way, if you know what I mean. But . . . '

Maggie is on her feet.

'I'm sorry to interrupt you, Roger, but I am just going to have to leave for a second. I'll be right back.'

He blinks at her.

'I'm just going to the bathroom. I'll be right back.'

He sits, affronted, listening to her quick steps in the corridor. This is typical, he thinks. She's late, she's hardly listening to him, now she's slipping out halfway through; it's not good enough, especially when you look at what he's paying. Imagine him in the middle of a meeting with a property developer, just excusing himself! But again, it's the way people are with Roger. This is it, this is where it ends. He steels his nerves for a confrontation.

Maggie slams and locks the door, trying not to think of the amused face of the glossy receptionist. She tears off a wad of paper and shoves it into the bowl to dampen the sound, then sits down hurriedly and realizes how fast her heart is beating. Everyone, everyone judges her. The way he looked at her as she went out of the room. The way the model talked to her earlier, contemptuously eyeing Maggie's rat's-tail hair and washed-out skin, as if Maggie's age were not down to the inevitable working of time but to a perverse and regrettable choice on Maggie's part. The MP who regards her more like a hired hand than a serious professional. All of them. Last week a client, who cried for twenty minutes into her shoulder, ended the session by saying, 'What the fuck do you know anyway?'

In the consultation room Roger waits for four minutes, five. This is preposterous, he's paying good money. He won't pull her up on it straight away. He'll wait until the end. But he will do it.

Maggie, red-faced and disarranged, tramps back across the corridor, feeling hot at the back of her neck as the receptionist, still with that pursed, know-all mouth of hers, smiles her consoling smile. Why is there such a stigma, thinks Maggie, attached to going to the

165

bathroom, for Christ's sake? Maybe there's a paper to be written on it, a book even. That's what I should be doing. Back to writing books. Enough of this. I don't need this.

Roger refuses to meet her eye as she re-enters the room. They get to the end. Maggie suggests some strategies that might help Roger. She might as well be reciting a recipe for an omelette. They agree Roger is going to continue with St John's wort, he's more comfortable with something non-prescription, he doesn't like the idea of pills, blah blah blah.

'Now, do you need to arrange payment,' asks Maggie, the usual euphemism for 'Give me my money now', 'or . . . ?'

Roger clears his throat, fiddles with his cuffs.

'Dr Reiss, I . . . '

What? Maggie thinks, beyond exasperated. Is it not over even now, this stupid, endless day?

'Dr Reiss, I haven't been entirely happy with the service I've received today.'

'You what . . . I'm sorry?'

Roger swallows. This is it, he's standing up to her.

'I've found you unprofessional. You were late for the session — seriously late — your mind seemed to be elsewhere, you left for some time halfway through, and now we're finishing a good three minutes short. I mean, I understand that we all have an off-day . . . '

'An off-day!' Maggie echoes, almost laughing. This ridiculous man, who the hell does he think he is, with his customer-relations phrases, his terrible trousers, his shocking breath?

166

'What I'm saying is . . . ' Roger hesitates, what *is* he saying? 'I'd like there to be an improvement next time.'

This is too much. Maggie raises her voice.

'You know what? Don't pay me. Keep your money. Keep it. And don't bother coming again. Find someone else.'

'Dr Reiss . . . ' Roger is alarmed. He'd thought it was going well, the speaking out. He was pleased with the way he expressed himself. This is why he avoided counselling for so long, this is what he feared, scenes, fuss.

'Dr Reiss . . . '

But Maggie has pushed open the door and marched, with the addled purposefulness of a drunk, out into the corridor.

'Cancel it all,' Maggie says briskly to the receptionist, whose perma-smile fades for once.

'What?'

'Cancel it all. I'm done with this.'

She doesn't wait for the lift but strides to the fire-escape door and almost runs down the three flights, her footsteps, hard on the seldom-used stone stairs, echoing down the stairwell. Maybe she would have carried on for another fifteen years, hating the job; maybe she would have quit tomorrow anyhow; but now is the moment, because Roger got angry over her bathroom visit, because he's upset over a text, mis-sent because of an unfamiliar phone, used because another phone was stolen, because a boy was sacked after a tantrum provoked by a review, which was fuelled by anger at a beating-up which Xavier failed to stop on that cold day a few weeks ago.

167

★　★　★

As Maggie boards the tube, mentally preparing a speech to her husband ('We need to enjoy ourselves, we can afford to leave all this behind, let's go anywhere, do anything'), Xavier is preparing his Wednesday-evening show. They're going to be talking about 'Brushes with Fame' — a lighter topic, tonight, as callers on a Wednesday, the sagging middle of the week, are often noticeably less sparkly and energetic than on other nights. Their boss Roland is always happy when the subject is more playful; less risk, as he remarked to Xavier earlier in the week, that Murray might say something jarringly inappropriate.

Towards the end of the show, at a minute to three, Murray flicks the switch to cue the penultimate news broadcast. The show has slipped by in a pleasant stream of celebrity-related reminiscences, perhaps the most interesting coming from a caller who was trapped in a lift with Terry Waite, some years before Waite's far more extensive captivity in Beirut. 'Murray's Musings' went fairly well: he avoided, on Xavier's advice, any reference to the recent trial of the man who kept his children locked in a basement, instead returning to the motif of the pirates, who fortunately came into the news again this week.

'Anything planned for the wer, for the weekend?'

'Not really.' Xavier sips his coffee. 'Couple of films. I've got some work on, columns and stuff. You?'

Murray plays with a frizzy strand of his hair,

168

which is, at the moment, particularly bouffant.

'My, er, my sister's having a per, party Saturday night. Do you want to come along?'

Xavier looks out of the window at the car park with its slow dumb-show: the caretaker, fag in hand, eyes bloodshot, counting down the minutes of his final hour on duty; the fox down there among the recycling crates, half a discarded McDonald's box in its teeth. He recognizes that this is less an invitation than a request from Murray, who, again, wants Xavier to serve as foil and support in his efforts to meet women. He's got better at not introducing Xavier by saying, 'We do a radio show together,' or (as on one ghastly occasion), 'This is the well-known Xavier Ireland.' Even so Xavier has little appetite for the idea of the party.

But the thought of Murray on his own, mooching in corners, inelegantly jutting into conversations, overeagerly quoting film lines or catchphrases from comedy shows in lieu of his own bons mots . . . Xavier finds the image as painfully easy to imagine as ever. He particularly hates the idea of people talking about Murray behind his back, exchanging wry glances of relief as he goes off to another room.

'Sounds good,' says Xavier.

'Brilliant.' Murray sounds relieved. 'It'll be a blast. She's got this friend who's just joined as a locum or something, and hopefully she's going to be there. Honestly, Xavier, you would not believe . . . ' He shakes his head and works his hands in a vague mime meant to evoke a large pair of breasts.

169

'You're a real romantic, Murray.'

Murray laughs.

'So I was thinking of getting a cab, so I can . . . ' This mime, hands tipping imaginary cans of beer back towards his throat, is easier to decode. 'So if I cer, cer, come and pick you up at, maybe . . . '

Xavier suddenly remembers.

'Ah. Shit. Actually, mate, I'm . . . I've got someone coming round Saturday night.'

'Someone coming round?' Murray raises his eyebrows, baffled. 'Like a . . . like a wer, woman?'

'No, no, er, well, yes,' Xavier blusters, 'she *is* a woman, but it's not . . . it's just a . . . ' How is he meant to explain that a lady is visiting, to carry out scarcely necessary cleaning, on Saturday night? 'She's just a friend.'

'Well, bring her along.' Xavier can see Murray's hopeful eyes converting this problem into an opportunity. 'Is she . . . is she . . . ?'

Xavier makes a rueful face.

'It would be awkward to bring her.' The lie, if it is a lie, is already becoming more complicated with each second of its existence. 'It's someone I haven't seen for a while, so, I think, I think she'll want to, er, stay in.'

Murray's amiable face clouds.

'I mean,' Xavier placates, 'we could always come along afterwards. Later, I mean.'

'Yeah. Of course.' Murray makes a good stab at a nonchalant wink. 'That'll be cool.'

There's a pause.

'Back in ter, two minutes. Coffee?'

Xavier hears his friend's footsteps in the

170

unoccupied, strip-lit corridor outside, the steps heavy and rather sad, he thinks, but overrules himself: there's no such thing as 'sad footsteps', it's just the sentimental weakness of the late night, and anyhow, what is he meant to do, attach himself to Murray twenty-four-seven to steer him away from every potential embarrassment? Xavier feels flustered and somehow irritated with himself; he knows he handled the conversation as if he had something to hide. A couple of emails come in at once and he slides into Murray's seat to read them, grateful for the distraction.

★ ★ ★

Saturday is mild, at last: the cold has finally loosened its grip on the year. Xavier wakes early, not because of Jamie, for once; not wholly because of bad dreams either. The walls of the house are running through their litany of creaks and sighs, the muttering to nobody.

Xavier spends the day quietly, writing two of his columns for next week. He listens to the football scores starting to come in at ten to five, and then at five exactly the final round-up of results, intoned by the announcer as gravely as a list of casualties. The sky outside scrolls through a limited palette of greys. Darkness is falling and listless rain greets Xavier when he walks to the corner shop for provisions.

The Indian man is in a good mood: his daughter has announced her engagement, he tells Xavier.

'Very nice man, very rich. *Very* rich.' The shopkeeper cackles suddenly, flashing white rows of teeth.

'I don't need . . . ' Xavier begins, because he's brought his own bag, but the shopkeeper, packing for him, pays no heed, continuing instead to discuss the startling salary of the man who will, in three years' time, make his funeral arrangements.

Pippa rings the doorbell right on time today; he sees her coming down the hill, watches her from his window, a big, aged colourless raincoat wrapped around her. Her head is bowed, as if she is studying the rain-darkened pavement in front of her. She moves slowly, without the usual sense of vigorous purpose.

Xavier rushes down to the door.

'You're wet!'

'It's raining, pet.' Her voice is rather flat, he thinks.

Xavier steps aside to let her past.

'You don't have an umbrella?'

'I don't like them.'

She ascends the stairs, still heavy-legged, removing her raincoat. Underneath it she is wearing a jumper with blue and white horizontal stripes, and jeans, above which the top of her knickers catches Xavier's eye as he walks behind her: they have a pattern of bright-red lips.

'They just get in the way, umbrellas, you bash people with them, they flip inside out at the first bit of wind, you have to find a place to prop them to dry, and they drip everywhere,' she declaims from inside the flat as she waits for

172

Xavier to catch up. 'And *then* you forget you've brought the bloody thing and you leave it somewhere.'

Xavier grins, knowing before he even sees her that she is counting these irritations off on her fingers.

He goes into the kitchen to put the kettle on. Under the gathering roar of steam he pads stealthily into the hall and, looking into the lounge, can see that Pippa has sunk down into the sofa, head slumped again, as if asleep.

'Are you all right?'

Pippa flinches and jerks upright at the sound of his voice.

'Oh, yes, yes. Don't mind me, pet. I'm just a little bit tired.'

Xavier brings in a tray of tea and biscuits and sets it carefully in front of her. He has a hunch about the cause of Pippa's fatigue.

'How's your sister?'

Pippa looks up slowly, her pale, almost translucent eyes hooking onto Xavier's.

'She's gone and got herself pregnant. Or rather, some guy has gone and got her pregnant.' She gives her own joke a tiny wistful smile. 'Either way, it's . . . well, it's not a great piece of news.'

She puts a hand over her eyes and for an alarming second he thinks she might cry, however unlike her that seems; but all she does is slide the hand down and down from her eyes to the base of her chin, in a single, exhausted movement.

'I feel like me face is falling off, I'm that tired.'

'What's she going to do about the . . . the baby?'

Pippa shakes her head hopelessly.

'She can't have it. We've not got a pot to piss in, as I've said before. Let alone another pot for a baby to piss in.'

'So will she . . . ?' Xavier makes an inadequate gesture.

'You don't know my sister. She'd go mad if she got rid of it. Mad with guilt, or get freaked out by the operation itself, or whatever. She's much more sensitive than me.' Appropriately, her accent manhandles the word *sensitive*, chewing up the defenceless 't'.

'So . . .'

'So I don't know what to do.'

'Well, without wanting to be harsh, it's her that got into this position. Not you.'

Pippa shrugs, massaging one wrist with her other hand.

'Her having a problem is the same as me having one. She's me sister.'

For the first time in months Xavier thinks of his older brothers, Rick and Steve. They were always just a little too old for Chris, they had their standard jokes locked down for ten years before he appeared; they had their cricket games he was too small to join in with. They both forgot his twenty-first birthday.

Xavier pats Pippa's knee and experiences an unexpected bolt of feeling for her, somewhere between fear and exhilaration.

'Have you eaten?'

She rubs her eyes and looks warily at him.

174

'No, well, no, not really.'

'Would you like — I could get a takeaway.'

Pippa blows a blade of whitish hair out of her eye and her cheeks flush slightly. She looks like a kid for a moment, Xavier thinks.

'Really?'

'Yes, why not?'

'Because I'm meant to be cleaning your flat, on a professional basis.' She bites her lip to warp a coming grin. 'Not stuffing me face.'

'You don't have to stuff your face. You can eat delicately if you want.'

This time she laughs out loud.

'Do I look like I'm capable of doing that?'

Xavier fishes in his pocket, and is reassured by a soft bundle of cash.

'Do you like Chinese?'

'Chinese would be amazing. I'll still do the same amount of cleaning, by the way.' Her face is suddenly serious again. 'I'll do more afterwards.'

'Don't be silly. Just relax for once and we'll have some food.'

Pippa starts to protest, but her stomach interrupts, growling plaintively. Her freckles float on another brief blush.

Xavier laughs.

'See? You can't argue with that. I'll be back soon.' He reaches for his keys. 'Stay there and try not to clean anything.'

* * *

As he walks back down Bayham Road with two plastic bags from the Chinese place, where the staff expressionlessly gazed at a small wall-mounted TV, Xavier wonders what he is playing at. Neon rain streams down in front of the street lights. He goes into the Indian man's shop — 'Nice to see you once more, sir,' says the father of the bride-to-be — and comes out with a bottle of wine. Halfway back, he remembers that there's already one in the kitchen.

With a tightening of chest muscles he wonders whether Pippa has set the table, even lit candles or something. Has he been an idiot, essentially asking her to dinner? I didn't ask her to dinner, Xavier answers his own internal critic, she was here anyway, and I'm giving her dinner because she's obviously hungry and done in, and it's a bloody takeaway in a bag. When he gets back Pippa has, in any case, not made any arrangements for dining. She's in the bathroom on her hands and knees, spraying the porcelain sink and then swiping it with a cloth. The toilet is already champing on a mouthful of bleach, the bath gleams with a whiteness inconceivable just a few weeks before.

'I've done the bedroom and I've made a start on the study and I'll obviously do the kitchen once we've eaten and whatnot,' she says, as Xavier appears and catches her eye in the bathroom mirror. Her striped jumper has slipped down around her shoulders.

He quickly redirects his gaze to the gleaming fittings.

'I thought I told you to have a break.'

'This *is* a break. I'm barely doing anything.'

They sit at Xavier's little dining table, eating

176

chicken in lurid sauces, vegetables exhausted from boiling, straight out of the polythene containers. They don't talk; Pippa eats, thinks Xavier, as if she had just been released from jail. She piles forkfuls into her mouth, breaks prawn crackers in two and uses them to scoop up leftovers.

When Xavier reaches capacity, half a mountain of rice still on his plate, she looks at him as if at a Scrabble opponent who has made a scarcely believable tactical mistake.

'You're not going to eat the rest of that?'

'I couldn't.'

'*I* could.' She eases his plate across the tabletop towards her.

Xavier is pouring wine.

'Do you drink wine?'

'Of course. I'll drink anything.'

She pauses with a forkful of rice halfway to her mouth and watches Xavier fill her glass.

'Do I look really bad?'

'What do you mean?'

'Well, just coming into your house and — I told you I'd stuff me face. Just laying into the food like an absolute pig and guzzling down your wine . . . '

'You haven't done that yet.'

'So you're saying I *have* eaten like a pig?'

Xavier chuckles.

'Of course not. Just someone who is really hungry.'

'I'll be the size of a marquee tomorrow.'

'We'll see. I reckon you might find you're still the size of a normal woman.' How twee of me,

177

he thinks, the habits of the radio show encroaching into everyday life.

'Normal women don't have tits like these.'

'Maybe not, but the average dress size is 16, you know.'

'Who wants to be average?'

'Point taken.' Xavier sloshes the glasses full again.

'How do you know so much about dress sizes, anyway?'

'I'm a tailor,' says Xavier, and somehow it seems very funny to them both.

Looking back, Xavier won't be able to remember whether there was a conscious decision to open the second bottle, who fetched it in, who uncorked it; not that alcohol will destroy the memory — neither of them gets drunk enough for that — but it imposes its own narrative, it seems to oil the edges of the night so that one scene slips into another. The two of them sit on the sofa, side by side, like sixth-formers. Actually, probably *not* like sixth-formers, thinks Xavier; sixth-formers would just go for it. Whatever 'it' is.

Pippa leans across and touches his lips with a finger.

'Go like this.'

'What?'

'You've got wine all over your lips.'

Xavier does as he's told and cringes, briefly, thinking about Murray, who always sports a wine-encrusted mouth at parties. He remembers with a brief spasm of guilt Murray's sister's party — he will be there now, he's no doubt sent a text. Xavier doesn't even know where his phone is, probably down behind the sofa cushions. Well, Murray is going to have to look after himself.

'Are you all right, pet?'

'Yes, I was just looking for my phone. But, I, er, I don't actually want to find it.'

'I'm the same, I've sort of deliberately parted company with mine.' Pippa grimaces. 'I don't want me sister on at me to know when I'm coming home.'

'What did you tell her when you went out?'

'I told her we'd see what happened.'

'And what *is* happening?'

Pippa's eyelashes flicker.

The first kiss is short and diffident, the second exploratory, the third long, so long that, when they finally come apart, they look momentarily disorientated, like surfacing swimmers.

After a long silence, echoed outside, downstairs, everywhere, Pippa says, 'Well, speed dating isn't quite as quick as they claim. But it does seem to work.'

★ ★ ★

They spend half an hour kissing on the sofa, kisses that taste of wine. Xavier slides Pippa's jumper over her shoulders, over her head, stroking her strong, freckled arms, kissing the very tip of her cleavage, which is much firmer than he imagined, closing his eyes as she kisses his neck. No more than that, for now; neither of them wants to be hasty, each minute of this is worth many minutes of regular life.

Then something moves heavily upstairs, voices

179

are raised, and — nudged by the rest of the universe, which had briefly, discreetly turned the other way for a moment — the two of them look at each other as if only now conscious of what has just happened. Pippa runs her hands dazedly through her tousled hair. Xavier sits up a little straighter; his back hurts. Pippa wipes her mouth with her hand. Xavier gets up to go to the toilet. By the time he comes back, the springs which held in place the extraordinary atmosphere of the last half-hour — at the same time narcotic and adrenalized — have slackened, and the two of them look at each other, still excitedly, but with an edginess, like two people who have reached a dangerous agreement.

'I should, I should really be going back,' Pippa murmurs. 'I've not even done the kitchen.'

Xavier, amused, reaches out to take her hand.

'I wouldn't worry about that. If you start looking at it from a cleaning point of view, it's been quite an unprofessional visit.'

She doesn't smile at the joke; for a moment he fears he has offended her.

'Sorry, I didn't mean . . . '

'No, no, it's fine, I'm just thinking about me sister.'

As the pragmatic consideration of everything outside this room steadily reasserts itself, Pippa looks so tired that Xavier wants nothing more than to put her to bed and tuck her in. He smirks inwardly at the bravado of this thought even as it's forming: she's not the sort of person you 'put' anywhere. But he can at least get her a cab home.

He squeezes her hand.

'You know, it will be all right, with your sister. Things will turn out all right.' I'm still a little drunk, thinks Xavier, surprised; the words are marginally slower than usual in taking form, and once uttered they sit self-consciously in the air, like misspelled words waiting to be found out on the page.

'Well, we'll see.'

'People always find a way to manage, they can cope with anything.'

'I don't want to be 'coping'.' Pippa lets out a long slow breath. 'That's what everyone said when me knees packed up. 'You'll cope.' That's what I always say to myself when I have to do six cleaning jobs in a day and then I come home and Wendy's left the washing up. I'd like to get to the stage where life isn't always a struggle. Anyway. Don't listen to me, I'm terrible for it. Talking on.'

'You've done a great job so far. I mean, this is what life is, 'coping'.' Xavier labours to get the conversational point, which he's sure is a good one, to stand up. 'Not many people come through their lives without a fair amount of problems, sooner or later. My dad once said . . . well, anyway. Some manage and some don't. It's what life's about.'

Pippa's mouth twitches into a smile, the meaning of which he can't quite assess.

'Are you going to use that?'

'Sorry?'

'On your radio show. You sounded just like your radio show for a minute.'

Xavier's mouth is dry.

181

'How do you know about that?'

'I heard you the other night.'

He doesn't know why this makes him uncomfortable, but as usual the breach of anonymity is like a torch shining into his eyes, and the room suddenly seems too bright, the light from the bulb queasy and glaring, like the lights in a cheap hotel.

'You're very good,' she says, patting his arm, 'but you could really do without that other man.'

Xavier pulls himself away.

'I try to keep it pretty quiet.'

'I'm not an idiot. I thought I recognized your voice the first time, even, but I couldn't place it.'

Xavier gets up from the sofa, the booze heavy in his head.

Pippa is still talking.

'I couldn't believe it! Me sister's dying of jealousy!'

'What? Why?'

'What do you mean, why? You're famous!'

'I'm not famous.'

'Well, you're on the radio.'

Xavier's heart is beating too quickly. He feels horribly out of sorts.

'Is that why you wanted to — to do this?'

The remark dies nastily in the space between them.

Pippa looks at him, affronted.

'Is that really what you think?'

Xavier is tongue-tied. Pippa, briskly, pulls the striped top over her head, dusts imaginary dirt off her jeans, reaches for her shoes.

'I didn't mean . . . '

'It's OK. Look, I have to get going. Thanks for the takeaway.'

'Let me — let me get you a cab, then. It's late.' Xavier looks for his phone.

'Don't be silly.'

She walks past him in the doorway, where they breathe the same patch of tense air for a second before she strides away, hoisting her jeans up. She goes into the study, where the blue-and-yellow laundry bag has been waiting sentry-like, and he hears the ominously decisive sound of the zip.

Attempting to compose himself, Xavier goes after her.

'I've not even paid you.'

'You think you have to pay me?'

'I mean . . . you did the, the bathroom, you did all that stuff while I was getting the food. You were working.'

'I *was* working, yes, but then it became something else, didn't it?' She speaks with no bitterness now, just a quiet disappointment. 'Never mind.'

He puts out his arms and they hug, but as stiffly, all of a sudden, as two distant relatives parting after a trying family occasion. As he did after the brief tryst with Gemma, the Australian girl, some weeks ago, Xavier feels dizzied by the way the poles of joyous intimacy and mild distaste sit so closely together, can be visited within moments of one another.

He walks her out to the stairs, the mood between them still ambiguous, questions out-numbering answers. But as they're halfway out of the door, there is another sudden, startling noise from Tamara's upstairs — a crash of timber as if a desk has been violently overturned — then more: muffled angry voices, thuds, what sounds like whimpering, frantic footsteps, then nothing. They hold their breath, waiting for someone to come down from the flat, or for something more to happen, at least, but there is nothing. They look at each other. Xavier feels colour come pouring into his cheeks; he avoids Pippa's eye.

Pippa doesn't need to say anything, but, as usual, she does.

'So, I take it you didn't investigate what's going on up there?'

'No,' says Xavier, 'no, I didn't, and I didn't help the lady downstairs, I didn't do anything. You're right, I'm selfish.'

'I'm not looking for you to say you're selfish, I'm just wondering how you can just let things like that happen without getting involved.'

'It's not really anything to do with you, Pippa.'

'I know, Xavier.' The exchange of names is icy. 'I just . . . well, never mind.'

'No, go on, say it.'

'Well, it just seems a bit odd that you can be there on your show giving out all this nice advice, and being Mr Helpful and Reassuring, and you're always there as a shoulder to cry on and whatnot, but then in your actual life you just kind of turn a blind eye.'

'You don't know anything about me.' How did it get to this, this pointless bickering? Xavier wonders helplessly.

'I didn't say I was an *expert*.' Pippa's accent, exaggerated by the rising temperature, claws

184

harshly at the word.

She is propelled by a fast, unruly series of emotions: indignation at being spoken to like some sort of clingy fan, embarrassment at having said too much, as usual, and lost her dignity; weary anger at the fact that everything always has to be about Wendy, or her mam, or at any rate, someone other than herself. And then, seeping into the cracks between these bricks, a slow, gooey disdain for this man who sits in his radio studio, dispensing his bits of advice, comes back to his nice flat, can afford to wave money at a woman to make his bed and put bleach in his fucking toilet, who clearly can't imagine what it's actually like to have the sort of problems he smugly counsels people on. Or the sort of problems Pippa herself has: surviving with no money, making fifty calls a day to ask people if they need a cleaner, propping up her sister, talking her mother down, falling asleep with her clothes on.

'I just think it's a bit, it's a bit *convenient* to be always on the radio saying it's good to talk about what's on your mind and all that, and then just shutting yourself away — '

'I've told you, I don't butt in, because — '

'Yes, because you think everything just happens of its own accord. Well, like I say, that's convenient.'

'Do you want to know something!'

Xavier doesn't recognize himself; he might be watching this scene from somewhere outside his body. He corners Pippa, thrusts out a finger, trembling slightly.

185

'Do you know what! I used to get involved in every bloody thing in the world! And everything went fucking wrong!'

There is a long silence after these melodramatic words: they could hardly be expected to provoke anything else. Xavier knows that they will have heard him downstairs, he could have woken Jamie. He tries to modulate his voice, but it wavers up and down, out of his control like a kite tossed in the elements.

'So don't ever come in here again and tell me that I should be running round doing people favours. Because the less I'm involved, trust me, the better.'

'I'll not come in here and tell you anything,' Pippa says quietly.

Xavier watches, aghast at himself, as she leaves. He still thinks she might come back, that they can somehow reset this awful, messy conversation, but after a pause that raises hopes for a moment, the front door clicks into place below.

* * *

Xavier finds a bottle of vodka he'd forgotten he had, in one of the cupboards Pippa reorganized, and sits on the sofa with the TV on. He drinks straight from the bottle, taking a grim pleasure in the three-second lag between swallowing and the burn in his throat. The takeaway cartons are still on the table, the air still smells of Pippa. He moves into the bedroom, leaving the late-night news to report

186

breathlessly to itself: *GIRLS WERE IM-PRISONED IN INHUMAN CONDITIONS, EMIRATES JET MAKES EMERGENCY LANDING.* He drinks until he can almost believe that tonight went perfectly, consoling himself with the thought that he didn't, at mild provocation, break his vow to never talk about what happened with Michael, and then drinks some more until his mushy brain can almost be persuaded to confirm that it never happened at all, that it's still six years ago and there is still everything to play for.

7

Xavier sleeps until three the following afternoon — or lies in bed, at least. Each time he regains consciousness, all he wants is to lose it again. He hears or senses the day going by, like music played in a distant room: Mel taking the squawking Jamie somewhere, footsteps on the stairs around lunchtime, and then the distinctive, heavy silence of the Sunday afternoon outside. The Bayham Road traffic is just a trickle of cars taking couples to pub lunches, or families to early-year picnics provoked by the long-awaited sun.

Eventually he sits up in bed, throws the covers aside and begins to review the events of last night. I fucked everything up, Xavier thinks. For a second all he wants is to call Matilda, or Bec and Russell, just to hear one of those familiar voices, even if they only describe what they can see around them, what they've been up to. But it's night in Australia. Matilda is dancing with her fiancé in Kings Cross, Sydney. Bec and Russell, exhausted as usual, are asleep.

Xavier takes a few exploratory steps to the bathroom, but his head feels as if it is being squeezed in a giant fist, and the floor and walls play maliciously with his eyes, refusing to stay solid or static. I'm still drunk, he thinks, Christ, I drank so much. This memory leads back to the others, to the awful exchange by the door, and further back to the sequence of events which brought him here, which made him withdraw from the world to the extent he has, and made him shout, absurdly, at Pippa, for saying things which were probably true.

Xavier feels sick. He manages to find his phone in the lounge, on the floor by the sofa. The whole room, with its sauce-stained takeaway debris and disrupted cushions, with traces of Pippa on the furniture and her accelerated breaths still in the air, is infused with a regretful ambience, a sad nostalgia for what briefly happened there. Don't be stupid, Xavier thinks, toughen up, get a grip, for Christ's sake. It takes him three tries to find Murray's number on his mobile.

'Xav? I was going to call you in a couple of hours — I've got a zinger of an idea for tonight, basically we get them to call in to evict people from the TV, like, you can choose one person to banish for ever to — '

'Murray, I'm not well. I'm not going to be able to do it tonight.'

This knocks the words out of Murray for a few moments. Xavier has never cried off once in these five years.

'I've got some sort of virus or something. Sick.'

'Wer, wer, wer, wer,' Murray begins, but he fails to come to an agreement with the word. 'So have you told . . . ?'

'I'm going to call Roland now. They'll get one of those guys to cover.'

'OK.' Murray still sounds shocked. 'Wer, well,

189

I hope you feel better by tomorrow. Big week of shows coming up.'

There's no reason why this week is 'bigger' than any other, but Xavier lets it pass; he wants to end the conversation and be asleep again. 'I'll be fine. I'll be fine. How was last night?'

'All right.'

Xavier can picture Murray's wry face, can almost see him run his hands through the tangle of his hair.

'I nearly went home with this Polish girl. She was hot, you wouldn't believe. But I'd misread her body language. So in the end, well, she went home and I went home, but not together.'

Xavier calls his boss, Roland, who is also surprised, but accommodating. As soon as this conversation is over, Xavier makes his way back to bed, but the phone cries for attention.

It's Murray. Xavier sighs deeply, but picks up the call.

'Listen, I've been thinking. Could you put a word in for me to — to do the show flying solo tonight?'

'Solo . . . ? What, you want to present it? Just on your own?'

Murray's tone is beseeching.

'Xavier, I've . . . I've been there a lot longer than you and mer, mer, most people. Everyone else gets a shot at presenting. Because of the, because of the stammer and everything it's a lot harder for me. If someone came in your place, I don't know how well I'd click with them.'

'It's only one night, Murray.'

'Still, though.'

Xavier sighs inwardly at Murray's request. He knows it's partly inspired by Murray's ill-founded belief that he might be able to impress their superiors and improve his stock at the station with a blinding performance; and there's little he can do to cure his friend of that idea. But it's also partly the case, just as Murray said, that a newcomer might not make allowances for the stammer, he might go away and tell people about the copresenter who can't say anything funny, who can't actually say much at all. This thought is enough to prod Xavier into making the call.

Roland is sceptical.

'We had Murray do a couple on his own years ago, when Malcolm couldn't make it, and they were a disaster. I mean, that was why you ended up taking over from him in the first place.'

'He's got a lot better.'

'What, he can finish words now?'

Xavier is silent.

Roland apologizes.

'He's just not very . . . look, Xavier, I love Murray and you love Murray, he's wonderful, but he's just not very . . . he's not exactly what they call a safe pair of hands when it comes to presenting.'

'He won't let you down. Give him one go. I'll be back tomorrow, anyway.'

His boss reluctantly agrees. Murray is grateful and excited. He texts Xavier with an idea for a way to explain his absence, some nonsense whereby he pretends Xavier's been kidnapped, as an ongoing comic riff, but Xavier advises against it. Murray sends four or five more texts as the afternoon fades to a clear evening, running this or that idea past his collaborator. Xavier replies helpfully each time he drifts into awareness, out of the time-free, amorphous blur where he spends the hours from five to ten o'clock.

In what would normally be the hours of making final preparations for the show, having dinner perhaps, waiting for Murray to pick him up in the car, Xavier, less groggy now, puts on a coat and leaves his flat, with no particular destination in mind.

★   ★   ★

Three minutes from 11 Bayham Road is a series of steps half-obscured from the street by shrubbery, which lead onto a long stretch of woodland. The path through the woods extends a mile and a half to Highgate and beyond. It's part of a little-known green ring which slices through the city, behind and between people's homes, over bridges and round the back of main roads, a parallel London full of dog-walkers, joggers, cyclists and petty criminals. Normally Xavier would think twice about strolling along this route at night, but at the moment he's not even thinking once about anything.

Xavier walks. It's a mild night, with a large moon hanging over the woods. Around the fringes of its light, undergrowth rustles as creatures scamper away from Xavier's lone footsteps. It's only now he realizes that he has

192

been damming a rush of memories for years with a force of will he was only partly aware of. As he walks on into the dark, over a muddy track dotted with clumps of nettles, the memories begin to rise up within him.

He heads back the way he came and gets home at a quarter to three. The show will be in its late stages, but Xavier has no desire to check how it's going. He fills the kettle and makes a cup of tea in a new-looking mug. Sitting in the study, with a single lamp facing the wall to provide a patch of light, Xavier allows himself to retrieve from the vault the full memory of 11 July 2003.

★　★　★

Bec and Russell's cherished ambition to have a baby eluded them until it became more like an insuperable task than a dream; and of course, the more everyone else waited for an announcement, the worse things became. When it was well known that they'd been trying, without success, for three years, the subject became a sticky one. More and more often Chris found the usually unflappable Bec confiding her worries to him.

'What if we're just not able to do it? What if there's something wrong, Chris?'

'Well, you've had tests, haven't you?'

'Yes. They can't see anything wrong. But some people, it just never happens . . .'

Chris didn't say, 'You have plenty of time,' or, 'You're only twenty-seven,' or the other inadequate things that people were saying with the best of intentions. He gripped her hand and told her to keep going and not to panic. At parties, he ensured that jokes were put down, conversation was steered the other way. The gang of four closed ranks.

When at last Bec broke the news of her pregnancy at York Minster, the collective relief powered a six-month euphoria. Jokes were back on: new jokes about what would happen if the baby was ugly, what if it became a serial killer; stupid suggestions for names, comically awful childcare books from the fifties bought in second-hand shops. It went without saying that Chris and Matilda would be godparents, and, to all intents and purposes, aunt and uncle. It had begun to feel, as Matilda said one night, as if it were *their* baby on the way.

What became the worst night of Chris's life had begun with him doing them a favour. The gang of four had tickets to see a famous rock band in the Vodafone Arena: Bec had got them months before Michael existed properly, when he was only a prospect. Now Michael was two months old, a placid baby who was starting to smile like his father. The concert that evening would be the first time Bec and Russell had been out since the birth. Bec was taking a few days off from breast-feeding, so there was technically no need for her to stay at Michael's side; everyone agreed she deserved a break, just for a couple of hours, the strain of recent weeks was obvious.

Everything was planned, but a babysitter couldn't be found.

At first when Chris volunteered to stay

behind, Matilda was aghast.

'These are $60 tickets!'

'We can sell it. We'll get a lot more than that, in fact. You can be a scalper for the night.'

'But I want you to be there.'

'I know, but Bec needs to get out. You've seen her.'

Matilda kissed him.

'You're amazing, you know that?'

'I couldn't agree more.'

Chris was given a set of instructions, but really, what was there to do? Be stationed somewhere near the baby, who'd be sleeping in Bec and Russell's room. If he starts crying, go and pick him up, give him a bottle, just hold him, he'll be straight back off. Always lie him on his back, but you're not an idiot. You shouldn't have to change him.

'I can if it comes to it,' said Chris proudly; he'd done this once already, in week three, when Bec was asleep and Russell seemingly catatonic with fatigue. Matilda and Chris were hardly away from the new parents in the first fortnight or so, fetching, buying, doing errands of every kind.

'If he really starts crying, text me, all right?'

'He will not text you,' said Russell, whisking the mobile out of Bec's hand. 'You'll be back here before the first bloody song. You need a break.'

After all the talk, the endless hype around the pregnancy and birth, Russell was conspicuously keen to show how cool they still were, how little their lives would be impaired by this new helpless dependant. He started to sing, tunelessly. Matilda was wearing a T-shirt she'd bought

195

as a teenage fan, and a bag whose strap bisected her cleavage. Chris imagined someone else bumping against her down in front of the stage, in the forest of arms and the confusion of bodies, and briefly regretted his good nature as the three of them went on their way.

'Just text *Russell* then, if he starts really crying,' Bec called back through the closing door, but Chris was determined that he would not.

Chris sat in his friends' bedroom, decorated with photos of the four of them. There was the one at York with the 'looking down from the tower' gag. There they were at the zoo, Russell dressed as a gorilla during an unsuccessful stint as a children's entertainer. Russell getting his degree. For an hour and a half there was no action at all; Chris read one of Bec's books on ethical shopping; the quiet was almost eerie. Michael slept on in his tiger-striped babygro, small thumb clasped to his mouth, looking much like he was in a TV advert for bedding. His miniature lips twitched in teaspoon-shallow breaths. He muttered crankily to himself. Chris realized that, one day, impossible as it appeared, this tiny thing would be as old as him, and Chris himself would be a middle-aged man. They could have a beer together.

But then Michael started to scream. He began with scratchy screams which ebbed in and out of coughs. Chris decided to ride it out — this was what babies did. Michael's yells doubled in volume and intensity. Maybe he's in pain or something, thought Chris, worried for the first time. He tried to think himself into the role of father. Gingerly, he picked up the baby. Michael was startlingly light, insubstantial for a living thing. At the feel of Chris's hands he redoubled his yelling. The yells built one on top of another, as if they were snatches of music divided into bars, each time culminating in a raw, awful crescendo, the purest expression of pain Chris could ever remember hearing. Shit, thought Chris, his heart beginning to speed up, this is why you're not meant to give your kid to anyone, this is why parents always stay with their newborns for months and months, every single night. Still he didn't panic, but shards of fear were gathering steadily in his guts.

He began to walk slowly around the apartment, whispering to Michael. 'It's all right! Mum and Dad'll be back in a second! Won't they!' — and so on, more for his own benefit, he thought. 'It's all right, Michael!' Wasn't that what they said, just walk around with him and he'll go back to sleep? It's not as if I'm some stranger, is it, I've been with him almost as much as they have. 'Haven't I, Mike, you know me, mate, don't you!' appealed Chris. 'We hang out, mate, don't we!' He had lost his initial self-consciousness about talking to the uncomprehending bundle in his arms. 'We go way back, don't we, Mike!' But Michael was unmoved. He continued to scream. That was the only word for it now. Chris had never heard screaming until now.

Chris quickened his pace, walking circuits around the little apartment, out onto the cramped balcony and back in again, around the battered sofa,

197

the lounge room with its giant framed movie posters, *Jules et Jim, It Happened One Night* — Bec's favourites. *RoboCop*, Russell's. The burst of speed seemed to subdue Michael a little, and Chris sank down into a chair, his legs crossed, the baby in his arms. Michael's knife-like cries had now receded to small sobs. Compared with what had gone before, they barely registered, like the washed-out music that had just started to play at the end of the concert, six kilometres away, after the real band had departed in a haze of noise and light, and Bec and Russell had turned hand in hand to go, stepping across a carpet of discarded plastic cups.

I can handle this, thought Chris, this is fine. This'll be OK. He sat there, not daring to move for some time. The sobs died away. Michael's tiny eyelids closed, opened, closed as he floated around the boundaries of sleep. Chris inhaled deeply in relief, but still couldn't bring himself to untangle his legs or to shift into a more comfortable position. He sat, listening to the familiar noises from the street outside: the clatter and rumble of trams, voices raised in a friendly argument. His right leg was now completely numb; he tried not to think about it. Chris's index finger brushed against Michael's mouth and Michael, without opening his eyes, pressed his lips gently around the tip of the finger, sucking it like a dummy. A couple of minutes later, the next time Michael opened his eyes, Chris offered his finger again; but this time, it seemed to upset Michael. He began to scream all over again.

He's hungry, Chris thought, that must be why he's nibbling my finger. He wants actual food. Bec had left a bottle in the fridge.

'All right, Mike, mate, let's get you some dinner, shall we?'

He rose, sharply, out of the armchair. The sudden movement dismayed Michael, and as well as wailing he began to writhe in Chris's arms, kicking out wildly and with surprising force.

'Hey, it's all right, mate!' said Chris, but there was a sudden jolt of pain from his dead leg as it came to life, throwing him off balance as the writhing baby kicked ever more energetically at the air. It was then that he dropped Michael.

For several seconds his brain simply refused to process what was in front of him. This hasn't happened, thought Chris. I did not just feel Michael, for no reason, drop out of my arms. He is not on the floor.

Very quickly the thin screen of denial melted away, and Chris's body filled with choking waves of panic, and horror, a word he had never understood the real reach of till now. Michael lay motionless and silent on the threadbare carpet, his head slumped to one side and facing away from Chris, his small plump limbs splayed and hanging limp at his sides. He looked like a plastic doll left on a nursery floor.

Chris fell to the ground, his legs feeling as if all the blood had been let out of them. He tried to say something out loud, but no words emerged. Jesus, he thought, no. He already couldn't remember what had happened, how the baby came to be on the floor. How can you drop a

199

baby? How can you be holding it, then not be holding it? This was a question that Matilda would ask him, that Bec and Russell would ask each other hundreds of times, and of course, that he would ask himself for the rest of his life. But there was no answer.

He called the emergency number and screamed at an incongruously chirpy woman for an ambulance. I don't know, he said when she asked if Michael was still breathing, feeling as if he was about to throw up. She told him to check for a pulse. Chris thought he was going to faint. He didn't trust himself to touch Michael. 'Just send a fucking ambulance!' he sobbed again. He laid his hand on Michael's wrist, which was alarmingly cold, but couldn't look at him. There was a whisper of a pulse, he thought, but maybe he was imagining it. On all fours, next to the baby, Chris began to cry.

Barely able to focus his eyes on the handset of the phone, he called Matilda, then Russell, then Bec, then Matilda again — none of them could hear their phones for a while, above the din of the huge dispersing crowd. In the end it was Russell he managed to get hold of.

'Mate, it was awesome!' yelled Russell before Chris could say anything.

But then he couldn't say anything at all. He sobbed and shouted, he made noises he could not associate with himself.

'I can't hear you, mate!' Russell said, still jolly as hell, always the last to react to things, and he gave the phone to Bec to try her luck.

Chris made one noise at Bec, and Bec knew.

Somehow, Bec made it home before the others, before the ambulance. The moment she ripped her prone — though still breathing — baby away from Chris, actually ripped him away like a prized possession from a thief, was inevitably the beginning of the end of their near-lifelong friendship. Their shared past was pulped at a stroke.

Michael was in hospital for three weeks. For a while it appeared he might not recover at all. When he did, it was with severe cranial injuries and long-term brain damage. That was the phrase as Chris first heard it, from Matilda, 'brain damage', a phrase like a handful of wire. He had to hear everything from Matilda, for weeks. He couldn't go to the hospital; he couldn't speak to, or see, two of his three best friends. At this point he thought, in so far as he could absorb it at all, that this was a temporary situation — long-term perhaps, but temporary. It had been a shattering catastrophe, one that would no doubt overshadow all of them for the rest of their lives, but in the end, they had to forgive him, surely.

Fairly soon, though, he realized that 'forgiveness' had nothing to do with it. Weeks became months. The story attained local notoriety: there was an inquiry, there could have been a criminal trial, there were a lot of talks. Chris again and again had to explain, with no expression in his voice, how, yes, he had dropped the boy, he could simply not account for it, it was an accident, a terrible accident. Of course Bec and Russell didn't want anything to happen to him; they just wanted to do whatever they now had to do to survive. On one occasion, Chris's and Russell's paths crossed outside the offices of one of the lawyers involved. They looked away from one another.

In the end, there were no proceedings: Michael's injury was ruled an accident. People had their opinions. What kind of parents go out to a concert with a newborn baby at home? But then, how could anyone be so unimaginably careless as to drop the most precious thing in the world?

Chris stopped going out. He couldn't watch films or concentrate on books, or even the TV. He left his reviewing job and began claiming unemployment benefit. For weeks he only stepped outside the apartment to collect his dole cheque. The more inactive he became, almost with each day that passed, the harder it was to imagine returning to the things he used to do. The less he did, the more tired he seemed to be. He felt that, while everyone else's lives had resumed after the tragedy, or were barrelling on in complete ignorance of it, his had frozen where it was; he had become a spectator.

Matilda went to the opposite extreme, tearing into tasks with a cold-eyed and uncharacteristic efficiency. She went trampolining five times a week, rather than twice; she volunteered for more and more overtime; she took no notice of films, declined invitations to parties. Many of her most endearing quirks seemed to have been steamrollered by the events. Instead of her trademark crumpled T-shirts and joyously mismatched accessories, she had taken to wearing polo-necked sweaters and long skirts — dressing, in fact, like Bec. She picked at her food, never finishing a meal. She stopped walking naked around the house. She didn't swear as much. She took up smoking, having stopped as a teenager. She insisted on his calling her 'Matilda', not Mat, on the few occasions they met for long enough to hold a conversation. She often stayed at Bec's. When she was at home, she and Chris lay at opposite ends of the bed, eyes wide open.

Russell and Bec went for counselling, having been recommended a therapist by the same person they'd once consulted about their sexual problems. Matilda attended all the sessions, but would never discuss them with Chris afterwards. One day she came back much later than expected. It was a beautiful spring evening: planes buzzed lazily over their apartment, office workers in rolled-up shirtsleeves sipped cocktails in rooftop bars, and the faint strains of an open-air concert reached Chris from a couple of streets away. Buoyed by a momentary surge of positivity, he tried to hug Matilda as she entered. She shrugged him off and sat down at the kitchen table, toying with a bracelet which hung loosely around her wrist.

'How did it go today?'

She shrugged.

'How do you think it went?'

'Well, I . . . I don't know what I can say.'

Matilda was glancing into a pocket mirror, rubbing something off the tabletop, checking her phone.

'Please, Mat. Matilda. Please look at me.'

She fixed him with two big eyes.

'There you go. Better?'

'I don't know what I can say.'

Matilda bit her lip, scraped her hand violently across her eyes.

'You know, after it was over today, Bec just cried for, like, a fucking . . . more than an hour. More than an hour. I was just sitting there with her weeping on my shoulder. Bec! Crying like a . . .'

Chris sat helplessly opposite her, trying to picture this.

'And Russell is on antidepressants. You know?'

'I'm feeling just as bad, Matilda.'

'I'm not saying you *aren't*. This isn't a *competition*. I'm just saying — I just don't see how this is ever going to get better. That's all.'

Chris dug out his voice from somewhere.

'It will get better because . . . because everything gets better. Time . . .'

Matilda sat down next to him and took his hand, almost roughly, in hers. She gripped it with a fury he had never known before. He could feel her whole body shaking.

'You're going to have to move out,' she said.

'What?'

'I can't do this.'

'You think *I* can do this any better than you?'

Matilda swallowed and looked at him, and he relived, in a few moments, the whole twenty

204

years, all the way from the blood dripping from her nose onto the floor tiles.

'The thing is, Chris, you can't see them. Right? There's nothing you can do for them because you're not even able to talk to them. *I* can. So I have to be there for them. So that means — '

'It means you choose them, not me?'

'It doesn't help anyone to put it like that. It's not 'choosing'. I don't know what else I can do.'

'And me? What am I meant to do?'

There wasn't an answer.

'I need you,' said Chris. 'For me to get through this, I need you.'

She didn't deny this, but didn't accept it either. Within twenty-four hours he had begun moving out.

★ ★ ★

Nobody knew what to do for Chris. His father had died a couple of years before, of lung cancer. His mother had begun to recover from that, thanks to the three boys' collective efforts, and in any case it had been expected, it was prepared for. Nonetheless it was asking too much of the remaining family to be able to rally and tackle another crisis so soon. And this was a much harder one to understand. Rick and Steve put their big hands on his shoulders, muttered about it being rough luck and not to blame himself, that things happen and you move on, that his mates would have another kid. Chris nodded, dumbly, at everything they said. He sat in the corner, watching what went on in the house with

205

the confused detachment with which he now viewed everything.

Rick had a word one evening after a quiet dinner, enlivened only by the tireless capering of his five-year-old son, Jayden.

'Don't let Mum see you like this, eh. Try to make yourself useful around the house. Whatever you can do. Just, she doesn't need to see you in . . . you know, in all this strife. Not after Dad and everything.'

Chris knew this was true, and he did try. He volunteered for decorating, painting, odd jobs around the house, jobs that didn't really need doing in some cases, but which his mum eagerly encouraged, hopeful that this meant he was 'on the mend'. He did bar work, on and off, for a couple of months, in a Mexican-themed place in the City, a comfortingly anonymous setting. But still a single moment could shatter his composure, leaving him pale and shaking.

Once it was a bit of chat at the bar, three guys, harmless banter — 'Jesus, mate, someone drop you on your head as a kid?' and laughter. Another time it was the mere sight of a baby, and then one night he dropped the cocktail shaker while mixing up a pina colada, and, looking at the oozy mess on the floor, began to cry.

After the first couple of upsets, the manager, a Greek immigrant, was patient with him ('Toughen up, mate,' he said with a jocular thump of the back, 'it's not the end of the world').

But after the tears, he called Chris to his office at the back of the bar, a room barely as big as a wardrobe.

'For your own good, mate, I think maybe we give it a miss,' he said. Chris agreed.

Toughen up. Toughen up. It was what Rick and Steve said to him as well. It was the Australian motto for testing times. Even Matilda used that phrase once. She did her best to stay in touch after he'd moved out; they spoke a couple of times a week, then once a week, then things lapsed further until his main point of contact was her calm recorded voice: *You've got through to Matilda, please leave a message.* But I *haven't* got through, have I? he would think. Sometimes he would leave a message, politely asking her to call back, and sometimes she would. But, for people who had spent most of their lives together, this chillingly formal contact felt worse than total separation. And so it was towards total separation that they began to drift.

Chris went to three sessions with a therapist, making sure he chose a clinic where he couldn't possibly run into Bec and Russell by some malign stroke of fortune. When he described the incident, dropping the baby, the therapist did a good job of nodding attentively, but Chris was pretty sure he knew the story already: everyone in Melbourne knew about it, it seemed. The man told him that blaming himself would send him into a 'spiral of shame'. He had to be kind to himself. Chris tried to explain once again that being kind was not the point; the only point was that he'd hurt the baby and lost his friends, and life had taken a turn from which he couldn't see how it was possible to recover. The therapist said things might well look different in a year.

Toughen up. Be kind to yourself. Chris stumbled through a couple more months. Summer came and Melbourne was hot and feverish. The grass was yellow in the parks, there were water shortages, the air smelled of barbecues every night. Chris would see groups of high-school kids, students, friends everywhere, going to St Kilda Beach, to music festivals, off for long weekends by the sea. He had started taking pills to get to sleep at night. His world, which had shrunk to the area of his mother's house, was now essentially contained within his bedroom. He read books without taking anything in. Once or twice he found the nerve to call Matilda, but the pauses were now longer than the stretches of conversation. Once, he even called Russell, and to his surprise Russell answered, sounding guilty and hushed, as if at any moment the call would be brutally curtailed.

'Chris, look, you know I . . . I'm still your mate and everything. It's just a very bad situation and it's best if we, if we don't communicate for the moment, you know?'

'Is it because of Bec?'

'Look, Bec's really been through it, mate. She's still going through it.'

'Does Bec hate me?'

'Chris, don't, please. Listen, I'll call you.' He put the phone down.

Chris's suddenly cut-down life might have carried on this way for any amount of time, but, perhaps mercifully, two incidents within twenty-four hours persuaded him to leave Melbourne.

The first was Lisa, an old university friend,

getting in touch: she'd been away in Britain for some years and was throwing a big party for her return. She had obviously been briefed about the situation; her tone was careful and affectionate. It would be great if Chris just wanted to stop in and say hello. She understood if it wasn't a great idea, but she'd missed him. Chris hadn't had meaningful contact with anyone for some months, and the idea of someone's having missed him, and making a genuine effort to solicit his company, struck him in a vulnerable place. He decided to see it as a turning point, the latest in a handful of moments he'd attempted to see that way. A turning point was all he needed, he told himself, a change of luck. He got a haircut, shaved off the default-beard which had built up, bought a nice shirt. In the mirror he practised saying the sort of things people say at parties. 'Yeah, you know, some ups and downs.' 'This and that.' 'How's your brother?' 'Good to catch up.'

And for the first half-hour it went well. He found a quiet spot in the garden and Lisa went out of her way to put him at ease, devoting her almost exclusive attention to him, telling him all about London: so much fun, but so expensive. Then he looked up and saw Matilda on the porch, with a new haircut and a new man. He was patting and stroking her ostentatiously and she, clearly all too aware of Chris's presence, was shaking him off with a resistance that was only misread as playful encouragement to keep going. Lisa's eyes darted between Chris and Matilda as she became aware of the awful mistake of inviting them both. How on earth did she overlook this, thought Chris, after all this effort to get me here? But perhaps she hadn't known that Matilda was going to bring someone, or known the full story of the break-up. In any case it didn't matter. He waited until Matilda had gone inside with the man, who looked like a footballer, short-haired and broad-shouldered, and left as quickly as possible. Walking away down the street, past pretty old brick houses with faded yellow paint and wrought-iron balconies, he registered the cruel visual joke of a skywriting plane slicing through the sky, almost as if it was inevitable.

The next evening his mother made a bold but poorly timed attempt to broach the subject head-on.

'You know, Chris,' she said, nervously interlocking one set of fingers with the others, staring at her wedding ring. 'When I was a bit younger than you, and I was working nights at the hospital, we had a patient who I was very fond of, and — '

'Mum, I don't want to talk about it.'

She swallowed.

Rick and Steve gave each other warning glances.

'All I wanted to say was,' she persisted, 'everything happens for a reason.'

'What the fuck does that mean!' Chris said, far more aggressively than he had meant to, or even realized he was capable of.

'Let's leave it there, shall we,' Rick began, dishing out a look of vicious warning to Chris, which Chris overrode, because for once what his older brothers thought made no difference to him at all.

'What's the point of saying 'everything happens for a reason'! What, so I gave a kid brain damage, but never mind, because there must be a reason! That's meant to cheer me up? What if the 'reason' is that everything is fucked?'

'OK, that's enough, mate!' said Rick in a voice that Chris had last heard him use just before he punched someone in the face. Steve laid an arm on Rick's, but Rick pressed on regardless. 'You don't speak to our mother like that, mate! You need to go away and have a think about whether that's a good idea!'

'It's all right, Richard.' This was the outcome their mother most dreaded, to have the boys at odds with each other. 'It doesn't matter. I was just trying to . . . I'm sorry.'

'Are you going to apologize?' Rick, six foot four with huge, tensed biceps, leaned across the table.

'I'll apologize to her in my own time. I'm not going to apologize to you. You can butt out of it.'

'Oh, can I! Shall I butt out of the fact that you're just living off Mum here, wallowing in your own misery? Contributing nothing to the fucking — '

'It's not worth it, mate,' Steve muttered.

'I'm not being unsympathetic or whatever but this has gone on long enough!' Rick said. 'And do you want to know something else? I'll tell you something else!'

'Stop it, *stop* it, all of you.'

She was sobbing. Steve put an arm around her. Rick never did tell Chris what the 'something else' was. Their mother left the room, collecting up plates as she went, helped by Steve, and the scene fizzled out to a thick, sullen silence.

Chris knew then that he would never be able to dispel the memory of his mother crying like this: that it would, like a bully, supplant many happier, more representative memories of her. He also knew that he had to leave immediately.

★ ★ ★

Xavier watches as Monday morning dawns, a brief smudge of pink giving way to a cloudy sky, and hears the week's clockwork start up once more outside. Tamara trots down the stairs outside his door. Jamie, below them, has a tickly cough. The mug of tea is still in front of Xavier. I haven't moved for three hours, he thinks, getting slowly to his feet. The release of these memories, imprisoned for five years, feels as though it has cost him a physical effort. It's as if after relentlessly walking down a road he has looked back for the first time and only now realizes how exhaustingly long it has been.

It's about thirty-six hours since Pippa left. Xavier lies down on his bed and laboriously composes a text message. *I'm really really sorry* is too melodramatic, *Please accept my apologies* too formal. What's needed is an explanation of the fact that she set off something crucial but violent, that she somehow made him confront what he's been avoiding for years: in other words, not a text at all, but a full conversation, something he doesn't dare attempt just yet. In the end he types *It was all my fault. Please get in touch. Sorry. Xavier.* The fifty-odd characters take him almost twenty minutes. He stares at the phone for a couple of minutes in the faint hope of an instant reply, and then falls into a thick sleep untroubled by dreams of Australia or anything else.

A shrill, monotonous tone interrupts the sleep. Xavier feels as if he has to drag each eye open individually. By the time he's fully awake, the phone has stopped ringing. It starts again straight away. Hope speeds up his heartbeat momentarily, but the display reads *MURRAY*.

'Just checking up on you.'

'Much better, thanks, mate.'

'So yer, yer, you'll be coming in tonight? Good news all round.' As incapable of subtlety over the phone as in person, Murray betrays a certain disappointment with his wavering voice.

'I will. How did last night go?'

'Oh, not too bad, not too bad at all. Had some good feedback.'

They agree that Murray will pick Xavier up at the usual time. Only when the conversation ends does Xavier, with a sudden stab of nerves, realize that he should see whether Pippa has sent a text back. She hasn't.

There are a number of emails from listeners enquiring as to Xavier's health; many of them express the hope that Murray will not be left to present on his own again. Xavier tries to respond

213

to these, and to tackle various other tasks, in vain: even the paltry reminder of Pippa afforded by the tidy bookshelves in the study keeps pushing everything else out of his mind. There is also the sudden overload of formerly forbidden memories to contend with: he's aware that it will end up being a relief, but for now he feels groggy and confused.

As the evening wears on, it becomes impossible to explain the lack of a reply from Pippa by imagining that she might be too busy, or that she is weighing up what to say. He's irritated with himself for this adolescent nonsense, all this second-guessing, and decides to call her. The simple press of a button is far more nerve-racking than it ought to be. 'Sort yourself out,' Xavier mutters. But the call isn't answered, and there isn't even the opportunity to leave a message. 'Your call cannot be connected,' a prim voice gloats. 'Please try again later.'

★ ★ ★

The week crawls by at the same lethargic pace, and with the same sense of befuddled inertia in Xavier's brain. He sends more texts to Pippa, the tone beseeching, even pleading. *I would really appreciate it if you got in touch. I would never normally snap at someone like that, but you seem to have got inside my head. You've come to mean a lot to me.* He is surprised at this statement — both that it is true and that he's prepared to say it — but lets it stand. There are no replies, and each fruitless message feels like a

214

humiliating failure. At night, Xavier slips in and out of grey, threatening dreams.

On Wednesday afternoon Xavier meets Tamara on the landing outside his flat. They smile warily at each other, each aware the other heard potentially incriminating noises from their respective homes at the weekend. Tamara has dark glasses on, Xavier notices with a jolt. Isn't that what they do, people in violent relationships, to conceal black eyes? He tries to remember the ad campaign — they played it on his show for a bit; what were the other warning signs of an abusive relationship? He can only remember the message: *If you know someone who is a victim of domestic violence, don't keep quiet.* He peers at her as closely as he dares.

'So, you know that petition?' Tamara says.

'Sorry?'

'The one on road safety, the one we all signed. About putting speed bumps on this road.'

'Oh. Yes.'

'So it went all the way through to head office, and do you know what happened?'

'Er . . .'

'They're going to bring it up in a meeting in a month. A *month*!'

'Long time to wait,' Xavier nods. He really can't think of anything better to say.

'So everything is on hold till then. This kind of red tape. Bane of my life.'

Holding her briefcase down by her side, her handbag in the other hand, Tamara is on her way.

'I'll let you know of any developments.'

'Yes, do,' Xavier agrees faintly.

Pippa was right, of course. He doesn't know a thing about his closest neighbours. He hears Tamara's heels on the landing above, hears her door swing open on a room he has never set foot in. Perhaps some good will come out of all this — perhaps he'll make more of an effort with everyone from now on — but for the time being it's enough of an effort to think about tonight: the cold studio, the half-drunk mugs of coffee, and Murray with his oversized headphones dragging him towards four o'clock.

Halfway through the Wednesday night show — a customarily sluggish one, which Xavier in his current frame of mind is unable to revive — Murray turns to him during the news and weather.

'Wer, what's up?'

'Nothing, nothing's up. Still not quite feeling myself.'

'Who are you feeling?' Murray coughs. 'Sorry. Poor joke.'

Xavier tries to smile.

'I was thinking about wer, Wednesdays,' Murray soldiers on. 'We could maybe address the fact that everyone always seems a bit pissed off. We could make it a bit different, somehow. Try and really crank it up.'

'We could call it 'Wacky Wednesday',' Xavier says flatly.

Murray's uneven eyebrows shoot up.

'That's a great idea!'

'I don't think ... I wasn't suggesting it seriously — '

216

'But imagine! Wer, wer, wer, wer, wer, wake up, it's Wacky wer, wer, wer . . . '

'I might have to introduce it,' Xavier observes quietly.

After they've laughed at this, Murray gets up from his chair and, unexpectedly, puts his hands on Xavier's shoulders.

'You're tense as hell.'

'I don't feel any tenser than usual.'

'Let's get these knots out.'

Murray begins to massage Xavier's shoulders, neck and back. His thick hands lumber across the terrain like unwieldy vehicles trying to negotiate a mountain road.

Xavier sighs in discomfort, which Murray misconstrues as relief.

'Good to get it all out, isn't it! Didn't know I had this skill, did you?'

'I didn't.'

Murray moves his hands in rough circles over Xavier's shoulders, up and down his spine, his fingers straining fruitlessly for tenderness.

'Back on air in one minute,' he says, finally going back to his seat. 'Any emails? Let's have a look. Bet you feel better now.'

★ ★ ★

Saturday is a Scrabble day. By now it's clear to Xavier that Pippa won't be replying to any of his messages, and it seems plain enough that he has strangled what briefly grew between them. All the same something makes him leave a note on the kitchen table just in case she comes. *I doubt you'll read this, but if you do: I accept complete responsibility for what happened. Complete responsibility* is hopeless, he sounds like a politician. He puts a big line through the whole phrase and just writes *SORRY* in half-page-high letters. He leaves money in an envelope a discreet distance from the note, and keys in the flowerpot outside 11 Bayham Road. All this feels to Xavier like a foolhardy lowering of his defences, and he walks hastily up the hill away from the house as if to pretend it has nothing to do with him.

He's not surprised to find himself some way off his best form. After the mental turmoil of the past few days his brain has little interest in reacquainting itself with anagrams and suffixes, and he can't find the will to ignite the competitive edge needed when playing against even moderate opponents. He blunders his way past a couple of serial losers before being beaten by the semi-retired pop star, whom Vijay effortlessly crushes in the final. Once again, he gambles repeatedly on letter-swapping and, although only one gamble in every four or five pays off, the impact of each successful one is so striking that it doesn't matter.

As always, Vijay spends some of his winnings on drinks for everyone at the pub. The organizer tells a long anecdote about the minibus he drove to Torquay last weekend; overloaded with unhelpful details, it raises only polite laughs. There is brief talk about football, the forecast hot summer, youth crime. The pop star tries to get people interested in a second round of drinks, but the kayaking couple have to leave — off to

218

France tomorrow — and this takes the steam out of the gathering. Pretty soon Xavier heads for home.

Feeling in his muscles the weight of the week — ridiculous, he thinks, I've barely done anything — he gets on a bus and sits next to the door. After a couple of stops he's conscious of a woman's hostile glare like a torch beam shining in his face. He makes eye contact, hoping she will look away, but instead her expression crumples in disgust and she shakes her head.

'Are you not going to offer me a seat? How long do I have to stand here?'

Xavier clambers to his feet guiltily.

'I'm sorry, are you . . . I didn't realize you were . . .'

She takes the vacated seat, shaking her head again. From the side Xavier can see that she is, indeed, pregnant, but it's not conspicuous; it's certainly not enough to justify such rudeness to him. Or is it? Xavier wonders if he has suffered a loss of perspective over this long week reliving the past, especially as he's not sleeping properly. Maybe he *is* failing to connect with other people, maybe it's quite obvious to everyone else on the bus that he should have volunteered his seat. He looks at other passengers, raising an eyebrow for opinions one way or another, but nobody meets his eye.

The incident is enough to remind him of Pippa's sister, also pregnant, which reminds him of Pippa, which means that as he walks down Bayham Road he is forced to consider the question he'd resolved to put out of his mind:

will Pippa have come? Of course it seems very unlikely, they've had no contact at all. And she would have read the note and called or texted by now. And she has better things to do, surely. But the grain of a doubt is stuck between his teeth. She might have come and cleaned almost to make a point, to shame him or something. Or she might have come, all ready to make up, and left a note back. But then — his lunging brain topples in another direction — she might have come, knowing he would leave the keys for her, and taken some sort of revenge, done some damage, stolen something. I mean, this is a woman I barely know, thinks Xavier. I employed her, kissed her, then made her feel humiliated and more or less threw her out of my home. If she *did* do something like that I'd fully deserve it.

But he doesn't quite believe that, and in any case doesn't quite believe she will have visited at all. And he's right: he can see straight away that the keys are exactly where he left them. And Pippa is wherever she is, but it's not here.

To Xavier's surprise and horror, tears sneak into his eyes. Ambushed, he stands weeping for perhaps forty seconds, for the first time since he left Melbourne, spluttering as he tries to stem the flow. A boy with a nasty scar on his right cheek walks past and glances at him with some curiosity, as if at a strange animal. Xavier, half-recognizing him, flinches like a criminal caught in the act and hastens inside, sensing in embarrassment that Mel, with Jamie in her arms, is watching him through the window with concern.

★ ★ ★

In the window of one of Soho's many Italian bars, Maggie Reiss sits with her friend Stacey Collins, at the dusk end of an all-day drinking session which began before the lunch menus had been handed to them. Stacey is a journalist. The two of them have known each other twenty years. Maggie called Stacey last night to say that they were going out, she had something to tell her. They've tottered their way in a zigzag across these teeming streets; this is their fourth stop-off.

Stacey has a strange expression on her face, as if she can't decide whether to be appalled or overjoyed.

'Look, are you sure about this?'

'I've never been so sure about anything. As they say in the movies.'

'You do realize that if you tell me anything I can use, I will *have* to use it. I won't be able to resist it. And there'll be no taking it back, you know, once it's out there. And you never know what the consequences will be, who it might affect.'

'That's the whole point. Once I've told you this stuff, everything is going to go nuts. People will hate me,' Maggie hoots, amused. 'And I will be out of here! I won't give two fucks!'

'It's not as simple as that, Maggie. People will bear grudges. For a shrink to reveal a client's secrets . . . I mean, it doesn't happen. *Nobody* does it.'

'Nobody does it because they're scared for their careers. It's not out of respect for the

221

clients. OK, so maybe it is in some cases. But mostly it's fear. And I don't have that fear. Because I don't want to do this any more. More than that: I'm *not* doing it any more. It's over.'

'You must have some clients you . . . you know, you genuinely care about, or — '

'Sure. But I'm not going to tell you any of *their* secrets. I'm only going to tell you stuff about the arseholes. The ones who, if they didn't have a psychotherapist to help legitimize it — ' She breaks off, momentarily surprised by her eloquence, given the drink. 'If they didn't have me saying it's OK, you have this problem, you have that problem, they would just have to *admit* they are bastards, cheating on their wives, lying to people, hurting people. So don't worry about the moral high ground, Stace. You're a journalist.'

'I know that. It's not the moral high ground I'm worried about, it's you. Do you see that?'

'Yes. But you don't need to be.'

Stacey lets out a long breath and shrugs, resigned.

'OK. Just tell me again, when did you come to the decision that you were going to sabotage your entire career?'

'Literally while I was taking a dump.'

Maggie laughs. The two of them cackle, with the abandon of drunks, till a couple of people look round.

A blonde woman in a shapeless raincoat walks past the bar and makes frosty eye contact with Maggie and Stacey for a moment. Her disapproving expression sets them off giggling again. It's Pippa, on her way to do waitress work at a gay magazine's awards ceremony on Charlotte Street. As she frowns at Maggie and Stacey through the window she is not — as they imagine — looking at them at all, but catching sight of her own tired reflection and wondering whether she ought to get in touch with Xavier. The thought of it, the risk of more unhappiness, all the emotional hassle, redoubles her feeling of exhaustion, and she lets the idea go.

'OK. Come on, then.'

'OK.' Maggie rests her chin on her hands, a pose that for so long served as her paying-full-attention face for ungrateful jerks. 'Would you like to start with the politician who's fucking a married TV star, the model who does twenty grand of coke a week, or the very well-known sports star who is gay and bribing rent boys for their silence?'

'Wow.' Stacey is hooked, however reluctantly. 'Right. The politician and TV star, I think.'

Maggie leans in close and says a name, which prises Stacey's mouth open by a fingernail's length.

'Are you sure?'

'Am I sure? He's told me enough about the fucking thing! Every week for two years!'

'And the TV star, who is it?'

This time, Maggie presses her boozy lips to Stacey's ear to whisper, and this time, Stacey's mouth drops open so wide that she could almost fit her fist inside it.

★　★　★

Xavier sits in the kitchen with a glass of wine, exactly a week after he opened a bottle with Pippa, remembering his departure from Australia.

Almost as soon as he was committed to the decision, things began to ease, if only marginally. His mother seemed relieved; not, as she might have been in other circumstances, upset that he was leaving. Realizing this only shamed him into going through with it. He saw Matilda briefly for coffee; afterwards, they held one another tightly for a while. She told him Bec and Russell were doing all right. Russell himself called to say goodbye. He also said that Bec was all right, and that Michael was too. It was the first time Chris had heard the name directly for months. He couldn't speak for a few seconds. Russell said, 'God bless you, mate,' at the end of the call. It was not the sort of thing he used to say.

A few days before he left, Chris was wandering down Brunswick Street when he saw the eighty-year-old man at the tram stop. As before, the old guy was wearing an aged baseball cap and clutching a lager can which had probably been empty for some time. Chris was surprised that the man recognized him.

'Long time, no see!' he croaked at Chris. 'How's life?' He flashed his oddly well-preserved teeth.

'Er, yeah, good,' Chris muttered. 'Ups and downs.'

'Ups and downs!' The octogenarian cackled at this. 'Ups and downs is right, I reckon. You know, just remember this.' He wiped his mouth and coughed. 'Whatever's meant to happen, happens. Right?'

'I . . . ' Chris began, but his new friend wasn't looking for corroboration.

'Whatever's meant to happen, happens. Do whatever you want. Some stuff'll happen. Bunch of other stuff won't. Right? We can't do anything!' The man gestured broadly around. 'We think we can, but we can't! We're just a bunch of . . . of bloody idiots, mate!'

He asked Chris for a cigarette. Chris gave him ten dollars and, to the slight surprise of them both, the two men shook hands. Chris continued on his way, past the turning he no longer took towards Bec and Russell's, knowing there was no chance he would ever see the man again.

*　*　*

At the stopover in Dubai Airport, two-thirds of the way to England, Chris stood for a minute at the top of a great staircase, looking down at the swarms of people traversing the shiny floor below, weaving between the shops. It was soothing to think that he didn't know a single one of their names, and they didn't know his. Outside, by the side of a runway, were piles of crates stencilled with words: *CHINA SHIPPING, MAERSK SEALAND*. He couldn't begin to guess what was inside any of these dozens of crates, what they were for, anything about them. Again, the ignorance was comforting.

Chris Cotswold became Xavier Ireland two weeks after landing at Heathrow. He had a new name, a new home, and — already, unexpectedly — a job: it added up to a new identity. It was never a specific condition of this identity to let life pass him by as far as possible and to stay out of others' lives as well, but it has been his unspoken pact with the world, he now realizes, ever since he set foot in England. As Saturday night turns into Sunday morning — the dark draining from the sky, as if reluctantly — he's only very dimly aware that the past few weeks have begun to break the pact.

8

Edith Thorne, a well-known TV presenter, thirty-eight years old, and in an adulterous relationship with a notable MP, wakes in her Notting Hill house at seven o'clock, three streets away from where Maggie Reiss is about to enjoy her first Monday morning lie-in as a lady of leisure. Edith's husband Phil has already had a shower and is mentally halfway to work. She kisses him briskly at the top of the stairs. After he's gone, she sits in the open-plan kitchen, wearing a towelling robe and eating porridge with blackberries. She watches the breakfast news. Later, Edith plans to do an hour of yoga and visit the gym and then have lunch and go to film her show at four o'clock. A car will come and pick her up at two fifteen as usual.

Edith used to worry, right up to the age of perhaps thirty, that all her advantages — good looks, good health, smooth professional progress, money, popularity — would have to be paid for in the end, written on one side of a balance sheet, the other side of which would bear details of a huge setback still to come. As her confidence grew, she realized that this was mere superstition. Some people, she learned, are simply marked out for success, some for failure. And then, of those marked for success, some work hard to live up to that marking, others don't bother. Edith realized that she'd got to where she was by a combination of good fortune and industry. It was much more reasonable to think she would continue to succeed by the same methods than it was to fret that some arbitrary realignment of fate's continental plates might throw her from this perch.

Her confidence had always been justified but, when Xavier failed to save Frankie in the snow that day, things began to change.

Edith's phone pulses on the table. Her agent, Maxine, is calling. Edith picks it up.

'Jesus, bit early in the morning for this, isn't it?'

The brightness in Maxine's voice this morning is noticeably synthetic.

'Edith, nothing to worry about, but I need to talk to you about something.'

At the 'nothing to worry about' Edith's spine stiffens with a premonitory fear.

'What is it?'

'I've had a call this morning from a journalist. She also sent me an email.'

Edith's body is still a few seconds ahead of her brain. Invisible hands creep over it, applying little prods of pressure here and here. She feels her throat constrict.

'And ... ?'

'She's got some ... allegations about you, about you ... ' Maxine coughs. 'Having an affair.'

As if a large object had been knocked over in the hall, Edith fancies for a moment she can hear the toppling of the precarious tower she has built.

'Edith?'

Maxine's voice sounds very far away.

Edith swallows.

'How did she, how did she . . . ?'

'I don't know, Edith.'

Maxine's normally smooth voice contains a high, unprecedented note which Edith recognizes after a few moments as fear. This is the first situation, in their nine years of working together, in which Maxine's repertoire of tricks and blandishments, her coaxing and haranguing skills, are not going to be enough.

'She's going to publish something tomorrow.'

Edith breathes in and out twice, and only on the second outbreath do words emerge.

'Can we do anything?'

'That depends, Edith. Is it true?'

★ ★ ★

If Edith Thorne's week begins with the most violent shock of her life, Xavier's begins much as expected. There is an atmosphere of deflation which the flat seems to absorb from Xavier and reflect back at him; and, even in this short time without Pippa, it is also in physical decline again. The sink is full of cups, the bathroom worn-looking, layers of dust are massing on the top of a bookcase here, a window ledge there; all things he would never have noticed before she first visited. Any attempts Xavier makes to tidy or clean feel pathetically inadequate given the standard that has been set, and trigger additional pangs for the woman whom, he's increasingly

229

aware, he has no way of contacting.

Around eleven, Xavier goes to collect the mail and deliver it to his two neighbours. He hovers for a shifty second outside Tamara's door, but of course there is no sound from within; she left early for work as always, the high heels pattering across the floor above, just beyond the edge of Xavier's consciousness. Her post includes a brown package marked with the words *STRICTLY CON-FIDENTIAL*. Outside his own flat, he is stopped by a piercing wail from Jamie, followed by an unusually feeble, 'Please, Jamie, stop it,' from Mel. She breaks into an escalating series of barking coughs that are painful to listen to. Jamie yells and hits something. 'Because *Mummy is not very well*,' Mel answers. Jamie advances a counter-argument. Mel erupts in coughs again.

Xavier, after a second's hesitation, pads down the stairs and knocks on the door. It opens almost straight away. Mel's hair hangs like washed-out curtains around her face. There are deep creases under her eyes.

She smiles wanly at Xavier.

'Hello. I'm sorry, it's all chaos in here.'

'I was just . . . I just thought you might be ill. Do you need anything?'

Jamie appears alongside his mother, tugging fiercely at the folds of her jumper.

Mel's dulled eyes flicker in gratitude.

'That's really . . . thank you. What have you got?'

'I've got cough medicine and, er, headache things.'

'Paracetamol?'

Xavier grins.

'Yeah. 'Headache things' is the medical name for them.'

She laughs and sniffs.

'Is it all right for me to . . . ?'

'Well, yes. You're obviously ill. I'm not too bad. I think you should have them.'

It's easy to find what he needs in the bathroom cabinet, which Pippa effortlessly reorganized. Xavier scoops up a packet of paracetamol, two rolls of throat sweets, a bottle of cough mixture and an assortment of other helpful-looking items into a carrier bag and takes it back downstairs. Mel, still propping the door open with her elbow, looks at him appreciatively, her watery eyes moistening further. When she's ill she becomes rather embarrassingly emotional; she cried at a song in an advert earlier. Jamie darts out from under her armpit and makes a charge for the main front door, smashing at it several times with his little fists.

'Come back, Jamie. COME HERE, JAMIE.'

But at the shout, her voice curls up, succumbing to more coughs.

Xavier, suddenly bold, squats down to make eye contact with the boy, who's wearing a red-and-yellow jumper, fresh on this morning but already grubby.

'Hey, Jamie. Come over here.'

After a few moments' consideration Jamie toddles back towards the adults and takes a fistful of Xavier's shirt in his hand.

Mel grabs her son and eases him back over the threshold of the flat. Jamie, wrong-footed by

Xavier's intervention, makes no protest.

'Thank you. He's getting worse and worse at running off. I mean, he's getting better. You know what I mean. He got onto the road twice last week.'

'If there's anything more I can do,' says Xavier. 'While you're ill. Or, well, you don't *have* to be ill.'

They smile at each other and Mel shuts the door gently. Xavier, invigorated, goes upstairs to his study to work on his emails. Halfway through the task, to refresh his brain, he wanders into the lounge, which still feels cold and unwelcoming, pregnant with the memory of Pippa. He wishes she'd seen what just happened.

It seems pathetic to pine for someone who was barely even here in the first place, and absurd that — as is becoming increasingly apparent — he might never be able to get back in touch with her. London is so small in some ways: the smallest of big cities, he's heard someone say. And yet, thinks Xavier despondently, it's easily big enough for somebody to be lost to you for ever. Especially if they like it that way.

He glances out of the window and is suddenly reminded of the boy with the scar he saw, through those surprise tears, the other day. God, Xavier thinks, registering it properly for the first time, it was the kid I saw getting beaten up in the snow. He got that scar then. I could have stopped that.

With this thought in and out of his brain, Xavier turns back to his emails. He advises an economics student to relax and be himself rather than continue to send the object of his unrequited love a present every day. He recommends hypnosis to a man scared of the dark, assuring him that it is a common fear. He doesn't, however, open the latest email from Clive Donald, who at this moment is midway through a double-maths lesson with 11.2, his worst class, and is watching calmly as they catcall and clatter about, thinking that very soon there will be no more double-maths with this class, or with 13.1, Julius's class; very soon there will be no more Mondays.

★　★　★

By Thursday night Edith Thorne's unfaithfulness is a matter of general knowledge, keeping North Korea's experimentation with nuclear weapons off the front pages of three national newspapers. So well established is the topic that Murray adds it to his 'Musings' that night, with Xavier conscripted into the role of the politician. They read a little skit which Murray scrawled across some of his yellowy lined paper.

'And if anyone else out there is sleeping with Edith Thorne, we may as well know now,' says Xavier drily, to chuckling from Murray. 'Do call in.'

The £1.2 million house, which, a few days ago, Edith considered a refuge from the outside world, has now been crudely invaded; a photographer camps across the street, sleeping in his car. The biggest reception room hosts what the papers call crisis talks between the star and her bewildered husband. Equally bewildered is Alessandro Romano, the Italian barman on the other side of town with whom she had been conducting a parallel affair, and who thought she was in love with him, believed she was on the verge of leaving her husband for him. He pulls pints without looking the customers in the eye, and waits in vain for a text. The politician Edith was sleeping with has already made a full apology to the leader of his party, and to his constituents, as if they were the real victims of the situation.

At two o'clock on Friday morning most of London's night-regulars are at their posts. Julius Brown still dreams about being caught for the mugging, but he's come to understand that the dreams themselves are his punishment. He's still not certain how he'll get another £67 for the next month's gym membership, but — ironically, perhaps — the stress of the past few months has seen his weight dip slightly. Clive Donald, who taught Julius's trigonometry class earlier, lies awake with the radio on, imagining the announcement of his suicide in assembly. 'I have to give you some very sad news, some terrible news.' For once, silence in the room.

The road-safety officer at Haringey Council, Tamara Weir, tosses and turns, wishing she had somebody other than her boyfriend to talk to. There's a lot on her mind; it's so hard to get people interested in the speed-bumps campaign without more support, maybe if she could get a celebrity to speak up, but it's finding the energy . . . nothing's been right since her dad died. She can't believe she wasn't there. Outside Xavier's studios, above the car park, clouds rush across the moon.

'So, the joys of drinks on Saturday night,' says Murray, as the news and weather rolls.

Anthony, one of the directors of the company that owns the radio station — their boss's boss — is stepping down this weekend after thirty-three years; there are drinks in a dowdy pub just around the back of the BT Tower on Tottenham Court Road. It's the sort of event nobody looks forward to — probably not even the person leaving — but Anthony's successor, a bright young man called Paul Quillam with ideas to 'take things forward', is going to be there, and their absence would be noted more certainly than their presence.

'I can hardly wait,' says Xavier.

'Do you want to mer, mer, meet up beforehand? Have a couple of drinks before it starts?'

'Good idea. I think we should be at least two ahead of everyone else.'

'Ber . . . back on air in thirty seconds. There's a caller who says she's got something very important to tell you. Iris?'

The name rings a bell, thinks Xavier.

'Or maybe we should start a new topic? She could be a bit . . . ' Murray spirals an index finger towards his temple.

'No, put her on.'

No sooner has he heard her twinkly, paper-thin voice than Xavier remembers the caller.

'I was the old lady in Walthamstow. I called a few weeks ago . . . '

'Yes, of course. So, how is *The Decline and Fall of the Roman Empire?*'

'It's still declining, I'm afraid.'

'Is it indeed,' says Xavier. 'Well, let's hope they find a way to turn it around. Now then, Iris, last time you called, you told us a story about a gentleman called Tony. He'd been the love of your life, but got away from you for — what was it, fifty years? And then you saw him again.'

'Yes. You encouraged me to try to meet him again. Actually, you asked him to come forward, if he was listening.'

'So, Iris, don't keep us in suspense. Have there been any developments?'

Xavier pictures her in her ground-floor flat in East London, twirling the cord of her old-fashioned telephone around her bony fingers.

'Well, Xavier, there was nothing for weeks. He didn't contact me. I thought oh dear, obviously he doesn't listen to the show . . . '

'Well, I find *that* hard to believe,' says Xavier, deadpan. 'As far as we know, everyone in London listens to it.'

'That's what I would have hoped!' Iris giggles. 'So I started sort of *hanging about*, I suppose you would call it, near the place where we'd previously met. I can tell you, if you're an old lady it's not easy to just hang about. People keep asking if you're all right. Two different young men tried to help me across the road.'

Murray: 'Nice to hear cher, cher, cher, cher . . . '

'Chivalry isn't dead,' Xavier agrees.

236

'It *is* nice,' Iris says, 'but in this case, rather inconvenient. Anyway, I'd almost given up hope. But I remembered your encouragement, Xavier, and thought damn it, I'm not going to be beaten. I remembered that last time I saw Tony he'd been picking up a prescription for his wife, and it was a Friday. So on Fridays, I would find an excuse to go to Boots. Last Friday I went in, pretending to look at umbrellas — not much use a lady my age pretending to look at make-up — and there he was! And if I'm honest, well, he looked pretty chuffed to see me. We went for a cup of tea and a bite to eat!'

'This is tremendous news, Iris.' Xavier grins, genuinely pleased. 'And are you going to keep seeing each other?'

'Well, of course he's married and I'm widowed and whatnot, so certain things aren't appropriate . . . '

'No, you won't be running away to Barbados or anything?'

'Goodness me, no.' Iris giggles again, and there is no difference, Xavier thinks, between the young woman who met Tony in 1950 and the one calling in now; the high-spirited 1950 version is still serving people in the grocery shop, even though the shop no longer stands where it did; somehow, each individual moment goes on existing, somewhere.

'But you will keep seeing each other? And you will keep calling in and letting us know?'

Iris's voice, once more, has a dusting of mischief about it.

'Perhaps we will. Perhaps we will ask you, like

237

that Edith lady, to respect our privacy . . . '

Xavier and Murray both laugh.

Murray has started to set up the next caller when Iris adds, 'I must thank you, Xavier. I would never — without you, I . . . Well, thank you.'

Xavier can't help but smile as they say their goodbyes. Before he knows it, he has allowed the surge in mood to dictate his next, surprising words.

'So, we've heard a touching story of a reunion here on *Late Lines*, and now I'm going to try to initiate another one. Pippa, if you happen to be listening, please get in touch. What happened was entirely my fault. I'd very much like to see you again.'

'And next up, here is . . . er, here's another song,' Murray stumbles.

As soon as the opening chords fade up he speaks:

'Wer, wer, wer, where did that come from?'

Xavier shuffles in his swivel chair and stares into the layers of sediment at the depths of his coffee cup.

'Been on my mind.'

'Who the hell is Pippa?'

'A girl.'

'The girl you had that date with, the Aussie?'

'No, another one. The, er, my cleaner.'

Murray stares at him, tugging at his curly forelock in perplexity.

'You've been having it with your cleaner?'

'It's not that sort of situation really. It was a one-off thing.'

238

'You had a one-night stand with your cleaner?'

'We didn't sleep together. I screwed it up.'

Murray shakes his head slowly.

'I've only just got used to you *having* a cleaner, let alone fucking her.'

'Me too.' Xavier coughs. 'Anyway, we didn't. We didn't do that.'

Over the remaining hour, they receive an exceptional number of calls and emails and texts from the listeners. Who is Pippa? people demand to know. Tell us more. What happened? Is it a serious relationship? But there is no correspondence from the one person Xavier hoped to provoke, and by the end of the night the exhilaration of his uncharacteristic appeal has faded, replaced by the queasiness of having revealed too much of himself too easily. Murray and Xavier drive home without speaking, tangled in their respective thoughts.

★ ★ ★

As for Pippa, she gets up two hours after Xavier goes to bed. Her first appointment is at nine, at the rich lady's house in Marylebone; she's living in it with her partner and son until she finds a new tenant, and wants to keep it, as she puts it, 'spick and span'. The radio is on when Pippa comes down for breakfast: Wendy doesn't ever seem to learn to switch things off, to make these small economies. They're talking about the World Athletics Championships in Berlin, which Pippa, had things gone differently, might have been preparing for now. Perhaps Xavier was right

239

after all, reads the graffiti on a wall of Pippa's tired mind, perhaps everyone would be best off just accepting what they're given.

Pippa spends four hours scrubbing stains out of the carpet, dusting vases, hoovering around a teenager who avoids meeting her eye and refuses to pick up any of the clothes, magazines, bags or bric-a-brac littering his floor like jetsam brought in by the tide. The landlady makes several pots of tea but doesn't offer Pippa a drink. At the end of the session, Pippa has to take five black bags of rubbish out to a skip at the end of the street, her knees creaking each time as she bends to pick one up. Am I missing something, Pippa wonders, feeling light rain on the back of her neck, or was I always cut out for this?

Clive Donald also heard the report about British medal hopes as he got ready to leave the house this morning, but it failed to interest him. As Pippa dusts and scrubs, Clive drops a series of hints in the staff room that he 'may not be around for too much longer' and that there 'could be some news soon'. He has been stockpiling sleeping pills at home; he's been on websites where mostly much younger people discuss such topics as how many pills it takes to kill you. Everyone is preoccupied with the impending school inspection, and no real conversation develops from the hints.

At lunchtime, Pippa gets a sandwich from the garage across the road. She has to do another four-hour clean this afternoon, in Bayswater, not far away, and she's then waitressing down in Surrey. She'll have to get the overground from

Victoria or something. She can see in advance the squashed corridors of the commuter train, the kid with hissing headphones leaning back against her, the superior looks of the high earners heading home to their satellite towns.

★ ★ ★

On Saturday morning Xavier — having checked his inbox in vain for anything from Pippa — is boiling the kettle when he hears Mel's worn voice downstairs, and the usual thudding sounds of Jamie being dragged inside against his will. He goes downstairs.

Jamie is screaming, waggling his legs furiously like an octopus caught in a net.

'No! No! No!' Jamie protests.

He squirms out of Mel's grip and back towards the front door, and is about to escape, but Xavier bounds down the stairs and reaches over his three-year-old neighbour to slam the door just in time. Jamie yells in disappointment. The two adults exchange a look of triumph at their narrow victory over the tiny opponent.

'Thank you.' Mel wearily scoops her hair out of her eyes. 'This is becoming a habit.'

'You're welcome.' Xavier eyes her shopping bags. 'I could have gone to the shops for you.'

'Oh, no, you've already been very — ' Mel breaks into coughing. 'You must get the impression I can barely support myself.'

'You support yourself and a child. That's more than I can manage.'

Mel smiles. It's their second successful

241

conversation in the past few days. I'm doing well, Xavier thinks.

He makes himself some lunch and wonders what to do with the afternoon, before the evening's drinks. The only previous time he met Anthony was a few months into his partnership with Murray, when the old man, eager to meet the new talent, invited him to a 'liquid lunch' in Holborn. Xavier remembers Anthony's red-wine-and-meat face, the nostrils flaring uncomfortably wide.

He has almost decided to go for a long walk when the doorbell rings. He goes downstairs again. He can hear Mel explaining, 'No, it's for the man above . . . for Xavier, that's right.' The TV is on at high volume. Xavier opens the door and there, in her shapeless raincoat and with her blue-and-yellow laundry bag at her feet, is Pippa.

Xavier has to resist his initial urge to grab her. He can feel a frantic pulse in his neck, hear it in his ear.

'Aren't you going to invite me in?'

She's past him and on her way up the stairs before Xavier can respond. Following in her wake he makes a mental tour of the flat, scanning the rooms for order and correctness.

'I can't stay long, I've got to be in Kentish Town in an hour, which I know isn't very far, but the buses are totally unreliable round here, and half the time they don't let you on, or something goes wrong, anyway I can't be late, but I thought I might drop in because apparently me sister heard you refer to a lady on the radio who might be me.'

242

She turns to him in the hall and they stand and look at one another. Pippa drops her eyes away from his glance. Xavier brushes one of his hands against hers. He notices her chipped fingernails.

'I didn't think I'd see you again.'

'You upset me.' Pippa's eyes flicker around, predatory, in search of dirt.

'I know. I texted you, I called you — '

'My phone,' says Pippa imperiously, 'has been wedged down the back of your sofa since that night.'

Xavier looks incredulously at her as she leads him into the lounge and casually peels the cushions off the sofa, exposing its forlorn-looking frame. She plunges her arm into the gap and fishes out the phone which has nestled there since she left this room two weeks ago, undisturbed by messages since its battery petered out, and undetected by Xavier who's hardly been in the room since the events of that night.

'You've not had a phone for two weeks?'

'I have what is known as a landline,' Pippa says loftily. 'I give that number to all my clients.'

'But all *their* numbers and everything — '

'Well, yes, it has been inconvenient.'

He's about to ask why she didn't simply buy a new one, but remembers that this is the sort of question someone with a comforting amount of money might ask too glibly.

'That's why I've come back to get it. It took me a couple of days to notice it was gone, and then I had to work out where it would be' — she counts off on her fingers, he notes with an internal shiver of familiarity — 'and *then* I had to find time to come over here and get it, and then I had to work out whether I actually wanted to see you.'

'And . . . ?'

'And I did.'

She leans against the arm of the sofa and Xavier takes her hand, handling it like china.

'I'm really sorry.'

'You already said that.'

'Do you want a cup of tea?'

'I've not got time, pet.'

She coughs.

'But thanks for mentioning me on the show.'

Xavier feels the unstoppable kindling of a fire in his lower stomach, spreading into his groin, as he pictures her breasts, her thighs beneath the sack-like outfit, regresses to the half-hour they spent, on this spot, in each other's arms. He can almost summon the taste of her mouth.

'Can I see you? Whenever you can. I realize you have a lot on. Just, any time.'

She blinks a couple of times.

'That would be nice. Give me a call.'

'On the mobile or the landline?'

Pippa laughs.

'Whichever you like.'

She glances at her watch and is gone, down the stairs, out of the door. Xavier waves to her as she hauls herself onto the saddle of her bike, then watches her all the way up the hill, her raincoat flapping on either side of her, legs urging the pedals forwards.

★ ★ ★

By the time he reaches his pre-drinks appointment with Murray, Xavier is cushioned by a
mood so close to euphoria that he could imagine
he'd had a bottle of wine already. On the
underground he glances benignly at a mouthy
gang of girls dispersed around the carriage,
whose yells shoot like tennis balls over the heads
of the spectators trapped in between.

In the bar-restaurant where they meet, he
doesn't flinch at the officious waiter who asks if
he's planning to eat, and then says, 'No one just
for drinks, it's Saturday night. You have to eat.'

'OK, I'll eat something.'

'It's a bit of a bloody cheek,' laments Murray,
who has made the best of the situation by
ordering a huge plate of lasagne with side orders
of chips and olives, as well as a basket of garlic
bread.

'I guess they have to make a living,' says
Xavier mildly.

'What's put you in such a good mood?'

'I don't know. I guess I was in a pretty bad
mood for a while. This is a kind of comeback.'

'When you say "a while" . . . '

'About five years.'

They laugh. Murray doesn't immediately press
him on the subject, but Xavier soon feels like
returning to it. Maybe there's something about
this street that inspires confidences; it was a few
doors down from here last week that Maggie
Reiss revealed the secret affair of her politician
client and Edith Thorne.

Murray listens, his front teeth hooking down onto his bottom lip in a bite that suggests considerable envy.

'So it's on again? You're going to . . . ?'

'We've said we'll see each other next week.'

'So this is, like, a proper relationship?'

'It's much too early to say that. It's only just saved itself from being a proper disaster.'

But Xavier looks to Murray as if he's rather more confident than that implies. Disconcerted, Murray hacks up the lasagne, as if it were food he had captured himself, and studies his friend, trying to think of witty ways to tease him. Nothing comes to mind, and in the time it takes Xavier to order, Murray has finished an almost-full glass of wine, poured himself another, and drunk most of that too.

★   ★   ★

Once in the dowdy pub, they go off on separate socializing circuits. Xavier uncharacteristically takes his eye off Murray, who heads straight for the forest of elbows at the bar. The radio station has paid a tab of £200 which he immediately sets about depleting.

Xavier shakes hands with Anthony, whose nostrils are as unhappily capacious as ever.

'Excellent show, excellent show,' he says, pumping Xavier's hand like someone operating a well; his wedding ring presses hard against Xavier's finger.

Xavier can't tell whether Anthony has actually listened to the show in the past years, but it

246

doesn't matter. Before long he is introduced to the new man in the job, Paul Quillam, who is in his early forties with a boyish dimple when he smiles, and raffishly untidy hair. He introduces himself as a 'great admirer' of Xavier's, and with the practised ease of someone who is perpetually arranging discreet conversations, steers him into an empty function room adjacent to the main bar.

'I hope you don't mind me talking shop on a Saturday night, very dull,' says Paul Quillam, not bothering to sound as if he means this.

'No, it's fine,' says Xavier.

'Now here's the thing. I'm a big fan of yours, as I've already said. I think I can speak for pretty much everyone here when I say that we're very impressed with what you've done; you've made the overnight shift, basically a graveyard, into something really special.'

'Thanks.' Xavier's never sure how to respond to the routine flattery that comes before a conversation of this nature reaches its spike of importance.

Luckily, Quillam is ready to get straight to the point.

'What I'm wondering — what I've already been talking to people about — is whether we can harness what you've got, and bring it to a bigger audience. I know you're probably very happy where you are,' he says, pre-emptively raising a hand to bat away objections. 'I know you're very settled at midnight to four. I'm just saying — I'm aware others would like to poach you, but we see you as a prized asset, and I'd like

247

you to have a status which reflects that. Does that make sense? Do you mind if I smoke, by the way?'

Not waiting for a reply, Paul Quillam leads Xavier out to a paved area. He lights a fag, shielding it with a cupped hand. Xavier knows that at the end of all this smooth talk will most likely be a definite proposition.

After a couple of satisfied drags on the cigarette, Paul Quillam flashes him a grin, flicks ash onto the floor, and addresses him.

'What we'd like you — what *I'd* like you — to at least consider,' he says, reaching up slightly to rest a hand on Xavier's shoulder, 'is something like eight till midnight, nine till one; an evening show. Prime-time evening. Obviously, the money would reflect that. But also, as you probably know, we're revamping the way the station is organized. You'd go out not just in London, but nationwide.'

'Nationwide?'

'And with a much stronger online component and so on. You'd reach a lot more listeners. Which we think you deserve.'

Xavier's mind flickers over Iris in Walthamstow, over the depressed teacher Clive Donald, the lorry drivers, poets, unwell or uneasy people, all the midnight-to-four-in-the-morning crowd who, to whatever extent, have come to like the company of his voice.

'I've always been reluctant to think about moving slots,' says Xavier.

'Do you smoke, by the way? Rude of me.'

It was ruder to have interrupted, thinks

248

Xavier. He continues.

'Er, no, thanks. Because — the thing is, a lot of the people who call in to the show, they kind of . . . they're quite a loyal audience, and . . . '

Quillam nods.

'Sure, absolutely. Well, a couple of things. Firstly, I think you'll find that your fans will follow you to the new slot. Maybe they'll all get a bit more sleep this way.' His mouth twists in a handsome smile for a second and Xavier half joins in. 'Secondly, there's always the option of keeping the latenight show, but maybe just a couple of nights a week. You could do the big show five nights, then *Late Lines* on Wednesday, Thursday . . . whatever you liked.'

Xavier runs his tongue over his lips. The inflated pay packet isn't of great significance, although it wouldn't hurt either; but the idea of reaching a much bigger audience stirs something in his recharged brain, brushes against some small pressure points of ambition or desire which have been submerged.

'The other thing is' — Quillam presses on, sensing that a small step forward has been made — 'we've got a couple of really good people signed up, people I think you would like working with, who might . . . might bring more out of you.'

Xavier takes a moment to grasp the true meaning of this.

'Murray is, er, he's been a very important — '

'Absolutely. I know you two have a really good relationship,' Quillam says with studied respect. 'But I wonder if that could continue for one or two nights a week on *Late Lines*, while you perhaps forge new relationships with, with other talents on the station.'

Xavier knows where this is heading; Quillam's voice contains the same note of gentle common sense that numerous others have sprinkled into similar conversations before now. Look, seriously, it says, Murray is all very well, and he's your friend and everything, but he's not really up to it. You have to move on.

'I'd be wary of,' Xavier begins, 'I'd be reluctant to work less with Murray.'

'Well perhaps Murray could continue to help you with writing the show, and preparing it?' suggests Quillam diplomatically.

But Xavier winces, imagining Murray reduced to scrawling down his ideas on lined paper — ideas which are all too soon discarded — and watching as a younger, more eloquent broadcaster slides into the co-presenter's seat. Perhaps someone else becomes the producer, Murray's role diminishing more and more, until, essentially, it is just to pick Xavier up and take him home again.

'I really don't think I'd want to . . .'

Quillam looks directly at Xavier, with a suddenly intent expression, a flicker of killer instinct, the look which momentarily passes across the face of his Scrabble rival Vijay as he prepares to strike a lethal blow.

'To be franker still with you,' says Quillam, taking Xavier's elbow for a moment as if about to deliver upsetting news, 'a lot of people have concerns about Murray. This can't have escaped your notice.'

They stand there quietly for a moment, Xavier gathering energy for a rebuttal. Inside the pub, a barmaid drops a tray of glasses, which shatter messily on the stone floor, rousing the traditional ironic cheer from drinkers. She grins bravely and goes to get a dustpan and brush. Across town in Chelsea, a glass manufactured at the same factory in Stoke-on-Trent was broken only a few minutes ago by the barman who was in love with Edith Thorne. He is still waiting to hear from her, and can't concentrate on anything else.

'Listen, I know you have a lot of loyalty to Murray and to all your listeners, but, well, things do have to change sometimes. Things have to keep moving forward.' Quillam's air is still matey and respectful, but there is a faintly threatening edge to his words now.

'I'm just not going to leave Murray high and dry,' says Xavier.

Quillam coughs, discards the fag-end, nods, and slaps Xavier on the back; he's made the territorial advance he wanted.

'Of course, of course. I admire your . . . well, your whole approach. But do think about this. I'm sure there's a way.'

They go back into the pub. Quillam stops abruptly a few paces inside the door, there's a disturbance of some kind. Xavier follows his gaze and stiffens in dismay. Murray, who's waded knee-deep in drunkenness over the past hour, is squatting down to make hopelessly unwelcome remarks to the barmaid as she clears up the glass. Onlookers trade glances of either amusement or contempt.

'Are you sure you don't want any help with that?' Murray offers in a voice which is like a pop song played too loud. 'Are you sure you wouldn't like a . . . a man's touch?'

'I would leave it,' someone warns him.

Murray shakily offers a finger to the stranger, whose mates break into appalled laughter. The barmaid turns her face away, discards the brush and begins gathering up the tiniest fragments of glass with her fingers.

'At least allow me the privilege of — the *opportunity* to carry the, carry your dustpan,' slurs Murray.

There's more laughter. Xavier feels his cheeks burn in empathic shame for Murray, but also, tellingly, for himself. He sees Paul Quillam making a conspicuous attempt, for his benefit, not to notice the scene.

Xavier heaves an internal sigh, and — bracing himself physically as if for contact with cold water — strides into the middle of the bar and pulls Murray, almost roughly, to his feet. Murray's eyes begin to fill with a slow-acting awareness of his stupidity, but his dulled reactions still trail well behind his instincts.

'Wer, wer, what are you doing . . . ?'

'Let's get you out of here, mate.'

Xavier ushers his unsteady friend away from the grateful barmaid, from the sniggering drinkers, from the condescending glance of Paul Quillam, at the bar with a gin and tonic. Before Murray knows quite why, he and Xavier are outside. The wind is beginning to pick up; the wooden sign bearing the pub's name creaks in the breeze, unheard beneath the general hum and throb of the streets.

Xavier shakes his head. What is there to say? Murray stares at him, hair tossed like spaghetti in the wind.

Xavier takes his arm.

'Come on.'

'I . . . ' Murray gestures helplessly. 'I must have just had a bit too much to drink.'

'Why do you always do these things at precisely the moment when I'm trying to — '

'Wer, when you're trying to . . . ?' Xavier has said too much, and Murray — even reaching through the treacle of drunkenness — is able to grab some of his meaning. 'Shit. Was he watching me? The new guy, Quillam?'

'It doesn't matter. Come on. Let's go and sit somewhere. Somewhere quiet.'

'Oh shit. I think I was really making a ger, a ger, a good impression on him, too. I sent him some stuff, some ideas. Fuck.' Murray's thick fingers grasp his moist forehead in despair. 'Now I'm back to square one.'

Xavier steers his friend down a hidden thoroughfare, past a pair of stinking bins at the back of Chico's, the Spanish restaurant; past the rear of a sportswear superstore where pipes discharge murky water into a drain.

'You just have to watch yourself. How the hell did you get drunk so quickly? Were you pissed before we even met?'

'No.' Murray stares with exaggerated concentration at the drain as they pass, as if trying to understand its precise workings. He belches.

253

'No, I mer, mer, mostly started to get drunk when you told me about the girl, about the cleaner, Pippa.'

These words sit, heavy as a sandbag, in the air between them.

'Because I didn't tell you about it before? Or because — what?'

Murray shrugs as if it doesn't matter. The side street drags them across the east end of Tottenham Court Road, where a long queue of punters in feather boas and fishnet tights awaits admission to a club, and down another alley, where Xavier knows a club of a rather more upmarket kind.

'We'll just go in here and have a — have a coffee or something, and we can talk things over.'

Before Xavier can press the tiny intercom buzzer next to the club's brass nameplate on the wall, Murray coughs and takes a handful of curly hair in each fist.

'It just came as a surprise,' he says, staring at the pavement, 'because we don't really talk much about relationships, well, not about *your* relationships.'

'I know.'

'And I thought . . . ' Murray wipes his hand across his wet lips. 'I thought, I don't know, it had crossed my mind you wer, wer, wer, wer, wer, wer, wer, wer, wer, wer, wer, wer, wer, wer, wer, wer, wer, wer, wer, wer, wer, wer, wer, wer — '

Xavier watches ineffectually as, inside Murray's throat, the desired word thrashes about, resisting eviction, like a child defying attempts to lift it out of a car-seat.

Murray puffs his cheeks out.

'I thought it could be the cer, case that you mer, mer, mer, mer, mer, mer, mer, mer, mer. Mer, might be gay.'

Xavier almost laughs. Then his stomach twists as Murray turns away, hands on hips. After a twenty-second suspension of what feels like all activity in London, he shuffles a step towards Murray and lays a hand on his shoulder. Murray turns his head. His eyes are moist, his cheeks pinkish.

'I've been stupid,' says Murray, 'I'm sorry, this has been a stupid night. Let's go home.'

'Are you sure?' Xavier gestures weakly at the club with its demure brass signage and, inside, its scuttling waiters in black waistcoats, who know the clientele — among them, the MP who had an affair with Edith Thorne — by name.

Murray nods and buries his fleshy hands in his sleeves. He looks suddenly older and calmer; there's no trace of the stammer for now.

He nods again, resigned.

'Yes. Forget I spoke.' He's already making for the main road, scanning it for the approaching beacon of a vacant taxi. 'Let's go home. Let's just go home.'

9

The second week of April; a mild Tuesday morning, mild both in weather and, so far on Bayham Road, in incident. The buses weave through traffic, workers head for their offices. Xavier answers the front door, signs for a parcel on behalf of Tamara upstairs, whom he's not seen for some days now, and collects a heap of other letters, catalogues, assorted junk from the postman, whose daughter will later today compete in Mathdown, the London Schools' Maths Olympiad, against Julius Brown.

Xavier knocks on Mel's door. There is a short delay before their usual roles are taken up: Mel, hollow-eyed, opening the door and squinting wearily at her neighbour; Jamie dashing nimbly for the corridor and Xavier, almost as a matter of routine, blocking his path and shepherding him back to his mother. Xavier and Mel smile, like teammates.

'How are you doing?'

'Oh, I'm better, much better.' Mel blinks brightly. Behind her, the flat is a shambles, toys everywhere, washing-up piled high, the TV chattering in an attempt to pacify the overactive Jamie. 'He's starting at a daycare place soon. Just a couple of mornings a week. So that'll give me a bit of, er — ' Mel gestures at the door, at the outside world, looking as if she hasn't visited it in recent memory. 'And his dad's taking him this

Saturday and the Saturday after.' But this thought triggers more discomfort than satisfaction and her lips thin in an ironic grimace. 'No doubt he'll have his views on how I'm doing.'

'Well, anything you need.' Xavier hands over her letters, or rather, bills, by the look of them; her eyes flick, discouraged, over a forbidding brown envelope. 'You know where I am,' he adds.

Mel reaches out, as if to pat him on the arm, he thinks, but Jamie has found something not to his liking in the living room, and his yells summon her back to her post. Xavier watches her retreat and gently shuts the door.

He and Pippa have been communicating by text, Xavier taking the lead, Pippa replying after suitably nerve-racking intervals of time. He doesn't know whether to put the pauses down to her incessant work schedule, or to a deliberate campaign to unsettle him, as punishment for what happened before. If the latter, it's been successful; he's caught himself glancing at his phone far too many times, feeling odd little stabs of disappointment when the display offers no new message, followed by an embarrassingly strong reaction to her dispatches, which, when they do arrive, are phrased with the correctness of her handwritten notes. *I should like to see you at the weekend, but it may not be possible. Tuesday afternoon is no use as I have to clean for this ghastly madam in Marylebone.* Maybe he always felt this way when she contacted him, almost from the beginning; it's hard to say now.

In the two shows since the weekend, there's

been no acknowledgement of what took place, other than a very slight reference to it by Murray when he picked Xavier up on the Sunday evening.

'It's well and truly out of my bloodstream, you'll be pleased to know.'

'And are you . . . are you all right?' Xavier ventured.

'I'm in fine fettle,' said Murray, drumming on the steering wheel with his inelegant fingers, and in the process accidentally honking the horn at a startled man crossing the road. And indeed, the Sunday and Monday shows zipped past nicely, with 'Dream Holiday, Money No Object' on Sunday, 'Superpower You'd Most Like' exciting plenty of calls on the Monday. They'd used that topic before, but nobody seemed to mind: sometimes, longtime listeners even email in requests for old discussions to be reprised.

Even 'Murray's Musings' — featuring a rumoured pandemic and a return to the hot topic of Edith Thorne's infidelity — have gone pretty well the past two nights. Xavier hopes that, if that trend continues, and if Murray avoids reviewing the weekend for a little longer, perhaps all its pressing points can be deferred until they disappear from view. It's a cowardly hope, he knows, and probably a naive one, but then, it's worked well enough in so many other situations.

Xavier showers, shaves, examines himself in the mirror. He's lost a little weight recently, though not intentionally. It occurs to him that he ought to call home, call his mum. Maybe later in the week. It has certainly been too long. Or he could wait to see if it turns out that he is 'seeing' Pippa after all. She'd like to hear about that.

In other parts of the restless city, Julius Brown frowns furiously over a tangled equation at Mathdown, while his competitors, equally engrossed, pay no attention to him. Vijay, Scrabble champion, loses half a day's work as the university's computer system goes down. He raises his eyebrows, shakes his head, and goes out to get a sandwich. At Frinton, Ollie Harper — who finally has a new phone — hears that Sam has a new boyfriend; no wonder she's not been replying to his texts. He's irritated to feel jealous of them both. Roger, Ollie's boss, is experimenting with a new mouthwash. He's decided not to seek any more therapy: clearly, the whole industry is full of crackpots. Frankie Carstairs' scar is finally starting to fade.

In her Notting Hill home three streets away from that of Maggie Reiss, Edith Thorne receives the ultimatum breathlessly predicted by the papers, from her husband Phil. Swear never to cheat on him again, or say goodbye to their marriage now. He knows it's two-thirds her money, her house, her everything, but he can walk away from it tomorrow, if she doesn't think she can commit. No, says Edith, she wants to be with Phil, nothing else matters, she'll do anything. By the end of an hour's conversation they are both crying. Later Edith will attempt to get straight out of the door and into a waiting car, its tinted windows like admissions of wrongdoing, but even in the ten yards from door to vehicle she's caught: the gently accusatory sound of a shutter opening and closing, the photographer grabbing his bounty of shots. He shouts her name as she slams the car door. The chauffeur, professionally indifferent, acts as if he didn't notice.

Clive Donald is teaching a class on quadratics to twenty-nine mixed-ability students. Six of them, intending to pursue maths to AS level, concentrate and take notes; ten or twelve more face the front, at least, even if nothing he says is of any importance to them; the remainder are openly subversive, throwing things at each other, writing notes — *DONALD IS GAY* — shouting, eating snacks, counting down the minutes to the end of the lesson. The tired rattle of the bell is a relief to everyone. Clive watches the pupils disperse. It's not their fault. He remembers being a pupil himself; catching the bus home after school, wanting nothing more than to be far away from the relentless square brick buildings, the radiators with their chipped paint. It's not clear to him — maybe it's never been clear, he thinks, starting up his grey Peugeot with a halfhearted wave to a colleague — why, after thirteen entirely undistinguished years at school, he allowed his life to amount to nothing more than a shapeless streak of days in an almost identical institution. And for what? To produce more teachers. Five of the kids in his A level set will become maths teachers just as he's a maths teacher produced by his own maths teacher. It's like some infinitely replicating sequence of the kind he would be enthused by if he were a real mathematician, rather than a facilitator of endless future educators.

At the roundabout that feeds onto the ring road that will eventually cough him out on the new-build development where he lives, Clive Donald brakes sharply to avoid a collision, and is faintly disgusted by his goody-goody instincts: even as he fantasizes about his own death, he can't resist playing it safe, there's no genuine abandon about him. Maybe I won't go through with it, he thinks — maybe I am too much of a coward. What kind of miserable bastard needs to convince himself that he's up to the job of finishing himself off? He catches his reflection in the hall mirror — paunchy, paper-faced, exactly what he feared becoming; you could watch him commit a murder and struggle to give a single detail to the police — and notes with disdain the way he hangs up his coat. Still the same pointless observance of tasks, the same routines. It's as if one side of his brain can't take seriously the suicidal yearning of the other.

As night falls, or rather stumbles, a cheerless purple over the road outside, Clive continues to struggle to raise the sheer *balls* to do it — not the courage, so much, but the sheer self-regard involved in the act seems more than this indifferent life of his deserves. He thinks about the reactions of each of his three ex-wives to the news: Angie, genuine sadness, maybe tears; Polly, contempt, exactly the sort of idiotic thing he *would* do; Marjorie, confusion — she was never able to empathize with him, or with anyone. But Angie, yes, the first wife, she was the one. If she hadn't left. If they'd had children, perhaps. She will be sad when she finds out, she'll remember their honeymoon on the Norfolk Broads, laughing at a line of ducks. She was the one, all along; everything since then has been a horrible mistake.

Midnight comes; going to bed would be an admission that he's not going to do it, that he's going to get up as always and do the usual things in the usual order tomorrow. Out of habit, Clive puts the radio on and sits, with thirty exercise books in front of him, hundreds of scrawled numbers in the little squares maths books inexplicably substitute for lines. Xavier Ireland introduces the night's themes, opening a discussion on, as his annoying co-presenter puts it, 'The Joys of Political Correctness'. The first song begins. The little tower of maths books sits unimpressed as Clive reaches for the phone and taps in the only numbers, among all those on his kitchen table, he has any use for.

* * *

'He just keeps calling.' Murray, dustbin-lid headphones clamped around his red-tipped ears, ruefully holds up the phone like a malfunctioning kitchen implement. 'He's tried four or five times in the past half-hour.'

'Well, put him on.' Xavier thinks uneasily of the emails he's ignored from Clive.

The voice of the woman they never meet delivers, in smoothed-off consonants, the news and weather report.

'But he always says the same thing. He's miserable. His wives left him. He feels like he deserved ber, ber, better from life. I mean, it doesn't go anywhere.'

'But he probably needs to talk to me . . . to us more than most people.'

'Are we a talk show or a char, a char, a charity?' mutters Murray, half in jest, as he prepares to fade the song out. Xavier takes a sip from the *BIG CHEESE* mug. 'And now,' says Murray, with an aggrieved glance at Xavier, 'we're going to hear from one of our regular callers.'

Clive's point is even more flimsily attached to the night's debate than usual; after the most cursory of topical remarks he returns to the familiar ground of his misery.

'I have to say, Xavier, I'm feeling unusually grim tonight.'

'Any particular reason why tonight?' asks Xavier.

'Oh, there's nothing particular about tonight. I just feel, you know, enough's enough, really. Things haven't worked out. I can't really see a good reason to — you know. To keep plodding along like this.'

'I told you so,' say Murray's eyes to Xavier's.

'Have you spoken to anyone else about this?'

'I can't really see the point.'

'Because it's not good for you to carry these thoughts around on your own, Clive. That's why you called *us*, isn't it?'

'I think it may be too late for anyone to . . . I

263

mean, I'll go back to feeling like this.'

The conversation progresses in painful little steps, Clive evading any attempt by Xavier to lift the mood; but Xavier nonetheless tunnels on until Murray interrupts.

'Well, great to hear from you again, Clive . . . '

Clive, far off on the crackly line, sounds as if he's about to say something else, but he is gone.

In the next commercial break they glance uneasily at each other.

Murray breaks the silence with a shrug.

'It's not our responsibility to look after everyone in the wer, world.'

'I didn't say it was.'

'You obviously don't think I should have got rid of him, though.'

Xavier gestures in annoyance. In the car park, the fox comes briefly into view, nosing around a pair of black rubbish sacks.

'It was bad radio,' Murray persists.

An advert plays for the supermarket chain that employs Julius Brown's mother.

'It's not always bad radio when we just let people talk.'

'It is in his case.' Murray doesn't want to argue. He gets to his feet, miming coffee. Xavier nods.

As soon as Murray is in the corridor, Xavier makes a decision. He slides into his colleague's chair and brings up the full list of callers; their numbers, their locations. He finds Clive's number and dials it. After four rings, there is a hesitant answer.

'Clive Donald.'

'Hello, Clive, this is Xavier.'

'From the radio?'

'Yes.'

'Goodness. I . . . '

'Listen, Clive, I'm worried about you, mate. You sound a bit desperate.'

'Frankly, Xavier, I am.'

'Well, I haven't got much time, I have to go back on air, but I thought I could come and see you, if you wanted. Just to have a chat.'

'Come and . . . come and see me?'

'I could come tomorrow, or — if you just text me your address. I can give you my number.' What am I doing? Xavier asks himself with a bemused grimace.

There is a pause.

'Could you come tonight?'

'I won't finish the show until four o'clock.'

'I'll be awake.'

They're back on air in thirty seconds. Murray shoulders the door aside, an overspilling coffee mug in each hand.

'All right,' says Xavier hastily, 'all right, I'll come.'

★ ★ ★

Xavier sits in the back of a taxi heading north out of London, having told Murray he had 'some urgent stuff to do' and wouldn't need a lift home. What urgent thing could possibly take place at 4 a.m., Murray's brow wondered, but he didn't pursue it. There are barriers between them suddenly. Xavier felt the curdling of a slight irritation, almost a distaste, as they parted in the car park.

He watches out of the window as the third quarter of the night gives way to the last; the dark still hanging heavy but quietly resigned to its end, birds on branches starting to murmur their way through rehearsal. The silent cabbie has the radio on, the same station Xavier and Murray were just on; there's almost a solid hour of soul music now, and then at five their successors, the unnervingly awake breakfast broadcasters, will start to gabble at the early risers. The cab swings off a roundabout and deposits him at the end of a drab driveway. Xavier pays the man, who takes the money without a word, like the ferryman at the Styx, Xavier thinks vaguely, clutching at some near-forgotten memory from school. The pre-morning air is chilly and still. Xavier shivers as he rings the bell, wishing he were in his bedroom now on Bayham Road, or in front of the all-night news with a cup of tea. A dog barks a few doors down.

A balding man in a balding woolly jumper opens the door.

'I can't believe you're actually here.'

Xavier steps inside.

'See it as a kind of outside broadcast or something.'

Xavier follows Clive down the hall and into the kitchen, where a dismal pile of books sits on the table. The kettle and toaster stand bored beside a microwave oven which clearly does almost all of the cooking around here. A kitchen window looks out onto an ill-tended garden, fringed with nettles which sway restlessly in the wind, as if waiting in vain for the challenge of a gardener's shears, like a dog appealing to be chased.

'This place is a bit of a state,' says Clive, rubbing his eyes.

'Have you thought about getting a cleaner?'

Clive is surprised, as well he might be, by the directness of this response.

'No, well, no, it hadn't really . . . no.'

'Sorry, strange question maybe. It's just, it really worked for me.' Xavier cautiously picks up one of the orange books. 'You're a maths teacher? I was pretty average at maths.'

'So was I.' Clive smiles weakly.

'So, how come you listen to the show, if you have to be up for work at — what, seven? Half past six?'

'Well, I have a lot of trouble sleeping. So I started listening to — '

'To send you off.' Clive looks abashed, but Xavier grins. 'Don't worry, that's a familiar story. Most of our audience are exhausted. That's how we get away with Murray's bits.'

'You know, I don't want to speak out of turn, but Murray is really not — '

'I know.'

Clive puts the kettle on. As he's fussing around in cupboards, uneasily scanning shelves in the hesitant way of a man unused to entertaining, Xavier glances at the sink and spots a familiar logo.

'I've got a mug the same as that, in the studio. The *BIG CHEESE* one.'

'What? Oh yes. They bought that for me when I became Head of Maths.'

'Ah. So you're more than just a maths teacher?'

'Unfortunately, it didn't work out. I had to take two months off after my second wife — after we divorced. I wasn't in the right frame of mind. So someone took over as Head of Department and did a good job and, well, he sort of stayed in that role.'

'Don't you get two months off for the summer holidays? It's a shame she couldn't have divorced you then.'

Clive laughs out loud. It's the first time he can remember laughing, especially in his own kitchen, in recent months.

'No, the papers came through in March. Not even half-term. That tells you everything you need to know about my second marriage.'

'Tell me about the other ones.'

★ ★ ★

Clive met the first one, Angie, in a manner so effortless and delightful that he struggles to believe it really happened. It felt like a very short film. It feels as if the memory really belongs to someone else's life. He was walking through immigration at Heathrow as a young trainee teacher, after a week in Crete with some friends from the course. He had fair hair then, wore what used to be called a sports jacket, was in better shape than most of his mates, who had been getting drunk on the flight. A girl checked his passport. She looked at him twice, three times, looked between him and his black-and-white likeness. Clive's heart wavered; he'd always tried to avoid trouble.

'It's not a very good photo . . . '

'No, no, it's fine,' said the girl, whose name-tag read *Angela Pickering*. 'I was just thinking that you were very handsome.'

Nothing in the world could have prepared him for this, and he had no idea how to reply, but luckily Angela Pickering continued, 'Will you meet me in two hours, when I finish?'

In those days, things were simpler, or so Clive remembers, anyhow: they saw each other for a year — went to the pictures, dancing, to parks, museums, always her idea — and then they got married. When she lifted the veil, her cheeks were glistening with tears and he kissed her when instructed by the Vicar. They cut the cake and went off to Norfolk.

Perhaps it wasn't that things were simpler 'in those days', perhaps things were just very simple with Angie, because her impulsiveness sliced through decisions which would have detained anyone else. They bought their house after looking round it just once. She flitted from job to job and then, leaving him to bring in the money, from hobby to hobby: glass-blowing, jazz piano, cross-stitch. Once he came home and she had bought two chinchillas. She laughed as he stepped back in horror from the enclosure.

'What on earth did you buy a pair of . . . of these for?'

'I couldn't just buy one. They get lonely on their own.'

Opposites attract, they say: and it might be true, but over the long haul of a relationship similarities are a lot more useful. Angie's impulses and Clive's meticulous plans played out in an unlikely harmony for a few years, but they began to grate against one another. They never fought, just slid, consciously but helplessly, into the mire which had claimed three or four other couples of their acquaintance in the past year alone. Clive hated to see Angie unhappy, the emotion suited her so badly, and he was almost relieved when, impulsive as ever, she slept with a man she met at the supermarket, and then with a man at the sorting office, and with very little acrimony they began the negotiations which would end with Clive owning the house and Angie beginning a new life somewhere in Africa. Clive, who had scarcely believed how easy it was to get married, was now taken aback to write *divorcee* on forms.

The second marriage was even more traditional in the pattern of its decline. It began with each party, Clive and Polly — another maths teacher, they met at a conference — lonely, divorced, overeager for company; progressed from a series of days out to the registry office to a year and a half of bickering, and ended with the two them lonely and divorced all over again, and resentful at a settlement which somehow they both considered an insult. Clive was suddenly forty. He had lost a lot of his hair, most of his enthusiasm for work, and two marriages, both of which felt in hindsight like things that had happened to him, rather than things he had made himself.

By the time it came to the third marriage — to a woman called Marjorie, who proposed to him six months after they met at a party, but got sick of him pretty quickly, and now lived in a lesbian community — Clive had almost come to feel that his life in general could be summed up as a process he had been subjected to, a trick that had been played on him, rather than a chain of events he'd had any control over. It was someone else's idea, surely, not his, that he should end up a maths teacher with a string of failed relationships behind him, living in a featureless semi in Hertfordshire which was the least bad of the remaining options. Not that he felt unlucky, or in any way victimized; just stupid, as if in embarking on life he'd set his sights too high, and had his inadequacies exposed at once.

Over the course of the past few years, staring at blank or contemptuous faces across rows of desks, applying red penstrokes to minor errors in books, stumbling through the smallest of staff-room small talk, tiny, tiny talk, Clive's indignant confusion at having been tricked, at having failed to work out the rules of life until it was too late, has hardened into something grimmer, and more permanent: misery.

By the time Clive Donald comes to the end of this potted history of his disappointments, light has started to dawn — weakly, as if leaking through a hole in the sky. It's one of those mornings where it is hard to tell whether it is simply slow to start, or the beginning of a depressingly dark day. Xavier glances at the clock, and Clive's eyes automatically follow.

'Good heavens. It's a quarter to seven.'

Xavier has been in Clive's kitchen just over two hours, but he registers the time with no particular alarm.

Clive seems agitated.

'I've kept you here — '

'Not at all,' says Xavier. 'I came of my own free will, if you remember. It's been good to talk to you.'

'I should, I should,' mutters Clive, 'I should be sort of getting ready for work.'

'So when you invited me here, were you planning to go into work on two hours' sleep, or . . . or what exactly?'

Clive sighs.

'I was planning to, er . . . '

But it sounds too stupid to say out loud.

'I've been pretty unhappy, as you know,' Clive tries again, 'and I was thinking . . . '

Xavier nods; he's heard this kind of thing far more often than most people.

'And yet you're worried you might be late for work?'

Clive grimaces.

'You would have been quite a bit later, by the sound of it, if — '

'I'm embarrassed. It seems ridiculous, talking about it.'

'If I were in professional mode,' says Xavier drily, 'I'd suggest that embarrassment about your

272

emotions is part of your problem rather than part of the defence against them. But since I'm not, I'm going to simply suggest that you don't go to work.'

'What?'

'Call in sick. Give them an excuse.'

'I've got classes.'

'Well, of course you have. You're a teacher. But it's one day.'

Clive falters visibly. He runs his finger along his brow.

'You don't even like the job.'

'People can't just not do their jobs because they don't like them. The country would be at a standstill.'

Xavier grins.

'OK, maybe. But *you* can not do yours, for today.'

Clive hesitates again, and then he nods.

★ ★ ★

They walk in small circles on the dew-soaked lawn; it leaves a wet imprint on the hems of Clive's corduroy trousers. Beyond the fence which pens in the garden, traffic roars its way into another morning.

'I honestly think that talking to you has been,' says Clive, staring at his dew-darkened shoes, 'you know, it's very much like your show, I mean, er, a problem shared . . . '

Xavier thinks of Murray, who sometimes cracks a joke relating to this cliché — that a problem shared makes two people miserable, which is a cliché in its own right.

'I haven't really done anything.'

'Well, I'm very . . . I'm very grateful. I didn't mean to keep, as it were, brow-beating you by phoning the show. And all the emails, and so on. I just didn't honestly know what to do.'

'I'm glad to have been able to help.'

'You must be very used to this conversation.'

'Not really.' Xavier toes the grass with the tip of his shoe. 'Until fairly recently I tended to think that pretty much nothing I said had much of an effect. Or at least — that it was a kind of . . . theoretical exercise. You know. I lost touch with the idea that I could actually make a difference. It was just my job.'

'And what happened to make you think otherwise?'

'It's a long story.' Xavier rubs his nose. 'It's to do with a cleaner.'

$\star$ $\star$ $\star$

This is where the story could end, but it doesn't; life isn't so neat. The thousands of tiny consequences of Xavier's non-intervention in the bullying of Frankie Carstairs, eight weeks or so ago, continue to spawn thousands more, which spawn thousands more again, which run unchecked around London. Still, for now, Clive Donald feels differently about his relationship with the world. A virtual stranger, known to him only as a voice on the radio, has come personally to his aid. Without directly absorbing it, he realizes that every person is connected to every other, and therefore that every lesson he teaches — all those poxy graphs, those weary reprimands to the fat-necked youth eating crisps at the back — has its consequences. Everything has a chance of mattering.

'How are you going to . . . ?' Clive begins to ask Xavier, when they finally go back inside, stamping off the dew on the doormat. It is almost nine now, and too late for him to get to school even if he had a last-minute attack of conscience. This irreversibility is comforting. Already, the playgrounds will be full of blazers and ties and shouts, energetic cursing, accusations of homosexuality, football games descending into wrestling. Julius Brown, who secretly credits Clive Donald with his success, will be walking more upright than usual through the gates, bag slung over his shoulder, and an engraved maths trophy sitting on his desk at home.

Xavier orders a cab. The two men, never to meet again, shake hands in the hallway.

'Stay in touch. Email, or call. You don't have to call the show. Just stay in touch.'

'I will.'

Clive waves as Xavier opens the car door, crunches it shut. There is a bark from the dog three houses away, as if in deliberate bookending of Xavier's visit. The cabbie, too, is the same man who brought Xavier here. Xavier gives him the postcode of his flat. The car eases into the stream of just-past-rush-hour traffic sinking slowly into the city's digestive system. The earlier haze is gone now, and the daylight seems, to Xavier's eyes, unnaturally bright, almost showy,

275

like the light that greets afternoon cinemagoers when they leave the building.

As often happens, the night without sleep has left Xavier, not exhausted, but full of a confusingly unfocused energy. Home, he looks back on the hours just gone with a strange mixture of incredulity — did I really go to a stranger's house and act as his counsellor? — and an almost euphoric sense of having done a solidly good thing, the kind of thing he's rediscovered the joy of doing. He finds it hard to settle down to any other task, even one so simple as pondering what he will say to Murray tonight by way of explanation. He goes to the corner shop and ends up chatting to the Indian man for almost twenty minutes, eagerly learning details of the forthcoming wedding, the terrific wealth of the groom's parents, who have a house in Surrey with 'three cars and a fabulous garage'. Even though he'll be working until 4 a.m. again tonight, Xavier doesn't want to sleep; he wants to share what happened last night, not just the story, but the feeling that its aftermath has produced. What I really want, he realizes, is to be with Pippa.

★ ★ ★

'So this fella you've never met is depressed, and you go to his house?'

'Well, it was a bit more complicated than that . . . '

'The line's not too good, pet. I'm on a bus.'

When Xavier calls Pippa she is, of course, on

276

the way to work, or rather leaving work hurriedly in order to go to work somewhere else. The rich client in Marylebone has gone skiing with her partner and child, and Pippa is to give the place the usual three-hour clean in their absence.

'What, even though they haven't been at home? What does she expect you to do? Make a mess yourself just so you can clean it up?'

'She can afford it, though, so why not,' Pippa snorts. 'You know, she could probably afford to buy a new house each time the old one gets messy.'

'Where did she make her money, this woman?' asks Xavier, unconsciously imitating his mother. He can hear, down the phone, Pippa's irritated sigh: in her view it's a waste of time asking where people get money, some people simply have it and other people have to do things to get it off them.

'It's a pain that you have to go and clean it even when she's away, though.'

This is intended to be helpful but, again, it seems to strike a wrong note.

'It's not a *pain*. I'm lucky she's that stupid that she'll pay me. I need it.' The P of stupid disappears in the angry lick of her accent.

In the course of the conversation, conducted over a sonic backdrop of bus sounds — irritable voices, doors creaking open, the sigh of the engine, like an ageing pair of lungs — it becomes clear that Pippa has no time to see Xavier today, and can't really commit to tomorrow. He feels as if he's been back-pedalling since he dialled her number, and can sense the glow of the day fading.

It's time for another gamble.

'Why don't I come with you?'

'What?'

'Tell me where you're working and I'll come and help.'

'I don't think I want you to see me at work, pet.'

'I've seen you at work. Remember? You've worked in my flat.' But the memory is still somehow embarrassing, and he tails off.

Then: 'All right.' Pippa sighs, making a show of indulging him, and suddenly Xavier is encouraged again. 'All right. If you're stupid enough to come to fucking' — her voice dips a couple of volume notches — 'to Marylebone, just to see me looking like shit, on my knees with a dustpan and brush, then be my guest.'

Xavier grins.

'Great. I'll see you there.'

* * *

'So, he calls the radio show so many times you think he might be dangerous, and he talks about doing away with himself . . . '

'He just kind of hinted at it.'

'Hints about doing away with himself — hold this — and you decide the best way to deal with it is to go round his house in the middle of the night?'

'Well, I wasn't sure it was the best way, but it did . . . it did seem to work.'

'Hold this.'

Pippa jiggles the keys in the lock, muttering

278

idle curses to herself, 'Fucking double lock, fucking door.' Xavier stands, the blue-and-yellow laundry bag heavy in his hands (how the hell does she cart this everywhere, he wonders), feeling that he would have done better to tell his story when she was not distracted: it's been rather wasted. The door swings open and they are in a large, opulent hallway, a luxuriously carpeted staircase rising up and away to the right, and above their heads an enormous, glittering chandelier.

'Well, here it is.'

They stand in the hallway, Pippa surveying the wooden panelling, the expansive tiled floor, and the high arches above the doors, with something like affection: the strange affection of the hunter for the prey.

'Right. I'm going to start with the living room. Break the back of that.'

'I'm serious about helping, you know. What do you want me to do?'

She looks at him, her pale blue eyes amused and disdainful.

'Do you honestly think you're at the ability-level we expect in this company?'

'By 'this company' you mean yourself?'

Pippa throws a playful punch to his arm which, catching him on the bone, hurts only slightly less than a non-playful punch might. 'Remember what your flat was like before I came along?'

'Yes, I do remember, because it's getting that way again.'

'Exactly. *Grubby*. Do you think I can risk you

279

leaving even an inch of this place grubby? This woman is an important client.'

'At least let me hoover, or something. Anyone can hoover.'

'Not anyone can hoover, by any means. You might as well say anyone can play the piano.'

'Give me a probationary period.'

Pippa shakes her head despairingly.

'It's in that cupboard there. Try doing that room. You've got ten minutes.'

As he propels the whining machine over the heavy green carpet, Xavier remembers, as a nine-year-old in the passenger seat, being allowed to take the steering wheel of the family's old Holden as they drove along a country road on some holiday or other.

What would Dad think of this, he wonders, angling the nozzle of the Hoover into a corner made by the edge of an antique bookcase, housing antique books which are never read. I moved to England — almost fifty years after Dad, as he saw it, rescued Mum from it. I don't have a car; to him, that would have been as unthinkable as not having a roof on the house. And I'm hoovering a rich woman's house, in order to impress another woman.

'Stop, stop right there.' Pippa, her white-blonde hair now scraped back with painful-looking hairclips, sweeps into the room and jolts him out of these thoughts. She bends down and pushes a button to silence the machine. 'See what I mean? Look. You've missed a bit *there*.' Out come her indignant fingers for counting. 'A bit *there*. You've not even *gone* there. This is hopeless. I could have vacuumed this room better with my feet.'

'But I did go there. And there.'

'Then there's something wrong with your action, pet. Come on. Look.' She replaces the hose in Xavier's hands, and lays her hands on top of his, like someone teaching first tennis strokes to a child. 'We're going to walk through it.'

With a toe, she presses the button again, and the Hoover roars at the thick carpet. Xavier feels Pippa pressed in behind him, the fullness of her breasts against his back, her hands on his. She says something which he loses under the noise.

'What?'

'I said,' she says, louder, 'you are lucky to get this sort of training. I could charge for this. Look. Push down on it. Force it to take the dirt in. Don't just trust it. Force it.'

'Can you say that again, 'Force it to take the dirt in'?'

'Why?'

'It was kind of adorable, with your accent.'

'You are a patronizing fucker,' mutters Pippa into his ear, and the suddenness of the contact is one intimacy too far.

Xavier pivots and kisses her. She closes her eyes; her hands search out the buttons of his shirt.

In a stranger's house for the second time in twenty-four hours, Xavier, naked, stares up at the woman straddling him. His hands reach around to grasp her back, the curve at the tops of her buttocks; his fingers, as if equipped with

281

sensors, search for freckles, moles, every tiny detail of her skin. He feels, with a wild joy, the weight of her on top of him. Helplessness, in sex, is something he has never known. He starts to speak, but Pippa leans down and silences him with a kiss. Her strong hands are on his chest. He looks up at the ornate ceiling, a stucco, he thinks it's called. His brain focuses on whatever it can.

She grits her teeth and sighs deeply, as, inside her, Xavier moves. He is shaking; his whole body feels like a bag about to burst. He feels as if no one has ever done anything as good as this.

★ ★ ★

Edith Thorne will never have sex with anyone other than her husband again. She knows she has acted inexcusably and jeopardized everything. She broke it off with the politician instantly: it was in his best interests, too, in fact it was the only way he could maintain any sort of career, and he aims to be in the Cabinet in five years. Edith and her agent Maxine have won, with bribery and threats, the silence of a couple of other people who know things. But there is still the barman, Alessandro.

He won't accept that it's over. He's texted and called her almost non-stop these past five days. She has had to block his number from her phone, but the texts still arrive, and if Phil were to go through her mobile — which he's a lot more likely to do, in the light of recent events — there could be further disaster.

They met in the bar at a wrap party for a mini-series Edith presented, about people obsessed with celebrities. Alessandro, six foot three, olive-skinned, was done up as Clark Gable with a joke-shop moustache and bow tie, his hair gleaming with gel. He was well over ten years younger than Edith, and as soon as she saw him, she wondered what it would be like to fuck him, even if he *did* look ridiculous at that moment. Later, on her way back from the toilets, she walked past the staff room and saw him, clocking off, pulling his shirt over his head to reveal a smooth, muscle-bound chest, and wondered even more. The answer was that it was very good, extraordinarily good, that night and on several other nights, and yes, maybe she *did* tell him she loved him.

And so, although she's been putting it off, she owes him at least a goodbye. In the basement of the £1.2 million house — whose value, neighbours mutter bitterly, must be a bit less than that now, since the area became infested with photographers — she dials the blocked number, holding her breath, hoping for his voicemail. But no, she should have waited till tonight, when he'll be working.

As it is, he answers on the second ring.

'Edith, at last. Thank fucking God.'

His English is good, but heavily influenced by American cinema, and as a result — especially because of his accent — he often sounds like an actor in a TV movie.

'Alessandro, listen . . . '

But it's even harder than she expected to

283

explain; the silence on the other end is even chillier. Braced for an argument — she's in practice for those — she instead has to deliver her justifications into a wall of ice. *I have to think about my family. I shouldn't have said I love you. I shouldn't have led you on. It's been an amazing adventure. I think in life you have to just let things happen sometimes.* She speaks for two long minutes unchecked.

'So . . . so I'm saying goodbye.'

'This is bullshit.' Alessandro's voice is angry, but a quiet, measured anger, worse — thinks Edith — than hysteria.

'I know I've handled things really badly.'

'Yes. You have handled things really badly.'

Pause.

'I'm sorry.'

'Edith, I need you.'

She wasn't prepared for this. The guy is twenty-two, for Christ's sake; they met in a bar and had casual sex.

'Well, you can't *have* me.'

The muffled sound of sobbing comes shuffling through the phone.

'Alessandro . . . '

'Please, Edith, if you change your mind — '

She won't change her mind, she says. She ends the call, and vows to ignore the phone for the next hour.

Edith leaves for the show feeling somewhat shaken, forgets to lock the front door, and then on returning to it realizes she's left half of her gym clothes in a bag next to the washing machine. She sits in the back of the car — its driver professionally tight-lipped again — and thinks about Alessandro. She'd been familiar with the hazards of sleeping around, the scandal and shame that have now caught up with her, but she never expected someone to, of all things, *fall in love* with her. And of all people, a tall, masculine Italian who looked like the perfect caricature of a guy who would sleep with you and leave before you woke up, and yet is now crying himself through the afternoon. She feels sorry for him for a few moments, and then gets out a mirror and applies lipstick, and brings the notes for today's show out of her bag. It's a pity, but she can't be responsible for everyone's feelings. Really, you can't be responsible for *anyone's* feelings, thinks Edith, approving of her face in the mirror. You can't be responsible for what happens to other people. You just have to live your life.

10

While the nocturnal version of London sleeps, snacks, paces, sweats, shits, fights and breathes its way through another midweek night, events domino mercilessly on.

In a rented studio flat in Tottenham, Italian barman Alessandro Romano is heartbroken when he returns home from work at two in the morning, because he was dumped by his lover Edith Thorne, because she had to save her marriage, because she'd been exposed by the journalist Stacey Collins, because her friend Maggie lost faith in her job and decided to spread dirt about her clients, because an estate agent called Roger was ratty with her, because he'd accidentally received a nasty text message from his colleague Ollie who was using an unfamiliar phone, because his BlackBerry had been stolen by a fat kid, Julius, because the kid needed money for a gym membership, because he was sacked by egotistical restaurant owner Andrew Ryan, who was overreacting to a harsh review, which was penned by Jacqueline Carstairs, who was in a bad mood because her son Frankie was beaten up, because Xavier didn't stop the bullies from doing so. Alessandro, the eleventh person in the chain that began that cold day, looks around his poky flat somewhere between distaste and desperation.

Xavier has, by now, forgotten that original incident once again. At two in the morning, he lies with Pippa in the bed where they have spent a large portion of their time since that first, ungainly, wonderful sex in the home of one of Britain's foremost female entrepreneurs.

A fair amount of that time has of course been taken up with more sex. Xavier loves having sex with Pippa. He loves her superior, almost intimidating, bodily strength; the way she sometimes stands completely naked before they begin, next to the bed, looking straight at him, daring him to look straight back. He adores the fact that she is the hungriest, most visceral lovemaker he's ever known, and yet her peculiar sense of decorum, her faintly old-fashioned commitment to common sense and not making a fuss, keeps intruding; she flames a delicious colour, looks faintly appalled to find herself crying out, and afterwards forbids all talk of what has happened. There is no reviewing, it is briskly filed away with the rest of the day's completed tasks. Indeed, Xavier thinks wryly, sex is one of the only things she *doesn't* talk unstoppably about, though he feels guilty even thinking, let alone vocalizing, the joke. They often make love in the afternoons, between her cleaning appointments, before his evening with Murray and his listeners, and her return to the side of her needy, now heavily pregnant sister Wendy.

But even more than sex, Pippa has used the bed for sleeping. Since she started spending her

287

meagre free time at his flat, Xavier has become fully aware of how tired Pippa is, how much sleep she has missed. It's a debt accrued over the past five years and now stacking up interest faster than it can be paid off. Even when she does get a decent sleep, it only seems to remind her system of what it is properly entitled to, and it raises its demands accordingly. Xavier is getting better at persuading Pippa to rest properly between jobs, to take naps and lie-downs, to let him make her tea and toast, even to overlook small messes and imperfections.

'I'm not an invalid.'

'You will be if you continue like this, that's the point.'

In commanding Pippa's time, Xavier has two big opponents: her tendency to take on too much work, and her loyalty to Wendy. To tackle either subject feels as precarious as walking on marbles. The sister he will leave until he's collected more evidence, but the workload he has started to address, albeit tentatively, opening talks a few days ago in a café down the road.

'Look, you've got to let me . . . let me take some of the pressure off you a bit.'

'I have to work, Xavier. What, I'm just meant to let you pay bills for me? Do you think I've no pride?' Her blue eyes swoop down to look at the table.

She is serious enough about her pride for this to be a risky subject, but he still persists, even though money was one of the factors that caused that awful argument that awful night.

'I'm not saying you should . . . sponge. I'm

saying let's be practical. I've got some money. You don't have much. You are wearing yourself out and in the long run it'll cost you more work because you'll be — '

'So what are you suggesting? Next time I could earn twenty-five quid I just ask you for twenty-five quid instead?'

'No . . . '

'Or you pay me to hang out with you?'

'No. Just . . . oh, I don't know. Maybe just let me do nice things for you, sometimes, without complaining.'

'I'm letting you take me for tea, aren't I? In a café.' She shakes her head. 'My mother would never forgive me. 'Going out to a café! What do you think I buy teabags for!''

She did let him buy her a coat: a beautiful, floor-length, green floral affair — thick, almost a cloak — which she had spotted in a shop in Soho almost six months ago.

'Every time I go past my heart stops in case it's not there any more. I know it's stupid.'

Xavier went straight in and paid for it.

'That's that sorted. It would be a shame if you had heart failure over a coat.'

She blushed and thanked him, and kissed him on the mouth.

Last week, to cheer her up after a trying day, he bought her a box of chocolates. They go to the pictures, eat Chinese food, go for walks. They speak on the phone two or three or four times a day. In a couple of weeks he plans to buy her a new dress and take her to an art exhibition with a posh drinks reception beforehand.

He can remember how recently it seemed absurd to refer even privately to 'taking her' somewhere. He's not sure whether she has softened a little, or whether he's simply got bolder.

Tonight he watches her sleeping face, the eyelids that dropped down like sliding garage doors almost the instant she got into bed, the expression of absolute seriousness. Earlier, they played Scrabble.

The old green box caught Pippa's eye as she rummaged through a cupboard.

'Hey, why don't we play this?'

Xavier, glass of wine in hand, glanced up from the TV and cocked an eyebrow.

'Are we that desperate?'

'Shut up. I like Scrabble.'

'I don't think you'll like playing it with me.'

'Oh really? And why not?' She was already getting the board out of its box.

'Because I'm a tournament-standard player.'

'Oh *are* you!' She shook the velvet bag and mockingly ruffled his hair. 'Well, *I* used to be the UK's best young discus thrower but I don't wear a bloody rosette for it, do I!'

Sure enough he infuriated her, with 58 points for *JA, JAR, AA* and *AR* in one move.

'You can't have those! They're not words!'

Xavier reached into the box and casually removed a beaten-up little book.

'Fortunately, I keep a Scrabble dictionary for just this sort of debate.'

'*JA* is a German word!'

'If you look in this dictionary, it's also an English word.'

'*AA* . . . ?'

'It's a type of lava, with a rough surface.'

'So how am I supposed to win,' she asked a bit later, 'now you're this far ahead' — counting on her fingers — '*and* I've got shitty little letters *and* I know you've got good ones because of the way you're smirking?'

'You're not supposed to win. I'm supposed to win. I did tell you this when we started.'

She poured herself another glass of wine.

'You're not having one.'

'If you really want my advice,' Xavier continued, 'you need to either hit back with a Z- or X-type word of your own — '

'Which I can't as I don't have a Z or an X.'

'Never reveal your tiles. Or, get rid of all seven, get a Bingo, get a 50-point bonus. That'd put you . . . ' He scanned the meticulous column of pencilled figures in front of him. 'Well, within 120.'

Pippa elbowed him, fairly hard.

'Very short words and very long ones, that's all Scrabble is about. The rest is just filler. Do you realize that when you play-fight, it is as painful as real fighting?'

'Of course I realize.'

'So all in all, I'd advise you to swap tiles.'

'But then I miss a go.'

'It's not *missing* a go. The swap is a move in itself. Sometimes a risk is the only way.'

Xavier listened to the gentle clicking of the tiles against one another as she rummaged in the bag with a resigned groan. He wondered how Pippa would react when he put down *DZO*, a hybrid of cow and yak most commonly found in Tibet.

★ ★ ★

The following Friday, Xavier takes Pippa to a movie and then to a classy restaurant, where they drink two bottles of wine. Occasionally, Pippa laughs so loudly that people on adjoining tables, heads bowed over leather-bound menus like delegates examining the minutes of a meeting, look up peevishly from their deliberations. They walk dizzily home from the tube station, hand in hand, tracing loose diagonals up Bayham Road. Pippa, repeating herself, talking around in circles, and counting lists down on her fingers, outlines her objections to the film's intricate plot.

'And how would he even *afford* a gym membership, a bloke who works delivering pizzas? How is he going to get the money to ponce about in some fancy place with running machines?'

'I don't know. Maybe he stole it.'

'So what're you going to say in your review? Two stars?'

'Three, I think.'

She punches his forearm.

'It's not *worth* three stars.'

'It is. It was competently done. There were some good bits.'

'Are you going to discuss it on your *radio show*?' She puts on the haughty voice she uses for undermining him. 'Are you going to make

292

amusing remarks about it with your friend Murray?'

The mention of Murray's name provokes misgivings, the precise shape of which Xavier cannot trace.

'How is the show going, anyway?'

'You should know. You're one of our valued listeners.'

'I normally fall asleep before the end of it.'

He returns her punch on the arm.

'The show is fine, thank you, to answer your question.'

Murray has been bright enough on the show, but the atmosphere between the two of them is still somehow clenched and uneasy. In commercial breaks and during the weather, they make little conversation. Xavier looks out at the empty car park and Murray tugs and twists handfuls of his bushy hair.

Just before the 2 a.m. midpoint of last night's show, Murray remarked, 'No sign of that guy recently.'

'Which guy?'

'That miserable bugger who was always cer, cer, cer, cer, calling in.'

'Clive?'

'Yeah. The guy with the wives.'

'The guy *without* the wives,' Xavier murmured. 'No. He's been quiet.'

'Probably for the best.' Murray uncrossed his legs, scratched his left testicle with a thick finger, and grimaced. 'He was pretty much a cul-de-sac.'

'Mmm.' Xavier raised an eyebrow and let the

subject run out of air in the warm room.

Now, with Pippa's hand in his, he lets Murray disappear in similar fashion from his mind.

★ ★ ★

Even during sex she's in the mood for mockery.

'*Dear Xavier, please sort me life out. Dear Xavier, I can't live without you.*'

'This is not an appropriate time . . . ' Xavier's hands, sweatslick, clutch her sides. 'This is not an appropriate time to question my professional standing.'

'*Dear Xavier. I am currently having sex with you and want to know what you would like me to do next.*'

Because of his longtime habit of keeping peculiar hours, Xavier normally finds himself awake for some time after Pippa has fallen asleep, which she seems always to do immediately after sex. Tonight, as on previous nights, he watches her face and gently strokes her arm, admiring the freckles shown in a soft light from the full moon outside. Her breaths are slow, each exhalation a little longer than Xavier expects.

He's been asleep for only a few minutes when they both sit straight up in response to a resounding crash from upstairs.

'What is it, what is it!' mutters Pippa, still half-asleep.

He grabs her hand and threads his fingers between hers.

'It's all right. It's just . . . upstairs.'

She leans across and puts on the bedside light.

They sit, holding a joint breath. From the other side of the ceiling come raised voices, which Xavier and Pippa can't help but hear, like the overspill from the film in the next auditorium. Tamara's furious shrieks are countered by the nasal yelling of her boyfriend. There is a series of thumps, cries, another crash, and finally silence. Downstairs, Jamie wails; Mel can be heard hauling herself wearily out of bed and to his side. The silence continues. Xavier feels as though everyone in London must be listening as breathlessly as they are; but no, nobody else is aware of what is happening. The knowledge is suddenly frightening. Xavier still has hold of Pippa's hand. He remembers shouting for his mother after a nightmare, eight years old, on holiday in the outback. 'It's all right now!' she said, as his arms trawled the sheets frantically for imaginary snakes. 'They've gone now! I mean, they were never here!' she corrected herself.

Just when the silence seems as if it will swallow up whatever events it succeeded, the door of Tamara's flat can be heard swinging open violently, followed by a further exchange of shouts.

'Let's go up there.' Pippa's pale blue eyes shine in the dark.

'What?'

'Let's go up there and see if we can help.'

'But — '

'Something's not right, Xavier.'

Xavier starts to protest again, but then remembers the row they had about this before. Pippa is already halfway to the front door. She

295

has on a long T-shirt from an old athletics event, and knickers; she never sleeps naked. 'You can't,' she explained to Xavier, after they slept together in his bed for the first time. 'You never know what might happen.' Now, he thinks wryly, fumbling in drawers for something to wear, she's been proved right. He follows her out onto the landing where the two of them, half-dressed, watch Tamara's boyfriend come clumping down the stairs, a bag over his shoulder and his shirt, as Xavier's mum would say, 'buttoned all wrong'. He eyes them both.

Xavier looks back at him. He has a purple bruise by his eye, which his hand leaps too late to cover. There's an older cut on his lower lip. Xavier draws a long, shaky breath and feels his stomach plunge.

'Are you all right?' Pippa asks the man rather weakly.

He looks at Pippa, seems to consider saying something aggressive, and then decides against it.

'Oh, I'm fine, I'm fine!' he contents himself with saying, the bitterness in his voice leaving both of them somewhat at a loss. 'Nice of you to ask, finally!'

Xavier coughs.

Pippa asks, 'What do you mean?'

'Well, could you not at some point have come up to see what was going on? Could you not have taken some sort of interest?'

'We did take an interest,' Pippa begins.

'It's me, not her,' Xavier objects. 'She doesn't live here. It's me that lives here.'

'Well, all I can say is it would have been nice to have had some support,' says the man rather incoherently; it's not clear if he quite knows what he means. 'It would have been nice to have had someone come and say: what's going on here? Then maybe it wouldn't have been quite so easy for her to smack me around. What do you think?'

Xavier and Pippa stand dumbly, not looking at him or at each another.

'Yes, I know what you're thinking,' the man continues, 'so why did I keep going back? Because I'm a stupid fucking . . . because I love her. Well, I won't make that mistake again! I'll find someone who doesn't smack me in the fucking face!'

Xavier and Pippa watch him take the rest of the stairs in inefficient strides. He throws open the front door, which admits a puff of cold air in the hall below. Instinctively they both gaze up the stairs in case there is a glimpse of Tamara, but there is nothing to see, and nothing to hear, just the heaviest of silences, and the diminishing whimpers of the pacified Jamie in the ground-floor flat.

★ ★ ★

The next morning Pippa leaves early — she wants to go home and check on Wendy before her first cleaning job. The events of the night hang damply on their conversations; Pippa seems distracted as she kisses him goodbye. Xavier can't concentrate as he tries to prepare the show.

He replays in his mind the many times, at least half a dozen over the past three months, that there have been noises from upstairs. Could it all have been avoided? It's no longer satisfying to console himself with the thought that things just take their course.

Jamie is in a fractious mood — if he has any other moods — and splinters the air with an angry howl as Xavier collects the post from outside and knocks on the door. Mel looks as if she hasn't slept at all, and he notices how thin she's become; her jumper hangs roomily around her shoulders.

'What happened last night?'

Xavier glances sheepishly back up the stairs, as if the situation were still unfolding up there.

'The lady . . . Tamara's boyfriend stormed out. They'd had a fight . . . I mean, an actual fight — '

'BE CAREFUL, JAMIE. Sorry? An actual fight? He'd hit her?'

'She . . . she'd hit *him*.'

'God.'

'I think it must have been happening for a while.' Xavier clears his throat.

'God,' says Mel again. 'Do you think we should, you know, report . . . '

He's about to reply when Jamie darts past her legs and comes out into the hall, targeting Xavier's knees with his toy fire engine. He strikes Xavier an accurate blow on the kneecap with the little emergency vehicle, whose painted-on driver smirks as Xavier cries out.

'Shit,' Mel mutters to herself. 'Jamie, get back

298

here. Oh, I'm so sorry. I'm . . . he's just so full of energy . . . '

Mel clasps her forehead miserably.

'Are you all right?'

'I'm fine, I'm fine. You must think I'm always ill. Just a bit of a migraine. You must think I'm a . . . ' She smiles ruefully, her face off-white. 'Sorry.'

'Would you like me to take him out?' Xavier hears himself ask.

'Take . . . ? Take Jamie?'

'Just to give you a break. I could just take him down the woodland walk for an hour or something. If you wanted.'

Even as he's saying this, he hopes the offer will be declined. You're not to be trusted, says a voice at the back of Xavier's brain. Remember Michael, remember what you did? But he pushes this away fiercely.

Mel crouches down next to Jamie.

'Would you like to go for a walk with Xavier?'

Jamie nods.

'Are you sure you'll be good?'

He nods, tight-lipped, eyes reproachful, as though the question does him a disservice.

'You won't be naughty and you won't run away from Xavier?'

Jamie shakes his head of floppy fair hair, still with an expression of mild surprise that such questions should be asked.

He turns to look at Xavier.

'Can Valentine come?'

'Valentine is his rabbit,' Mel explains. Jamie holds out a grubby white toy to Xavier, like

299

someone declaring an item at Customs. Xavier gravely inspects the proposed passenger.

'Will Valentine be good as well?'

Jamie consults briefly with Valentine.

'Yes.'

'Then let's go.'

'Thank you so much,' says Mel. 'Are you absolutely sure?'

Well, it's a bit late to go back now, Xavier thinks as he takes Jamie's hand. They walk along the narrow stretch of pavement at the bottom end of Bayham Road, where cars pick up dangerous speed. When they've crossed the road, Xavier gingerly releases Jamie's hand, and allows the boy to totter in front of him along the canopied path through the woods. Birds chatter in the branches above them. It's a greyish, fairly cool midweek morning. A huge red-brown dog, seemingly taking its owner for a walk rather than the other way around, lopes up to them and Jamie pats its head. The dog snuffles delightedly at Jamie, its glistening nose in his palm. The owner exchanges an amused look with Xavier as they wait for their respective charges. Xavier realizes that anyone passing would take him for Jamie's father.

At the long-disused railway bridge which marks the halfway point of the path to Highgate, a teenager in a white hooded jacket is spraying a purple graffiti tag onto the wall. He glances at them without interest and returns to his work.

Jamie tugs at Xavier's sleeve.

'What's he doing?'

'He's, er . . . Well, it's called graffiti. He's sort

of drawing on the wall.'

'Why?'

'Well, some people do that. They like it.'

'But why don't they do it on paper?'

'Well, they . . . they like people to see their drawings as they walk around.'

'Why?'

'It's a good question,' Xavier admits.

They turn at the railway bridge and head slowly back towards home, Jamie's small shoes seeking out puddles left by the light rain of the previous night.

'Careful not to get muddy,' Xavier says. 'Your mum won't be very pleased.'

'No,' Jamie concedes.

'Do you think you could make her worry less, mate? If you were . . . if you didn't shout as much, maybe?'

Jamie considers this suggestion with seeming nonchalance, but he gives a half-nod before running off in the direction of a promising stick.

A long time from now, this walk will be one of Jamie's earliest memories; he'll wonder who Xavier was and how they came to be walking there, and what his mum was doing at the time. It will swim into his mind of its own accord as he lies awake one night, turning the results of an experiment over in his head, an experiment which will ultimately pave the way for the antibody which will ease the lives of many people, including the as yet unborn granddaughter of the Indian shopkeeper.

Xavier grabs Jamie's arm as they wait for a car to plough up the hill.

301

'Thank you for my walk,' says Jamie gravely.

'Thank *you*,' Xavier replies with equal seriousness. 'Perhaps we will have another one.'

'Perhaps,' the boy agrees.

Xavier hands Jamie back to Mel, who answers the door in a bathrobe, a book in one hand; she looks as if her hour of freedom was more like a whole day.

'Was he good?'

'Couldn't have been better,' says Xavier, and Jamie calmly rejoins his mother.

Back in his flat, Xavier suddenly feels drained. He sits heavily on the sofa, realizing that his heart is racing. It was, of course, the first time he'd been in sole charge of a child, or of anything much, since that night in Melbourne. He sits motionless for a long time, listening to the muffled TV downstairs.

★ ★ ★

It's late morning in London, night-time in Australia, and an hour after returning from the walk Xavier finally calls his mother. He wants to tell her about Pippa, there's a lot to talk about, but he senses that, whatever his intentions, the conversation will settle into the usual pattern: her questions will irritate him, they will somehow remain at right-angles to one another's meaning, especially with the distance, the time difference. All the same, he feels the call is overdue. The phone rings in the family home twelve thousand miles away, its single tone slow and hesitant; it sounds slower every time, he

302

thinks, as if it's getting older along with his mum. She doesn't answer. Xavier feels uneasy; this possibility hadn't even occurred to him. Where would his sixty-eight-year-old widowed mother be at ten at night? He doesn't know, because he hasn't taken care of her. She's probably out somewhere with Rick and Steve. Everything is probably fine. He counts thirty rings before admitting defeat.

Hanging up after a surprisingly unanswered call is a chilly feeling, especially a call made over such a long distance; it feels somewhere between a snub and a failure. 'Snap out of it,' he mutters to himself. Then, his fingers shaking very gently on the phone's keypad, he begins to call Matilda. He stops the call, tries again, stops it. This continues for a few moments. Finally, he lets it ring. The tone this time sounds almost incredulous, as if the call is being put through against everyone's better judgement. This time, he almost hopes not to get an answer, but it's picked up.

'Hello?'

'Matilda?'

'Yes.'

She has a fiancé now, she lives in Sydney, she will have a different haircut; she'll be slimmer, or curvier, she will have a whole wardrobe that he's never seen, she and Bec and Russell will have new catchphrases and gags, new friends they refer to, new favourite films and bands. There'll be new clubs and bars. The Zodiac, he knows from a petition he received by email, has been bought out by a company who have ripped out the balcony and put in a second screen. At best Matilda might occasionally glance at a photo of the gang of four, or find an old birthday card and remember for a minute before hastily putting it away. It's the past and it ought to stay there; it can't be returned to, this is stupid. All this passes through Xavier's mind in the three seconds before he speaks again.

'Mat? It's . . . I'm sorry to disturb you. It's Chris.'

'Chris!' She sounds surprised, of course, a little fearful, but maybe, just maybe, pleased.

'I'm sorry. I just haven't called for so long. I wanted to . . . I don't know.'

'Chris! Jesus.'

'Is it a bad time to call? I know it's late.'

'No, no, it's fine. We're just watching TV.'

'You and . . . your partner?'

'Me and Bec. I'm over at Bec and Russell's.'

Xavier catches his breath.

'Oh.'

'Hey,' she says, just like she used to, and he can picture her soaring on the trampoline, jumping off it straight into his arms so he staggers backwards, 'hey, are you on the radio over there?'

'What? Um. Yeah.'

'Fuck, Chris, that's great! There was a rumour you were. I couldn't find it. Someone said they listened online.'

'I go by a different name. Um. Xavier.'

'Xavier.'

'I know. It's kind of dumb.'

'Xavier! Fuck! You're a DJ! That's awesome!'

304

'It's pretty cool, eh?'

For thirty seconds they've been talking as if they still saw each other regularly, or were, at least, still in the same city. Suddenly aware that this is not the case, they falter.

'How are you?' asks Xavier.

'Good. Yeah, things are good.'

'How's . . . how's Bec? And Russell?'

'They're good.'

It's difficult again, but at least they've got this far. He takes a deep breath.

'Would she speak to me? Do you think?'

Matilda considers it for a while. Xavier starts to backtrack, but then she says, 'Hold on.'

There are footsteps and a muttered conversation which he longs to overhear. The phone audibly changes hands a couple of times.

'Hello, Chris.'

'Bec.'

'How are you going?'

'I'm good. It's good to hear you.'

'And you.'

Bec's voice has changed over the five years since he last heard it, in the indescribable ways voices are changed by time — the way experience, stacked up inside a person, weighs on the vocal cords. The tiny, careful strokes are enough to carve the first nicks into the ice that froze over everything. Or almost enough.

Xavier swallows an empty mouthful.

'How is Michael?'

Bec takes a breath, and her voice is unsteady.

'He's OK.'

There's nowhere they can go from there, and

the moment is cold and stiff, but it was a moment they had to pass together. Bec gives the phone back to Matilda and they say goodbye. He imagines Bec and Matilda mentioning the call to Russell when he comes back, and the three of them soberly discussing their old friend.

He knows that Australia is gone and these people are gone from him, that the life he had can't be returned to, but nor does it have to torture him any more. It is just what it is. Xavier puts the phone down. He looks out of the window at a bus labouring up the hill. In Sydney Harbour, the moon that beamed in on the sleeping Pippa last night is now a ghostly floodlight over the placid, lapping water. Matilda, on Bec's balcony, looks up at it and thinks about Chris for a moment.

★ ★ ★

It's raining by the time it gets dark: once again, London seems to be using the darkness to sneak in adverse weather. At eight, the doorbell rings. Jamie is quiet in the flat downstairs; Mel is watching TV. Compared with the boisterous programmes she normally puts on for Jamie, the overwrought yelps of her soap opera are almost soothing. Pippa stands on the doorstep with her blue-and-yellow bag, which Xavier takes smoothly from her. In her other hand sits the handle of a big black umbrella.

'I thought you didn't like umbrellas.'

'I didn't want to spoil the lovely coat you bought me.'

'I didn't even know you *had* an umbrella.'

'I invested in one for four pounds. Don't say I never take your advice on board.' She edges past him onto the stairs. 'Seldom, but not never.'

They lie together after a bout of sex which, in ten minutes, relieved each of them of eight hours' irritations and imperfections. Xavier's notes for the night's show are on the bedside table. He caresses Pippa's strong shoulder with his left hand. The covers are pulled up over her; he is stretched out naked on the sheets.

'That was nice.'

She rolls away.

'I don't know what you are referring to,' she says haughtily.

Xavier grins.

'Will you sleep here tonight?'

'You won't even *be* here. You won't be back till half past fucking four, excuse my language.'

'But I just like going to sleep next to you. I like it when you're there.'

'I need to look after Wendy.'

'Are you always going to look after Wendy?'

'What do you mean?'

Xavier's tongue runs over his lips.

'It's just, if you — moved in here . . . If you lived here . . . you'd have a hell of an easier time.'

She doesn't say anything.

'You could still work whenever you wanted. But you could relax more.'

'And me sister?'

'You could still see each other the same amount.'

'She'd hate it.'

'She could move in too.'

Pippa cackles.

'You can't have two Geordies move in overnight. You'd have a nervous breakdown. We make a lot of noise.'

'I'd quite like a lot of noise.'

She sits up, gathering the covers around her. Xavier glances down at his naked body.

'She relies on me being around all the time.'

'But do you think that's healthy?'

' "Healthy." ' She snorts. 'This is Xavier Ireland on *Late Lines*.'

'I know she's . . . I know you're sisters. But I'm not saying you should leave her to struggle. I just think it might be good for her to be more, more self-reliant. I don't know. Sometimes you have to be brave.'

She looks at him and he wonders whether she's going to bring up the Tamara situation, any of the numerous examples of his cowardice or passivity. But she just rubs her hand gently against his, then swings her legs over the side of the bed, and goes to the bathroom. As after so many conversations between people, it's hard to say what the outcome was.

After Pippa has left to go back to Wendy, Xavier thinks over what he said about being brave and taking action, reflecting that it is — as the English say — a bit rich for him to lecture Pippa on these ideas.

He gathers his notes for the show and pulls on his jacket, just as Murray honks the horn outside. He goes down to the door and sees the

Escort and the curl-topped head of his friend inside.

Clive Donald won't be tuning in tonight; he's already sleeping soundly in advance of another week at school. He saw his doctor, who prescribed a gentle tranquillizer to steady his sleep patterns. This evening he sent Xavier an email explaining this, and thanking him for 'helping to turn things around'. While this regular listener may be absent, twenty-two-year-old Alessandro Romano, the barman still in love with Edith Thorne, will hear *Late Lines* for the first time tonight. He'll turn it on at 2 a.m. when he returns to his unheated flat and plays with the radio dial in search of company. Still in a state of raw, heightened sentimentality, he will cry at the nineties rock ballad 'It Must Have Been Love'.

Xavier gets into the passenger seat. The air in the car is murky, as if Murray had either farted or been eating some sort of takeaway. There are empty sandwich packets at Xavier's feet.

'So, the joys of another Sunday,' says Murray.

Although he doesn't feel it at this point, an idea begins to occur to Xavier, one not firm enough yet for mental fingers to touch and pull from the pile of thoughts. It will take several days to collect itself, gathering whatever material ideas are made of. Then, soon, it will lodge heavily in Xavier's brain, forcing him into action.

★   ★   ★

The following Sunday, the 10th of May, Xavier arranges to meet Murray in the afternoon, before the show. Murray has been suggesting for some time that they 'sit down and have a chat'. From the officious way he says it, Xavier knows that the 'chat' will have something to do with work. They go to a pub in Crouch End, not far from Bayham Road. Pippa is disappointed to learn that he's going out on one of her free afternoons, and Xavier wishes that she would stay in his flat, treat the place as her own, and be there when he comes back from the show. But Wendy has to come first. Choosing not to rake the embers of the awkward subject, he leaves in a substandard mood.

In the pub, young families buzz messily around long tables, well-behaved children in fashionable striped jumpers, tiny designer jeans; couples sit with pints of beer studying the bloated Sunday newspapers, the sections stored inside one another like Russian dolls, spilling out when the paper is lifted up, as if to mock the reader's attempt to make sense of the whole universe.

'So, ner, next week is Quillam's birthday drinks,' says Murray.

Xavier had forgotten this, but indeed the new boss has requested the pleasure of their company — as the invitation puts it — at a floating restaurant on the Thames next Saturday.

'So we're going, right?'

'I was thinking . . . I don't know. It depends what Pippa's doing. If she's working.'

Murray grimaces.

'Are you just going to get more and more boring, now you're with her?'

'That remains to be seen,' says Xavier.

'So, look.' Murray thoughtfully kneads his hair. 'I don't know if we're going to get to talk shop with Quillam. But it's a good chance.'

'Last time he saw you, you were pissed, harassing that barmaid in the pub.'

Murray shrugs impatiently.

'That's all behind us now. Here's the point. If you look at what we're getting and what other people are getting — I've been talking to a couple of people. I think we should be pushing for a better deal.'

Xavier looks down at the table. The thought which was born in the car a week ago now sits poised in the back of his throat, like food waiting to be expelled.

'I just think wer, wer, wer, we're one of the most popular double acts on the radio, and wer, wer, we need to give them a bit of a kick up the arse from time to time.'

Xavier, still looking at the table, says, 'Look, mate. Quillam spoke to me recently, at that party. He's been talking about a slightly earlier timeslot.'

Murray shakes his head.

'I don't think we'd work in an earlier slot. Our thing is connecting with the late-night crowd. You know. Wer, wer, we're too unusual for . . . '

Xavier looks into Murray's brown eyes and sees them change, second by second, as if a chemical agent were being fed in drop by drop.

'Hang on. Der, der, do you mean us or just . . . just you?'

Xavier toys with the cuff of his shirt.

'He was talking about shaking it up a bit. Pairing me up with other people. You know.'

Murray doesn't say anything at all.

Xavier says, 'People have offered things before, and it's never seemed right. But, you know. We've had this show for a long time. I kind of feel that the time might be right to try something else.'

Murray gulps and his Adam's apple visibly wedges itself in his throat. He takes a large swig of beer and wipes his lips with his hand.

'I mean, they'd keep you on as a producer.'

Murray's face is a little red.

'They wouldn't. The, the, they only have me because of you.'

'I'd make sure they kept you.'

'But I wouldn't be able to present. They wer, wer, wer, wer, wer, wouldn't have me as a presenter. They only keep me because of you.'

Xavier feels the flush from his friend's cheeks spreading, like a germ, onto his own.

'I'm not stupid, Xav. I . . . ' He takes his run-up to the sentence. 'I wouldn't be on the radio at all.'

'We can't have a relationship that's based on . . . on that.'

'On what?'

'On me doing you a favour. It's not fair on either of us.'

Murray's big head swivels to look around the pub, as if seeking some dramatic intervention from a third party, some revelation that this is all a stitch-up. Then he looks at Xavier.

'Is this the girlfriend's idea?'

'What?'

'Well, it's funny,' says Murray, nodding slowly,

'funny that you mer, mer, meet her and you've never had any problems with the show, and then suddenly now that you've got her in your ear — '

'She's not in my ear.'

'Well, you've certainly changed since she came on the scene.'

'I know.'

Murray drains the rest of his glass. Outside the pub, people walk dogs, inspect second-hand books, queue in the supermarket, call after kids.

'And you've made your mind up about this?'

Xavier's surprised to hear it put like this, because there was no real process of 'making his mind up'. But it feels no less definite for being so sudden.

'Yes.'

'Well, there's not much else to say, then.'

Nonetheless Murray looks for a moment as if there are all sorts of things he might say. He gets to his feet and walks quickly to the Gents, catching his hip on a chair as he goes past a family group, and interrupting their conversation. As he continues, one of the children makes a remark; the parents laugh and then look guiltily around.

★ ★ ★

In the bar where only a few weeks ago he thought he had fallen in love with Edith Thorne, Alessandro Romano has been drinking with an Italian friend since shortly after they closed at 1 a.m. Having got everyone out and locked up, and made sure the premises were absolutely

313

empty, he called Marco, and by twenty-five past they were raiding the bar. They've had a bottle of gin, some wine; Alessandro even made a cocktail, expertly cradling and shaking the silver vessel, thumping it down on the bar, sloshing it out, as his friend cackled in the silence. It was only frightening for the first half-hour, this; now, he doesn't give a shit what happens. He doesn't want this job, he doesn't want to stay in this country. He'll keep drinking and then Marco can drive them back to Alessandro's in his car, or if he refuses Alessandro will drive the damn thing himself, who cares?

★ ★ ★

The journey back to Bayham Road after the show is a quiet one, but as the Escort crunches to a halt alongside the kerb, Murray says, 'Good show tonight.'

'It was,' Xavier agrees, grateful that the silence has been broken. He clears his throat. 'Thanks for driving me home.'

'I always drive you home.'

'Yes, but . . . after the — the discussion in the pub.'

Murray's big hand reaches around and pats Xavier heavily on the back.

'There's ner, ner, ner, ner, ner, no . . . '

'No hard feelings?'

'Exactly. No hard feelings.'

Xavier gets out, slams the door shut, waves to Murray, who waves back. All is quiet in Mel and Jamie's flat. When he opens his own door, Xavier

314

tenses. Something is different, the air is rearranged. He goes cautiously into the bedroom. There under the covers sleeps Pippa, her face turned towards him, drawn into the pose of absolute solemnity that marks her sleeping hours. Her lips, parted a quarter of an inch, admit long, slow, even breaths. Above the line of the covers, her pale shoulders gleam in the light of the two-thirds-moon.

On the bedside table is a note:

If you are reading this, it means I am asleep.

In light of the way you handled the Murray situation I thought I would also stand up to my sister for once and stay here. Some of the language she used would have made a miner blush, I'm afraid. I wrote minor the first time I did this, and had to start the whole note again.

I was planning to stay up and be here to say hello when you came back, but that bloody floor this morning nearly killed me and I have to be up at eight. So I'll probably try to let you sleep and slip out. But at least we'll have had these three hours, eh?

Love, Pippa.

PS I have taken the liberty of binning that bread.

Xavier watches her sleep. Wind stirs the branches of the trees in the little wood behind the flats and from the bottom of the garden floats the faint typing sound, the tapping of light rain on the shed roofs.

315

11

Pippa must have gone at about a quarter past eight. Xavier can remember foggily registering the blur of her body as it swept past the edge of the bed. When he comes properly to consciousness a little later, Jamie is making a commotion downstairs, so Xavier doesn't bother going back to sleep: he sits in the kitchen and read his emails. Iris, in Walthamstow, has just worked out how to use a computer, she tells him proudly. She is seeing Tony, the gentleman, for a cup of tea this afternoon. She signs it *Yours faithfully*.

Still early in the morning, the bell rings. Xavier goes out onto the stairs, but by the time he's got there, Mel is talking to someone at the door.

'I was here a couple of weeks ago,' he hears a girl say, 'and I was talking to a man about a great way to help people less fortunate than ourselves.'

Xavier sighs and continues down the stairs. Jamie is frisking about behind Mel's legs, driving his toy fire engine up and down the bottom stairs, grabbing her clothes, telling her to be quick.

'This is for me, I think,' says Xavier.

Mel turns thankfully, swatting her unwashed hair out of her eyes, and gives way to Xavier at the door.

'Hello again,' says the girl with the clipboard, a lanyard around her neck, the look of professional

316

hopefulness. 'We met a couple of weeks ago, when . . . '

Jamie takes advantage of the situation and makes a break for it out of the door, past the girl, propelled forward on his small, restless legs.

'Come here, Jamie! COME HERE, Jamie!' Mel commands automatically.

But Jamie has seen something on the road — a stick, or a feather, something he would really like — and this time he doesn't stop.

'JAMIE, COME HERE!' shouts Mel again, and her voice rises in a shrill panic.

Xavier follows her gaze. Mel screams a scream so terrible that the hapless fund-raiser takes several panicky steps, as if thrown backwards by the force.

Alessandro Romano, many times over the legal limit, and his friend Marco roar unstoppably down Bayham Road in Marco's car. Alessandro, at the wheel, is dazed and nauseous, well out of control of the vehicle. The engine is rattling; they clatter over a tiny pothole which jolts both men in their seats.

'Slow down, for fuck's sake, stop, for fuck's sake,' Marco shouts, but he is inarticulate, Alessandro's hands unsteady on the wheel, and they career past the spot where months ago Xavier walked away from Frankie Carstairs.

Alessandro, the eleventh link in the chain, sees a movement up in front of him and blasts frantically on the horn. At the bottom of the hill the Indian shopkeeper, walking back from a doctor's appointment, stops still, his mouth slack in horror.

For Xavier, there are two seconds of life between seeing Jamie charge into the road and realizing that the car, which tears towards them suddenly in a metal blur, will hit and kill Jamie. In the first second his mind alights on many separate thoughts, seeing them all at once, like a card player with a hand fanned out in front of him. He thinks of Michael, not prone on the floor as he last saw him, but as he must be now, walking around on little legs. He registers Mel's animal howl, feels as if Pippa is in his arms somehow, and visualizes a Scrabble bag into which he is about to delve for an exchange of tiles. He remembers his dad saying that nobody really knows what they are doing, and, like George Weir in the throes of his heart attack some months ago, has a memory from school: Russell lumbering on all fours on the floor, Matilda on his back with her hair in her eyes, traces of dried blood around her nose.

In the other second, feeling as if hands are pushing him from behind, Xavier sprints wildly into the road. He grabs Jamie and shoves him, with all his might, out of the way. Mel, her hands clasped to her mouth, and the Indian shop-keeper, statue-still, watch from their different vantage points as Xavier is flung up into the air by the impact of the car.

It may look as though events have come to a head at last, as though this is the end of the chain. But Xavier, floating above the ground for a few instants, feels very differently. Perhaps he senses that, when his body hits the road, it won't be the end of him; he will survive somehow,

318

because for all the cold logic of the world it is also fond of handing out last-minute reprieves, defying its own rules. Perhaps he is looking ahead to a different kind of life, a life of consequences: new opportunities for Murray and for Pippa, new paths shooting into the future from the present moment he helped to create. In any case, as he falls to earth, Xavier feels that all kinds of things are just beginning.

We do hope that you have enjoyed reading
this large print book.

Did you know that all of our titles
are available for purchase?

We publish a wide range of high quality
large print books including:
Romances, Mysteries, Classics
General Fiction
Non Fiction and Westerns

Special interest titles available in
large print are:
The Little Oxford Dictionary
Music Book
Song Book
Hymn Book
Service Book

Also available from us courtesy of
Oxford University Press:
Young Readers' Dictionary
(large print edition)
Young Readers' Thesaurus
(large print edition)

For further information or a free
brochure, please contact us at:
Ulverscroft Large Print Books Ltd.,
The Green, Bradgate Road, Anstey,
Leicester, LE7 7FU, England.
Tel: (00 44) 0116 236 4325
Fax: (00 44) 0116 234 0205